THE DEVIL TO PAY

AN EM RIDGE MYSTERY
BOOK THREE

LINDA HALL

WILD SEAS PRESS

THE DEVIL TO PAY

Formatting by Rik – Wild Seas Formatting
http://www.WildSeasFormatting.com

Editing by Rogena Mitchell - Jones Manuscript Service

Cover design by Elaine York – Allusion Graphics

Published by Wild Seas Publishing
Linda@WriterHall.com

eBook ISBN: 978-0-9949550-2-9

Print ISBN: 978-0-9949550-1-2

09242019

A Note to Readers

This book has been three years in the writing. I was writing about a hurricane hitting the Bahamas long before Dorian blasted his awful self into the islands ravaging Abaco and Grand Bahama Island. As I write this, hundreds of people are still missing and the devastation is horrendous.

The Bahamas are a chain of more than 700 islands off the coast of Florida, thirty of which are inhabited. They are no stranger to hurricanes. Throughout history hurricanes have wreaked havoc. In recent years, building codes have been ramped up to withstand very high winds.

Unfortunately, Dorian was a Category 5 Hurricane with winds exceeding 156 mph. According to reports, the Caribbean has not seen a storm of this strength before. Ever.

I have set much of the action of this book on the Bahamian island of Eleuthera, a place we visited some years ago and fell in love with. It is a gorgeous spit of land with pink sand beaches and an amazing bridge. The Glass Window Bridge separates The Atlantic Ocean from the Caribbean Sea.

As authors do, I took great liberties with the island and added marinas, and homes and resorts where there are none. Like an artist, I am merely creating an impression of the setting and not a realistic view.

I have also taken the same liberties with Portland, Maine. There is no island near the city connected only by tidal road. I modelled this mostly after Minister's Island in the Bay of Fundy, near where I live in the province of New Brunswick.

I hope you enjoy this third instalment in the Em Ridge sailing series. If you have any questions, I would love to hear from you.

Linda@writerhall.com

DEDICATION

TO RUTH

To pay the deck seams meant to seal them with tar. The devil seam was the most difficult to pay because it was curved and intersected with the straight deck planking. Some sources define the "devil" as the below-the-waterline seam between the keel and the adjoining planking. Paying the Devil was considered to be a most difficult and unpleasant task.

Smyth's Sailor's Word-Book

PROLOGUE

To my mother,

I'm finally here on Eleuthera. I couldn't believe my luck when I got called for this job! Hopefully, I will figure out what happened, and you and I—we won't have to hold this awful memory anymore. I will finally understand, and we both will be at peace.

You'd be surprised to know how much I think about you, Mom, how helpless I have felt through the years with so many questions, so many guesses with no answers.

I have decided, finally, to get everything down on paper. All of it, every little bad bit of it. For me. For Terrance. For Francine and Marilou. But mostly for you. I like to believe that someday, you'll even get to read this. I want you to know that at least I tried.

It has taken me a long time to get to the place where I even wanted to remember, much less write it all down. All those years. All those long years of not knowing. Those years when I was called "troubled."

"She'll be trouble when she grows up." I heard the whispers. I saw the way the middle school teachers looked at me.

In high school, a guidance counsellor gave me a blank notebook and told me that it might "benefit me" to write out my anger, my emotions, all my feelings. The book was one of those plain lined notebooks that I'm sure schools purchase by the boatloads. (This book that I hold in my hands now is a fancier one that I bought at Office Depot.)

Back in high school, I laughed at the idea. Everybody was stupid back then, teachers, counsellors, everyone. I threw the book in the garbage can in the office on my way out of my appointment. I made sure the school counsellor saw what I'd done.

But now it's time, and I have this new blank book.

It's so beautiful here in the Bahamas, Mom. You would love it. (I remember how much you loved the lake!) The water here on Eleuthera is so blue. Well, it's this blue-green color, which is amazing and unusually warm for swimming. I have a room down here, right behind an outdoor restaurant called the Tiki Bar. My place is kind of small and utilitarian, but that doesn't bother me. Those rooms don't even have air conditioning, but if you want, you can leave all your windows open at night, and the door, too, and then you arrange this big mosquito netting over the bed to keep out bugs. It's not too bad. I guess I should get used to living like this. If I become a boat captain, I'm sure I'll be all over the world and living in many, even worse conditions.

But for now, I'm sort of used to a hot place with no AC. Skip and Sue, who I live with in Florida, have AC in their big house but don't use it much. It can be like 95 in the house, and there they are, not even noticing how hot it is, but with all the windows open, and then with Skip walking around in a jacket!

Right outside my door is a small porch with a metal chair and table. That's where I am now, sitting and writing. In the distance is the beautiful ocean. In the far distance are sailboats. Soon that will be me out there.

That's the good part. The bad part is, of course, Terrance's death by some stupid, stupid accident! When I think of his senseless death, I can't help it. I think of you and Francine and Marilou. And it all comes back to me, and I get this catch in my throat.

I have yet to meet the owners of the boats who hired me. They're supposed to come by later today. I'm excited, Mom, I really am. But I'm also a little bit afraid. What if I can't do this? What if I screw this up like I screw up everything?

Your daughter,
Janice

CHAPTER 1

He died here. Right here on the ocean floor where shards of sun gashed through the blue layers of the Caribbean Sea. As I swam down toward the bottom, I tried to ignore a dime-sized blot of condensation on the inside of my mask near my right eye. I'd live with it. This wasn't a pleasure dive. Sunny and I had come here to find something, anything, one thing to prove that Sunny's Dive Shack was not the reason the victim had drowned.

"Em," Sunny had said to me that morning. "You have to help me with this. Please."

Sunny was my friend. I would. Of course I would.

I maneuvered my gloved hands around a rock that might have been the one that had grabbed onto the victim and held tight, imprisoning him until he choked out his last breaths. I tried not to think about that part of it—the suffocation, the gasping, the flailing of arms and legs, the instinctive pulling off the mask, which only makes death come that much sooner.

I grabbed a beer bottle that was lifting and falling on the bottom in the soft swell, and several small crabs scurried away, looking for a new place to call home. I tucked the bottle into the mesh bag I always carry—part of my "clean up the oceans" plan. So far, two cans, one bottle, a black plastic cable tie and a piece of plastic wrap. Yay for plastic. I'd like to come diving just once and not find plastic.

I turned a stone over. No. This smooth stone wouldn't have caught that diver, even as inexperienced as he most surely was. Sunny was right. It had to have been a submerged anchor or length of rusted chain, something with a sharp edge, something that would've caught quite suddenly and unexpectedly and held. Why wasn't it down here? Why weren't we finding anything?

A few feet from me, Sunny was working his knife around a bit of vegetation. Even though it's a challenge to read expressions through face masks, I had the feeling he was frowning. Sunny seldom frowned. He needed to find that piece of something that had snagged the victim and caused him to die. Sunny needed it not to be a defective tank, not a defective reg. Not his fault. He was my friend, and he needed not to be sued.

The problem was, practically the only things down here were swathes of seagrass, schools of translucent bluefish and acres and acres of bottom sand rippled into doll-sized mountain ranges by the action of the waves.

I had arrived on Eleuthera late last night and was staying in one of Sunny's eco-tourist rooms behind the Tiki Bar. When I came out to the deck this morning, ready for coffee and eggs, Sunny was up and waiting for me. Not sitting and waiting but pacing and waiting. "I might be sued, Em. I might get sued." Those were his first words.

Sunny is a big Bahamian fellow with the kind of glistening dark skin that you only see down here. A handsome guy, a gentle fellow, one who you could genuinely describe as having a "heart of gold." His continual smile and cheerful demeanor are how he got the nickname "Sunny." Apparently, his mother called him that almost from the day he was born. She might be the only one who knows his real name. Sunny has a pretty wife named Delia, who grew up in Nassau and whose family still lives there. They have a child, a baby daughter named Marybelle. He proudly posts pictures of her on his Facebook site.

He had sputtered out the whole story this morning while I polished off coffee and bacon and eggs prepared for me by Tina, who has worked here forever. Three Americans had rented equipment from Sunny's Dive Shack here on the

Bahamian island of Eleuthera. They had headed out on their own inflatable to the reef by themselves. They anchored the inflatable and dove off it. All was well for a while. But somewhere during the morning, they turned around, and their friend wasn't there.

When they couldn't find him under the water and saw no little air bubbles to signify his presence down below, the two returned to the shore. They'd beached the inflatable and ran wildly up and down the sand looking for him. Was he here? Had he somehow become disoriented and swam all the way to shore by himself, impossible as that seemed? Had someone in a boat picked him up? Was he here? Was he here? He had to be here!

Tourists and locals gathered along the beachfront shaking their heads. No. No one had seen him. Some offered to help look. One of the divers climbed back into the inflatable, pushed it back into the water. "I gotta go back out," he'd called to the other one. "You wait here in case he comes back. Go call the wives."

"Why didn't you go after the guy?" I asked Sunny while I smeared more guava jam on my slices of Tina-made bread. "Why didn't you get in your boat and go right on out there?"

The main dive boat was out, he told me. Plus, his secondary boat was having engine problems, and a couple of other boats would have been too slow.

"But, I shoulda gone," he said over and over. "I shoulda just gone out there, but I didn't think it was anything to worry about. I thought he'd be back any minute. This sort of thing has never happened here."

A full cup of coffee sat in front of him. He wasn't drinking it. He was sure—he kept shaking his head—it was merely a case of getting separated, and if the divers were as expert as they claimed, the three of them would be up on the deck drinking Kalik beer and yukking it up by lunch. Then the merriment would go on all night. Like it had for the past three nights. The drinking. Sunny had told me that. "The drinking."

"Drinking?" I asked. "Did they go out diving while they were drinking?" The thought alarmed me.

"They weren't drinking when they rented the equipment," he told me. "I made sure of that." He paused. "But I never should have let them go alone. That's not my policy. I know better...but..."

I knew what he was going to say, and I stopped him before he did. It was for the money. He needed the money. I could relate.

The fact that Sunny had waited before taking them seriously was to be his undoing when the police finally did come and question him, especially when the lawsuit threatened. "Also," he added, "why would anyone be swimming so far away from the reef anyway? That's the part I'm not getting." Sunny pushed his cold coffee mug away from him. "The reef is a good half mile from where they found the body."

"Maybe he just got confused. It happens."

Sunny scowled, wiped a hand across his face, and looked out to sea. "Something about those guys." He shook his head. "Something's not right."

Sunny told me the inflatable had slowly returned some time later. The dead friend lay prone on the bottom of the inflatable. He told the police he had anchored the dinghy and gone in. He still had a bit of air in his tank. His friend was at the bottom, snagged on a piece of chain. In his frenzy to get free, he had used up all his air.

"That in itself seems strange to me." Sunny placed his closed fist on the breakfast table.

I asked, "If he used up all his air, why is he suing you?"

"Because they are saying that there should have been enough air. That I didn't fill the tanks properly, that there was some leak or something."

"Doesn't sound right to me," I said.

He grunted and added, "They were all three of them sailing in here on some fancy vacation, and yet the three of them, well the six of them if you include their wives, didn't seem all that happy about being here or even being together. There were many arguments between them. Like huge arguments."

"Arguments? Really?" I drank more of my coffee. "Do the police know?"

"Police don't care."

"Sailboats are small," I said. "Close quarters at sea. Even the best of friends can part as enemies."

He let out a sigh. Out beyond us, the ocean was so blue that it seemed bewitched. Several local children were running down the length of the sand calling each other.

"I need to figure this out," he said. "My business depends on it."

Sunny knew about divers. Sunny had been taking groups of them to the best reefs and wrecks off the coast of Eleuthera for as long as I've known him, and that would be coming on fifteen years. When the local police had arrived and assessed the situation, they contacted the Nassau force. By the time Nassau arrived, the five of them, according to Sunny, would have had plenty of time to "get their stories straight."

"Really?"

He looked on down toward the children on the beach and didn't say anything. The police came and grilled the locals, he told me. They grilled the two remaining divers. They talked to their wives. They took the widow aside and spoke at length with her. They took notes. They looked at Sunny's equipment long and hard, photographing everything and examining every piece. That's when Sunny started to get nervous.

"Was all the gear yours?" I asked.

"That's just it. It wasn't. The suit was his. Mask and fins too. The only things they got from me were tanks and buoyancy compensators. And…and…the police aren't even going out there." He pointed out toward the water. "No dive team. Nothing. You know why? You want to know why?" He leaned toward me. "Because the guy that died? American.

Police over here don't want to mess with Americans. Now, if the group of divers were Bahamian, they would be all over everything. All over it. Even now. They'd be talking to everyone. There would be arrests. There would be justice!" Sunny banged his fist on the table. "But an accident with American tourists? The police won't touch it beyond giving it a cursory look. If I get sued..." He looked me straight in the eyes. "If I'm sued, how will I take care of my family? How will I? And now that the big resort's going in..."

I nodded.

This dead diver was the reason I was here on Eleuthera. I would be returning their boats across the Gulf Stream to Florida one at a time. Three couples on two sailboats had been sailing the Bahamas. Five of them, the three guys and two of the wives had gone on several supervised dives with Sunny's nephew Kenny who worked for Sunny and is a certified dive master himself. The sixth one, the widow of the victim, was not a diver and, instead, usually sat drinking wine coolers on the deck of the Tiki Bar, either drawing in a sketchbook or reading.

"She seemed different," Sunny told me. "The widow. By herself a lot. Not overly friendly. Even with the other two women. They would all come over for beers, and she would just sit there. It seemed like they didn't even include her."

"Maybe she didn't want to be included," I offered.

Since they'd showed themselves to be experienced divers, when, one morning, the three men wanted to rent equipment from Sunny and take it out on their own, he saw no problem with it.

"They had all the certification, Open Water and one had Rescue Diver," Sunny told me. "I don't rent out equipment unless I can see some certification."

"Right."

"I'm cautious that way."

"I know."

"Still, I shouldn't have done it, shouldn't have let myself

be talked into this."

I nodded.

After the accident, a rumor started floating around that the widow of the dead man was planning to sue Sunny.

"That's what they do, those Americans." He balled his hands into fists. "They sue all the time. This'll ruin my business. It's my business that'll suffer. My company. My business. Divers will hear about this and think I'm incompetent. They'll write it all out on the internet." His voice had risen dangerously high at the end. "I keep all my equipment in perfect working order."

"I know you do."

"He got caught on something. It's the only explanation."

"Right."

"But I know those waters. There's no chain out there that I've ever seen. And now they're going to sue?"

I picked up a piece of toast and said, "I wouldn't worry about it, Sunny. Half the time these lawsuits are nothing but threats anyway. That's the way it works sometimes."

"It doesn't seem right. It's not right. It's not my fault. How could this be my fault? There has to be something out there."

"There probably is."

"But the police aren't even looking."

"Maybe they should be."

"Maybe *we* should be."

"*We?*"

"You and me," he'd said leaning toward me over breakfast.

My only conclusion now as we swam and examined the bottom was that all that stuff had by now floated away, the bits of his wetsuit, any signs of a struggle. Water, and especially sea water, doesn't have a great reputation for preserving crime scenes. Things dislodge themselves or drift away. Things get eaten by other things. Things get moved around by waves and currents. But solidly embedded anchors and chains don't. That's what we were looking for, and that's what we didn't find.

I had met Sunny fifteen or so years ago when I'd crewed on a sailboat from Florida. It was my first time across the Gulf Stream, and it was quite invigorating especially since we went out when the waters were a bit iffy. But we were on a large boat, a Swan 52 if memory serves, and the captain had assured us that "the boat could well handle it."

Invigorating, yes, but soon after, I made a vow. I would never attempt crossing the Gulf Stream in a small boat unless it was calm, calm, calm. Because even then it can be quite choppy. And me? I'm prone to seasickness. I think I'm the only boat captain in the history of boat captaining who gets seasick on a more or less regular basis. You want to know about every seasick med known to humankind? Just ask. I've tried them all. Got a whole drawer full of them on my own boat. I've got the pills, the patches, the wrist bands, the things you put behind your ears, the mindfulness meditations on my iPhone. You name it, I've tried it. But with me, the beauty of the water and being out there is worth all the throwing up over the side.

When I first met him, Sunny was here on Eleuthera working at a run-down dive shop. Much to the consternation of my parents. I had recently dropped out of college, deciding that what I really wanted to do with my life was sailing. I was sure that if I looked hard enough, I'd be able to find some sort of life's work that included only sailing. Sunny could identify. All he wanted to do was to dive and look at things underwater. His parents wanted him to go to college. They had one all picked out in Florida, even. We both wondered if they made adult jobs that included sailing and diving. We laughed a lot. I remember we laughed a lot.

Now both of us have found our adult careers. Sunny owns and manages Sunny's Dive Shack and Tiki Bar as well as several eco-tourist rooms on this beautiful island of Eleuthera. And me? I'm a boat captain and get to be out on boats all the time.

I mostly see Sunny online. Someone told him he needed a Facebook page for his business, so he set one up where satisfied customers write accolades and post the gorgeous underwater pictures of reefs, coral, and fish. Sometimes I go into Facebook and see how he's doing. That's where I'd seen the photos of his wife and baby girl.

So, after breakfast we had suited up. I always carry my personal equipment when I go on boat delivery jobs, my own snorkel and mask. Maybe it's me, but I don't like to use a borrowed mouthpiece that a million other people have sucked onto. Besides, my mask has prescription lenses for my bad eyes. I did borrow a BC, (buoyancy compensator) reg, and other gear from Sunny, however.

"Sunny," I protested, "I really should meet the boat owners before we head out diving."

"They're not here."

I looked at him. "Where are they, then?"

"Flew home day before yesterday, I think. Whole crew of 'em."

"Really?" I stared at him. "They're hiring me to take their boats back, and they don't even want to *meet* me?"

"Told you they were a strange bunch. Janice met them though. Maybe they thought that would be enough."

"Yeah, I'll have to talk to Janice, then."

I was beginning to wonder what I'd gotten myself into.

Sunny had the foresight to note the GPS coordinates from the dead man's dive computer. It turned out to be this long space of smooth, pure sand, where we were diving right now. Yet the entire bottom of this part of the ocean contained nothing that would snag a diver.

With my gloved hand, I swept away a bit of a dark spot on the ocean floor now, but it wasn't anything, just a trick of sunlight through the layers of water. Nothing. Nothing. Nothing.

The only anchor I could see anywhere was the one holding Sunny's boat to the bottom. Through the clear water above me, I could see the underside of his boat.

I followed the black neoprene form of Sunny as we swam around and around the accident scene in ever-widening circles. Nothing. No signs of a struggle. No little pieces of plastic goggle where the guy had flailed and struggled to breathe. No little torn black bits off a wetsuit where he'd tried to break himself free.

We were venturing further and further away from the place where we started. In the distance was the reef. I wondered again how the dead man had been so disoriented. It's kind of hard to get lost. The shore is that way. The reef is that way. Out to sea is that way. It's not rocket science.

I made my way over to where Sunny was examining another bit of something dark on the ocean floor. It turned out only to be a greyish stone. He flipped it over. Nothing. Nothing even crawled out from underneath. Over and toward the reef, thousands of sergeant majors, surgeonfish, and clown fish schooled past and momentarily gave me pause for the beauty of the place.

Sunny shoulder tapped me on my wetsuit and pointed up to his boat. I glanced down at my dive computer—time to head up. We were shallow enough that we only needed to stop for three minutes at fifteen feet. Soon we were back on his open dive boat and heading fast toward his dock.

I was surprised at the oppressiveness in the air. In the scant hour that we'd been under the water, the wind had completely died. Something about this bothered me. A storm was brewing way out in the Atlantic. The weather forecasters had assured everyone that this hurricane, big as she was, would be staying well away from the islands. Still, it troubled me. The air felt wrong, smelled wrong. There's never a time without a breeze here.

One of my guilty pleasures is reading sailing memoirs and adventures about the early days of sailing, the days of the square riggers, way before GPS when sailors relied entirely on the compass, the ship's clock, the stars, and their wits. This was back when weather forecasting was more art than science. Back then, captains felt the storms. A good captain could sense it in his bones. A captain would go out onto the foredeck of his ship, stare into the sky, gaze at the sea, and instinctively know when the storm was coming, how severe it would be, when it would hit, and from which direction. Nine times out of ten they were right. This was part of being a captain back then. This was a part of the job.

Now, it is all science — weather reports, weather monitoring buoys, satellite images, faxes, sat phones, emails. Somehow, I think we've lost something. I was sensing something now, and despite what the science was telling me, I didn't like what I was feeling. The sky was an odd shade of blue, like a painting where the artist had run out of the correct shade and had simply grabbed all the blue tubes, thrown them together onto the palette and threw them up there without rhyme or reason.

I pulled the top of my wetsuit down over my tank top and put a towel around my shoulders.

"I don't like the weather," I yelled over the noise of the enormous outboard.

"I checked the forecast this morning," he said. "Should be okay for taking those sailboats to Florida. Storm's not even supposed to hit here."

"Hope so. Where are the boats anyway? Do you know?"

"New marina over near the gas docks. Just past the Glass Window Bridge." I noticed he'd frowned when he spat out the word "marina."

"That the new resort you were talking about?"

"Yeah. They want to turn the whole place into something with five stars and condos. We're already losing our island way of life."

I nodded.

Closer to the shore, I said, "I'm assuming I get the keys from Janice?"

"Good luck with that one."

"What do you mean?"

Sunny yelled, "She'll probably still be sick when we get back."

"Sick? She's been sick?" *Had Janice been sick?*

"You may as well know what you're getting into. Kenny thinks she's been drinking too much. But I'm ready to give her the benefit of the doubt and just say she's sick. Or nervous. Just acting weird."

"Really?"

"When she first met the couples who own the boats, she fell over onto the sand in a dead faint."

"Are you kidding me?" I hadn't heard this.

"That's what Kenny told me. He took her to her room then."

I didn't know Janice all that well, but the young sailor had seemed capable enough when she helped me take my uncle's sailboat *Wandering Soul* from Florida to the Chesapeake a year earlier.

Minutes later, Sunny and I arrived at his dock. On the deck of the Tiki Bar, Janice was leaning into the railing and hugging her arms and frowning.

When I cupped my hands around my mouth and called her name, she fixed me a look, turned and walked away.

CHAPTER 2

I fixed Sunny's bowline to a cleat and looked up to where Janice had been. "I wonder what that was all about," I said to Sunny.

He merely shrugged. "I told you. I don't know what's wrong, but something is."

"I think she's just embarrassed, maybe," I said. "That she couldn't do the job. That she had to call me to take over from her."

We talked as we made our way along the short dock, across the sand. I would rinse all the salt off me and my equipment at the outdoor shower next to the dive shop before I went to look for her.

Kenny was washing out some gear at the shower post when I got there. We chatted our hellos while I turned on the second spigot. I told him I was on my way to find Janice when he said, "She really a boat captain?"

"I think she's working on it. We crewed together once."

He eyed me. "How was she then?"

"Good. Capable."

Kenny was placing the rinsed snorkels and masks into a plastic bin. "Why would they hire her if she's not a real captain?"

I shook my head. "I have no idea."

He said, "Janice wasn't like this when she first got here."

"Like what?"

"Acting all weird and hiding in her room."

"Really?"

"No. It seemed like she really wanted to do the job."

I pulled off my shorty, leaving me in my tank top and

board shorts. "I told Sunny I think she's got cold feet and is embarrassed."

"Yeah. Maybe."

Kenny reminds me a lot of his Uncle Sunny, big and dark-skinned, and handsome. There's definitely a family resemblance, although, unlike Sunny who smiles all the time — and I do mean all the time — Kenny has a more serious side.

"Something's going on with her," he said. "She got here, and everything was fine, and she was going to meet the people who hired her to take their boats back, and she's all excited. And then she meets them. After that, she completely changes."

"Sunny told me she fainted."

"Yeah, sort of. We were all at the Tiki Bar. Me and Sunny, Janice and Tina. And down on the beach they were all coming ashore in their dinghy. I'm watching, and she's smiling, but then, as they get closer to the shore, she's getting more and more agitated. And when they walk up the steps onto the deck, she stops. She just stops, and all of a sudden, she's shaking, like really shaking, and backing away, and I happened to be standing behind her, and she backs right into me like she saw a ghost or something. Then she fell. Fortunately, I was there. I sort of caught her. I thought she might be sick. That's what Sunny keeps thinking. Like maybe food poisoning or something. I took her back to her room where she sort of came to. Meanwhile, they're at the Tiki Bar just waiting, I guess. She goes out and says to them, 'I'm so sorry. I'm just sick. All of a sudden. I'll be fine for the trip, I promise, I promise.'"

Kenny dragged the plastic container of rinsed off scuba gear and hung the pieces next to the entrance to the dive shack where they would stay until they dried off. I stood under the shower for several more minutes until all the salt was off me.

Two days ago — *had it only been two days?* — I'd been walking the aisles of my favorite organic grocery store in

Portland, Maine, deciding what I could and couldn't afford when I'd received her frantic call. Since I have a job where if I miss a call, I might miss a potential pile of cash, I always answer. No matter where I am, I answer. Concerts, meetings, lunches with friends—I'm the one everyone hates because I always grab my ringing phone from my pocket, put up my hand, and yell "sorry. I have to get this," and make a quick exit. So when my phone rang, I scurried me and my half-full shopping cart to a quiet place in the back of the store and took the call.

Who am I kidding? There was another reason I was so eager to get to my phone. I was hoping to hear from Ben, my police friend. We had parted the previous evening not on the best of terms—my fault this time. I was trying to figure out how and if I should call him back and apologize. Maybe he was calling to apologize to me. Then I'd apologize to him, and we'd play the whole apology game until everything was fine. Who was I kidding?

It wasn't a number I recognized. Before I was barely able to blurt out a hello, I got, "You gotta help me! I'm in over my head. This is Janice. Do you remember me? I'm in way over my head. Way over. You're the only person I can think of to call. I'm drowning. Scared out of my wits, more like."

After Janice and I had said our goodbyes in the Chesapeake last year, I never expected to hear from her again. From time to time I wondered how she was doing. She was about fifteen years younger than me, this energetic, outgoing, extrovertish little pixie of a young sailor who wants to make sure everyone remembers her name. She has a bit of an odd little quirk. She always wears pins emboldened with her name, Janice, like she's perpetually attending a conference. I noticed this when I crewed with her but never asked her why. It had never felt entirely appropriate. She owns many. Some are ceramic, some wood. Some have her name JANICE all in capitals, and some are cursive. Some are tiny. Some are huge. But she always wears them.

"Of course I remember you. What's up?"

"I'm desperate. I've definitely taken on more than I can handle. I need your help. They're paying me. Pretty good, too. I'll give every cent to you. I swear. I don't want any of it. It's a crewing job. Can you come? Can you bail me out of this situation I got myself into?"

"Where are you and what's the situation?"

"I'm in the Bahamas. On Eleuthera. You heard of it?"

"Been there many times. Lovely place." A young mother with several children sitting inside of her grocery cart glared at me as she wheeled past. I tried to keep my voice as unobtrusive as possible.

She told me the story. Three couples had sailed to Eleuthera on two boats. After one of the guys had died in a scuba accident, she'd been hired by them to take their boats back to Florida one at a time while the five distraught vacationers flew back to their homes near Boston. In the middle of her story, I wondered why they had hired Janice. When we were together, she talked about getting her captain's license, but no way could she have logged the requisite hours and taken the courses since then.

I didn't want to be mean, but I said as calmly as I could, "Are you working on your captain's license then?"

"No. Not yet. I mean. I plan to. But not yet."

Nosy as I am, I was going to ask why they hired her, how they got her name, when she blurted out, "No way in hell should I ever have said yes to this. I need you. Oh, I'm such a loser. Can you come down right away? Like today? Tomorrow at the very latest? I'll give you the plane fare, too. That's part of the payment."

Getting myself immediately into captain mode, and intrigued by the request, I asked about the boats and the fee. I learned that one was a 34 foot sailboat and the other was a 37 foot. She didn't know the makes, just that they were sailboats. Two couples had crewed on the 37, and the other couple had sailed alone on the 34.

While we continued talking, I wheeled my grocery cart back through the aisles and unloaded all my organic produce and organic ketchup and pastured eggs and grass-fed butter and farm-raised beef onto the appropriate shelves, put my cart back and walked out of the store. If I were leaving, I wouldn't need any groceries. Soon I could be eating fresh fish and mangoes and drinking Kalik beer.

At home, I booked a plane ticket and packed. In the morning, I dropped off my dog and cat with my neighbor EJ and flew down here. My elderly neighbor never minds looking after my animals, which include my uncle's cat, Bear, and my old dog, Rusty.

There were any number of people I could have called to drive me to the airport. Jeff and Valerie who live a few doors down from me would have, and of course my two friends Dot and Isabelle who were two doors away. Dot would have for sure.

And then there was Ben, of course. There was always Ben. I probably should have called him. At least to tell him I was leaving for a bit. Maybe a bit of space between us now would be a good thing. I needed time to think. Perhaps we both did.

I had ended up not asking anyone for a ride. Sometimes I'm just too independent for my own good. I'd parked my car in long-term parking. How dumb is that? Racking up all those parking fees.

I took my scuba equipment to my room now and laid the pieces over the small table and chair just outside of the door. Two doors down, Janice's hoodie was hung on the back of her outside chair. I knew it was hers because I could see her signature name tag hanging vertically down the right front. I went over. On her table were two books. A novel she was probably reading and what looked like a notebook or journal. As I stood in front of her door to knock, I saw that the front cover of the journal was lying open.

I looked down and read what she had written on the first page. How could I not? It was right there and wide open."

Mother:

I'm finally here on Eleuthera. I couldn't believe my good luck when I got called for this job! Hopefully, I will figure out what happened and you and I, we won't have to hold this awful memory anymore. I will finally understand, and you will be at peace...

Mom,

I can hardly write this; my hands are shaking so badly. I am pressing too hard with my pencil, and I keep ripping the paper. Why did I think this was a good idea coming here? Where did I ever get it into my head to say yes? Even if it *was* Terrance! I'm in my room with the door shut and the windows, too. Even though it's hot in here, so hot, I feel safe. No one to ask me any questions. No one to know that I just can't do it. Can't do it.

I'm sick with embarrassment that I had to call Em. I couldn't do this thing on my own. When I came down here, I was so happy. I was going to help Terrance. I wanted to do this. And then they showed up. Then I actually met them.

I'll try to get it all down exactly the way it happened. I was sitting here writing. I was thinking about some of the good times we had and trying to figure out the best way to write about the lake, and then Kenny came over and said the boat owners were coming up the beach to talk to me. Two guys and two women. Terrance's widow was back at the hotel.

Great! I closed my journal, put it away, and I headed down, all smiles, to meet the people who'd hired me.

I can't even explain what happened next, but when I looked into their faces, something snapped. I suddenly felt fear. They told me I fainted! I've never fainted before in my life. Fortunately, Kenny, one of the dive masters, was right behind me. He caught me before I fell right onto the beach with everyone there to watch me, guests, tourists, everyone! And me trying to be this super cool big shot sailor in front of them all. Failure. Loser. That's me. All my life. Such a screwup! All my teachers were right. Whatever gave me the idea I could do this?

I remember only bits and pieces of the conversation above and around me.

Someone said, "Is she drunk?"

Someone else asked, "Is she sick?"

Another said, "Maybe it's the heat."

"She's just dehydrated."

"It's just the heat."

"Get her some water."

"Get her to her room."

And now, just the thought of those boats makes me want to throw up. I needed to find someone to take my place, and I needed to do it quickly. I need to get the hell out of here.

It was a stroke of genius that led me to Em Ridge. When we lived with Francine and Marilou, I always tried to keep my side of the room we shared pretty neat, but since then, I've gotten really messy. I'm so glad I found her business card in all the wreck of my wallet. Just before I came to Eleuthera for this job, some sixth sense told me I should take her business card with me. Maybe deep down I knew I didn't have the skills or the courage to take two boats across the Gulf Stream. Maybe I knew that all along. But I had to come. It was Terrence who had died. Of course, I had to come! I know you would want me to.

It was pure good luck that Em Ridge was able to come at the last minute! Not only is Em a good captain, but she has connections to the police! And that's important now! I know I keep putting in all these exclamation points, but that's how I feel.

I want to be successful. I want you to be proud of me, Mom. But I keep screwing up. The monsters are always there, right below the surface of everything. I try to forget. I really do. I try to put it all behind me, underneath me. Hide it all under the bed. Then something happens. Something like this. And it all comes back—every damn little bit of it.

Jannie

CHAPTER 3

I knocked at her door, surprised that it was closed and shut on a hot day like this. Down here, people mostly leave everything wide open.

"Come in." A faint, small voice.

I pulled opened the door. Janice was sitting on the edge of her bed, holding a hairbrush. She looked thinner than I remembered, if that were even possible, her shoulders like pink, chapped doorknobs under the skinny straps of a bright orange tank top. A flowered sarong was wrapped double around her waist as a skirt. When she turned to look at me, her eyes were red.

"Hey."

"Em," she said. "Thank you. Thank you so much for coming." She looked near tears.

"No problem." I stepped closer to her. "You okay, Janice?"

She shrugged. "I will be. Now that you're here. Now that it will all be settled."

She was small, an entire miniature person sitting there, holding a pink hairbrush in her hands.

I said, "Didn't you see me coming in just now on the boat with Sunny?"

"I must not have."

I didn't believe her but decided to ignore it.

"Okay, tell me the lay of the land," I said. "I need to get the boat keys and information from you, and then you can head home as quickly as you want..." I could tell by the half-packed duffle bag on her bed that she was ready to leave. "Sunny said the owners flew home already. I should get their numbers from you and call them."

Her entire body went rigid. She said, "It's okay. Just take the boats."

"I need to speak to them."

She sighed. "I thought maybe you could just take the boats and go, and I could meet you in Florida."

I shook my head. "For insurance purposes, for a whole lot of reasons, I need to talk with the owners. Boat captains don't just pass jobs around willy-nilly. You cleared it with them, didn't you?" When she continued to look at me with wide eyes, I said, "You didn't tell them I was coming, did you?" I asked. "They don't know you called me to take over, do they?"

She swallowed and shook her head. "I meant to talk to them... I just... I couldn't... It's an a...an embarrassment. I'm so embarrassed by the entire thing."

I took a breath and said as gently as I could, "Okay, give me their phone numbers, and I'll call and explain." Her eyes brimmed with tears. She looked fragile sitting there, folded in upon herself.

By this time, I was even second guessing myself. She hadn't told them. I was already here. What if they didn't want to hire me? How had she not at least talked with the owners before I flew down here? Would I even get my flight reimbursed? This is the sort of stuff I never do. I felt anger begin to boil up inside of me. I looked at her. She was scared, small, and had clearly gotten herself into a situation she didn't understand.

I tried to reassure her. "Okay, Janice, I'll smooth the waters. I'm good at dealing with all shapes, sizes, and stripes of boat owners, believe me. My whole sailing résumé is online plus references. I'm sure we'll be fine."

"The numbers are in my book." She looked around for several seconds before glancing through the open door. "It's outside. On my table. Let me get it."

I waited while she fetched the journal and then opened to the back and read me off names and numbers, which I copied into my phone contacts. "Wes Rhorson," she said. "Wes has been my contact person. He's the one who called me. He's the one with the larger boat. The other one is Marcus Downey. I never talked to him. It was mostly Wes. He seems like the nice one. And their wives are Beth Rhorson and Michelle Downey."

"The one who died. Which boat is his?"

"He didn't have a boat. That would be Terrance. Him and his wife Audra were on Wes and Beth's boat. Audra has already gone home, I think."

"Okay then. I'll call Wes right away."

"Yes, call Wes, not Marcus."

"Got it."

"The keys for the boats are at the marina."

"I'm going to head there today. As soon as I get all of this squared away, you can go home. Janice don't worry. It'll be fine. You'll be fine. You get home and start working on your captain's license. You're a good sailor, Janice."

She swallowed and said, "They told you, didn't they?"

"Told me what?"

"Kenny told you, I bet. Or Sunny, that I had a meltdown when I met the owners. Fainted right into the arms of Kenny."

I tried to keep it light. "Well, Janice, I can certainly think of worse arms to fall into…"

She sighed, and shoved a strand of hair behind one ear. "It was when I saw them that the whole thing just got to me. I knew I wasn't up to the job." She paused, looking down at her hands. Outside, a dog barked. "That's when I knew…" she said.

I nodded. "You did the right thing. This kind of fear can happen to anyone."

Very quietly she said, "I knew Terrance. The one who died."

I stared at her. "You knew the victim? You were friends?"

"Not exactly. Our families were…um…connected."

I thought about that. An old family friend. "That's why

they called you?"

"Probably. That's all I can think. Terrance must have told Audra about me."

I nodded.

"I don't know Audra very well. Well, just from being down here. She's very nice. An artist." She paused. "There's something else. There's another reason I called you."

I waited.

"I know you have a cop boyfriend, and I remember how you and him figured out that murder a year ago. I think something happened to Terrance. I don't think his death was an accident."

I thought about Sunny's suspicions.

She scooped up another handful of her hair and put it behind her ears. "Maybe you and him could figure out what happened to Terrance. That's part of the reason why I had to come. I feel I owe it to Terrance to figure out what happened."

I didn't say anything. I could picture Ben's reaction if I asked him to look into this. First of all, he would say it's out of his jurisdiction, and second, he would tell me to keep my blinkin' nose out of it.

"Janice, I don't know. Ben's such a by-the-rules kind of guy..."

"Just ask him, please?"

I sighed and told her I would but that I couldn't promise anything.

Later, I went down onto the beach to make my call. Usually, when I cross national boundaries—which often happens in my work—the first thing I do is to I put my phone into airplane mode, relying on Wi-Fi where I can get it, to text or email people. This time, I'd suck up the cost of an actual phone call.

When Wes answered, I introduced myself and told him about the change in plans and asked if it met with his approval. I gave him a bit of a rundown of my sailing résumé and the link where he could read it online.

"So, she couldn't do it, could she?"

"She decided she just needed a bit of help."

An audible sigh. "Well, maybe that's for the best. She seemed a little spaced out to me when we met her. To be honest, we didn't know who to call. Audra found her name in Terrance's contacts, so I made the call. We got to get those boats home any way we can. Marcus and I are still in Florida, but the wives flew back to Boston. We're thinking of staying here until the boats make it back."

I said, "Just curious. Why didn't you just take the boats home yourselves?"

"None of us want to get on the boats again. It's all pretty upsetting."

"I understand. I'm so sorry about your friend."

I told him I planned to leave with the first boat asap. "There's a storm out there. I hear it's going to stay well offshore, but to be on the safe side, I want to head out right away. Maybe even tomorrow. If we can get this done right away, so much the better."

"I agree."

"This thing could all be wrapped up in less than two weeks."

"Good then."

I asked him to tell me about the boats, and he did—a C&C 34 named *Sea Chanty* which belonged to Marcus and Michelle, and *On Our Way,* an Irwin 37 which belonged to him and Beth. Audra and Terrance had been on the 37 with Wes and Beth. Nice boats, I thought, nothing spectacular, but perfectly adequate. I told him I'd take the larger of the boats across first. Then I'd take the fast cat ferry back to the Bahamas and pick up the second one.

"Sounds like a plan."

Next on my agenda was to get to the marina and have a look at the boats. I glanced up and saw Janice out on her table hunched over her journal, writing. She didn't seem to see me. I'm not sure why I felt a sudden unease. But I did.

CHAPTER 4

I headed over to the dive shop to see if I could borrow Sunny's car. He wasn't there. Tina at the Tiki Bar told me that he and Kenny were down on the dock with a bunch of divers.

"I want to see if I can borrow his car," I said. "I need to head over to the new marina and check on the boats."

With her wet rag, Tina was going over the already clean counter with angry swipes.

"Did you meet them?" I asked. "The boat owners?"

"Oh yes." Her expression was grim.

"What does that mean?"

She stopped and placed her hands on her broad hips. "Just odd. That's all. Demanding. And if you're working for them, good luck to you. That's all. That's all I got to say."

"What do you mean demanding?"

She was back to harrumphing and cleaning up the outside counter at the Tiki Bar and shaking her head. Tina, who's been on Eleuthera for twenty plus years, is a big, pink-skinned blonde. The story goes that she and her "bum of a boyfriend" — her words — were sailing around the Bahamas on his "junk of a boat" — her words again. When they anchored just outside Nassau, she feigned sickness — made herself throw up over the side of the boat so it would look authentic — her words, and so didn't join him for a drinking binge on shore. Instead, she grabbed all of their money, both his and hers, packed herself a sack of clothes, and since he had the dinghy ashore, she stood outside on the foredeck of the sailboat and waved and called until a passing fishing boat picked her up. Once ashore, she got on the first ferry leaving for anywhere. That place happened to be Eleuthera.

I'm not sure how much of the story has been embellished through the years, or how much was truthful, to begin with — maybe none of it, but all I know is that Tina has been cooking, frying, mixing drinks and dispensing Kalik beer forever. Her conch fritters are second to none.

"Sunny doesn't have a car anymore." She pointed to a bicycle leaning against a palm tree. "Just that."

"What happened to his car?"

She hiked up a tank top strap on her fleshy sunburned shoulder. "Broke down. Doesn't have the money to fix it. He's been biking. Take it. I'll tell him you borrowed it. He won't mind. He won't be back for hours. He's got a bunch of Danish tourists heading over to the reef."

I hopped on the bicycle and headed out onto the Queens Highway, the main — and only — highway which goes from one end of the island to the other. The marina was a few miles away. It wouldn't take me long. Eleuthera is a long spit of an island. From the air, it looks like nothing more than a sandbar, a gorgeous long strip of pink sand, the kind of pink sand that isn't found anywhere else on the planet. From above, it always looks like one good wave could wash the whole island to kingdom come.

The marina was further from the dive shop than I had realized, and not even halfway, there I rued my decision to bike. This old 18-speed bike of Sunny's was too small for me, and no matter how I tried, I couldn't raise the rusted seat any higher. It only had one workable gear; the rest having been salt-corroded into oblivion. The only gear that functioned had me peddling too fast, and I felt like a little kid on a tricycle racing to the party.

It was hot, dreadfully so, and the sun pierced down like a series of fireplace pokers on my already sweaty back. How had I managed to come out on this bike and forget to bring even a bottle of water?

Tina told me that the new marina was on the Caribbean side just across the Glass Window Bridge. I peddled across, always marveling at the deep blue Atlantic Ocean to my right and the calm, green water of the Caribbean to my left, completely different colors, moods, and personalities, and yet not more than fifty feet from each other.

Like some people, I thought.

Like Ben and me.

The bridge road was a bit iffy, and in desperate need of a full refit, so I kept to the middle as much as possible. When cars would come, I would move to the side, get off the bike, and stand and wait. Almost to the new marina, my cell phone vibrated in my shorts pocket.

I'd already made one expensive phone call down here. I couldn't afford to make another. I'd wait until I had a stretch of Wi-Fi and text back whoever it was.

At the first safe spot I could find, I leaned the bike up against a palm tree and—again cursing my stupidity for not bringing water—I pulled out my phone.

Ben!

I looked down at his name there on the small screen. He had no idea where I was. He thought that when I picked up my phone to answer, I would be sitting on the old corduroy couch on the front porch of my little house at the end of Chalk Spit Island in Maine. What kind of a person leaves like this without telling the most important person in her life where she was going?

Maybe the marina would have Wi-Fi. When I got on the bike again, I began composing a text in my head. I'd have to tell him I was sorry. I'd have to tell him where I was.

I'm really sorry. This job came up suddenly. I tried to contact you before I left but couldn't get through.

No. That would be a lie. I hadn't tried to contact him. There had already been too many lies between us. Maybe just the truth this time.

I'm sorry. I got scared. I'm afraid of my feelings for you.

Truer. But even that wasn't the entire truth, was it?

You're still married. I need space to think. This sudden job came up. I took it. I'm here. Again, not the whole truth and nothing but, if I'm honest with myself.

That brought my rambling thoughts full circle to my Uncle Ferd who has spent the entirety of his whole life living on boats. When life gets too complicated for him, he weighs anchor and leaves. There used to be a girl in every port for him. That's what my mother used to say about her brother. Well, it still may be true, but recently, he had discovered a daughter he never knew he had, and a granddaughter. I thought he would settle down after that discovery, but no, that hasn't happened.

His boat, *Wandering Soul,* was still moored in the small bay in front of my home, and I have no idea where he is.

The trouble is, I'm doing the same thing now. When life gets too hard, I run. But this planet gets to be a small place after a while. There are only so many places to hide. Sometimes, you just have to quit running. Sometimes, you just have to go back to where you started.

Maybe. I just don't know if I'm ready to do that yet.

Ben is a detective with the Portland City Police Force, and he and I have been friends for about three years. I met him shortly after he moved from Montana to Maine. I sort of work as a consultant for the police at times, as well. When Ben wants information on boats or all things nautical, he calls me. We have lunch together, always in the same small café. I answer his questions as best I can while he takes notes. Lately, though, we've been gradually growing to be something more than just friends. Something way more.

I met him shortly after my husband Jesse was killed. Ben helped to figure out why he died, and he was there for the aftermath when I couldn't get my mind to fix around anything solid. While I nursed a broken ankle, he came up and sat with me on my porch couch. We talked. As the months—years now—wore on, we became even better friends.

Here's the problem—we both pull around a whole lot of baggage behind us, he more than me. He's married. Did I already mention that?

The story of how and why Ben came to Maine is all online. I've read all about the botched drug bust, about the boy who was killed. Fourteen years old. It's all there. Just Google it. I've also read how Ben and his team were exonerated. His team had received incorrect information. It wasn't his fault. Social media, of course, had a field day. I went through a lot of the sites and comments, until I couldn't stand it anymore, until my heart had started breaking for him, for his whole family.

It wasn't a case of police brutality of the kind caught on random cell phones and posted nationwide on twitter feeds. No, it was him seeking out this innocent person, thinking this fourteen year old, big for his age, was a notorious "Most Wanted" armed criminal—they wore the same shirt!—and then shooting him down in cold blood, when all the young boy pulled out of his pocket was a pack of gum.

What I need is for him to tell it to me in his own words. He's told me parts of it. Not all. Not the part about his wife and son. That's the part I need to hear.

After a time of counselling, after a time away, he came out here, which is about as far away from Montana as a person can get and still be in the same country.

I saw the picture of his family, too. I even know his wife's name—Cindy. And his baby son. In my mind, I still see the three of them in that grainy online picture, the proverbial happy family photo—handsome father, pretty little mother, a cute chubby baby boy with one blue slipper shoe half off and dangling from that little foot.

Ben never told me any of this during those first couple years of our friendship. All he said was that this was his first job after a few years of "stress leave." He must've known that I would Google it, yet he never mentioned it.

Until, finally, he did.

It was a clear evening, three months ago, blessedly free of mosquitoes, and we sat close together drinking glasses of

Guinness on my old front porch couch. He had something to tell me, he said. Something important.

I didn't move a muscle.

He started from the beginning. He and his departmental team had worked long and hard to set up an elaborate sting. It was going to be major. For too long, a drug gang had held their city hostage. It was time to end this. Time to take the city back for ordinary folks. Those were his words — ordinary folks.

Ben said, "What ended up happening was more stupid and tragic than anything I've ever been involved in. What ended up happening, a child could have done a better job."

Strange choice of words since it had been a child who was killed.

I held my cold beer with my cold hands. The police had the wrong address, he said. It was a case of a couple of digits in the address being reversed.

"A stupid, stupid mistake." Ben shook his head. Kept shaking his head.

For several minutes, neither of us said anything. He looked away and stared out at the bay where *Wandering Soul* gently bobbed in the bay.

"He was fourteen. Someone's son. Just fourteen." Ben's voice broke as he kept saying this over and over. Just fourteen. Only fourteen. Someone's son. Fourteen... Fourteen....

He took my hand then, his fingers twining around my own.

"I'm so sorry," I said.

"I need to tell you about my wife."

I waited.

"Her name is Cindy..."

I knew this. When Ben didn't speak for a long time, I said, "What happened?" My voice was so quiet that I could scarcely hear my own question.

"She couldn't stand the threats, the protests, the letters to the papers, the online criticisms, the spray paint on our house, people accosting her in the stores, coming right up to her, telling her she was married to a child killer, the protesters right outside our house, our church. She couldn't live with it. She didn't like what we'd become. What I'd become."

But I was stuck on one word. "Your *church*?"

He nodded. "My wife...the church is her lifeblood."

"Ah... but I take it not so much for you?"

"You might say not anymore."

Maybe we had more in common than I thought. High in the trees above us was a breeze. Wafting in on it was the smell of roasting meat. My elderly neighbor EJ would be preparing another huge slab of beef out on his barbecue rotisserie. Usually, I love the smell. Typically, I was right over there exclaiming and admiring his cooking skills. Normally, I waited, mouth-watering, for a sample, a foil-covered plate to take home. But today, the smell was overpowering, cloying. I wished it would go away.

Ben said, "It's time I told you more."

I waited.

"Because of what we're becoming to each other."

What *were* we becoming to each other?

"The envelope..."

A year ago, I'd been to his house, and while he went into a far room to grab a jacket, I decided to straighten his mail, which had come through the door slot and lay heaped in piles all over the floor. In the course of being Miss Helpful, I'd picked up a large manila envelope addressed to Cindy Dunlinson. "Return to Sender" was scrawled over the face of it in thick, black Sharpie. I'd stuffed it back in the pile, but I always had the feeling he'd seen me do that.

He said, "It contained divorce papers that I wanted her to sign. She wouldn't. She sent it right back unopened."

I swallowed. A spider was seeking access to the side of my sandal. I kicked him away. I said, "You're still married."

Ben got up from the couch and went and stood at my porch

rail and faced away from me, looking out at the water. I stayed where I was. When he turned back to me, he said, "Cindy. My wife, Cindy. She doesn't believe in divorce. You have to understand a bit where I come from. Cindy and me. Our families. We were church people, devoutly so—way back in the generations. Her grandfather was one of those old-time preachers. That's where we come from..." He let that sentence peter out.

I said it again. "You're married."

"Technically, I guess yes."

"*Technically*." I pondered that word, the way he said it.

"She doesn't want to live with me anymore. She's made that clear." He didn't look at me when he said, "According to the church, one of us has to commit adultery before a divorce can be granted."

I felt my entire body go still. A tsunami of thoughts began pushing and shoving all around in my head. Is that why he was here? With me? Did he intend to "commit adultery" with me? Was that his grand scheme to get that divorce? When he came over and sat down beside me, I stiffened away from him.

He said, "That came out wrong."

"Yes."

"I like to think I'm an honorable man. I have a Christian wife who won't divorce me, but yet who wants nothing to do with me. Will not even speak to me. And she is happy to live out her days like this, the ever-married martyr. I think she likes the status that gives her at church, the good one, the betrayed one."

Now would have been the perfect time for me to ask about his son. *Do you get to see your son much*? I could have asked. *Do you miss him a lot*? *I saw his picture. I know.*

"But I can't do that," Ben said. Then, he took my face in both of his hands. After a long while, he drew me to him. I didn't resist. The kiss was long and sweet, passionate and pleasing. For a moment, I could forget.

"Em," he said when we broke away.

I dabbed at the tears on my cheeks.

"Em." He repeated it.

We grew closer after that—a lot closer. Our "police consulting" lunches would last a couple of hours. We talked. I told him about my own religious background, how my younger twin sisters were so involved in church with their perfect husbands and perfect piano-lesson, soccer-playing children. I told him how I didn't fit in there. Never could. Never would. Even though I was the oldest, I was the odd one out—the non-twin.

He told me he understood.

Often, we talked about other things, things not so deep, not so personal. Ben told me about a canoe he had his eye on. He'd seen it on Craig's List, and I made this weird comment about too bad he hadn't met my husband, Jesse. He and Jesse would have been good friends. Jesse could have built him one. I told him that Jesse had made two matching kayaks for us and that I had a perfectly good kayak under my house I hadn't looked at since Jesse died when his kayak was hit by a powerboat.

"After his death, I never wanted to see it again," I said.

"That's understandable." Then, "It's under your house, you say?"

"Right."

"You might want to bring it out to the light. If it's as beautiful as you say, it should be kept up."

"I know. I know. I'm probably ruining it." Then, "Maybe there's a part of me that doesn't even care."

"Em..."

"Or maybe you could come have a look at it sometime."

"I'd love to. Be honored. I like working with wood myself. But I'm just a hobbyist."

"I'm sure you're more than that."

When I'm honest with myself, I have to admit that the marriage thing isn't the only reason I fled when I got the panic call from Janice. Not even the son. There is another reason why I run every time we get close, and it doesn't have to do with his wife and son.

It has to do with me.

Mother,

I'm sitting here at the little table outside my room, remembering things. As I look out at the gorgeous calm water, it's funny the things I think about. The lake. Do you remember the lake? Do you remember back to that time when we lived in a tent all summer at the edge of it? As I sit here, I'm seven years old again, and it's so beautiful, and there's that little boy on the sailboat.

I remember so clearly that day when you came to me and said we were going camping for the summer, the whole, entire summer. It looked like you had been crying, and I couldn't understand why if we were going camping all summer. It was only years later that I understood.

We packed up our things—we didn't have much—into the car, along with a big, leaky tent. I learned later that you found it at the end of someone's driveway wrapped up in a bundle and waiting for the garbage truck. We camped in the woods, just up the wooded path from the lake. "No one on the lake will even see us back here," you told me.

We were there for the whole of the summer. We ate from the jumbled piles of canned food we had brought from the Food Bank. Weekly, you would make the trip in, leaving me to look after our campsite. I was to stay inside the tent when you were gone and not come out for anyone.

It was there that I became fascinated with sailing. Across the lake was a real campsite with big trailers and buildings and a noisy beach with slides and children and a wooden raft that kids swam to and jumped off of. They had a lifeguard who sat on a high, white chair and blew a whistle. From where I sat, I could watch the campfires. I used to wonder what it would be like to be there, roasting hotdogs and marshmallows over the fire and sliding down that big slide into the water. Long hours during the day, I sat on a rock and watched.

There was a boy that I watched, too. He had shaggy brown hair and wore a blue life vest. He sailed the whole of the lake all day long. I think it was a little Opti he sailed, but at the time, I didn't know one boat from another. I watched for hours. I memorized the way he moved the sail from one side to the other, and I noted how that moved the boat. I watched the way the boat behaved on calm water, on rough water. I watched and memorized each move of the sail, each grab of the tiller, each movement of the sheet. I watched during the high winds when he would lean way back, the boat practically up on its side. I watched during the dead calm, when he had to rapidly move the tiller back and forth, back and forth just to get the boat moving at all.

Once toward the end of the summer, he sailed close to where I was sitting and said, "I see you there all the time. Do you want to come for a try?"

But I was little and shy and shook my head and ran away.

It wasn't a day later that I realized the mistake I'd made. I should have said yes. I decided that if he ever asked again, I would say yes. I planned what I would say. I waited and waited. But it was the end of the summer, and he never came back.

Eight years later I got to try it for real with Uncle Clifford. And it was just as I expected—I loved it. I could do it. It somehow felt completely natural. I can't explain it. It just was.

When the summer was over, we moved into an apartment with Francine and Marilou, two friends from your new job at the restaurant.

My hand is shaking as I write that last sentence. Your two friends. And you.

Why did everything have to turn out the way it did?

Jannie

CHAPTER 5

I almost biked right on past the entrance to this new marina. There was only the most meagre of signs that read,

RESORT/CONDOMINIUMS/MARINA/SERVICES

A hand drawn arrow pointed down a narrow road chunked with stones and dust. The gravel gave way to a large area which included trucks and equipment and piles of wood and cement blocks and supplies of all sizes and descriptions. Dozens of half-constructed buildings jutted out of the shoreline.

Ahead, out on the water, were several lengths of new docking. Not a lot of boats, but through the palms, I thought I could pick out the boats I would be delivering. They floated side by side on either side of one of the dock fingers, two sailboats. Several powerboats were tied up behind while numerous smaller boats were pulled up onto the sand.

My tires crunched as I cycled my way toward the sailboats. I tried to think back to what this place was like before. I seemed to remember it as a few semi-floating wooden docks, a whole bunch of iffy moorings (most sailors anchored), a ramshackle wooden convenience store, and a gas bar that had fuel provided they hadn't run out by the time you got there.

Scaffolding and cement blocks were everywhere. I also saw plenty of workers, Bahamians happy and eager for the wages. I took it all in. Sunny was right. This complex was going to be huge.

As I got closer to the building, which looked like it would eventually be the new dive shop, I could understand Sunny's concern. If you're visiting the island and decide to go for a dive, which dive shop do you go to, this newfangled resort with its dive shop, qualified instructors, all the best and fanciest equipment and new, shiny, fast dive boats, or with some local with a slightly rusty dive boat who was already being sued?

Even though the entire place was abuzz with activity, everyone mostly ignored me, which was fine. I leaned the bike against a palm and made my way down toward the boats. These docks were not made of boards, but of that new wood-grained non-rotting dense plastic stuff that southern climes are beginning to use for decking. No rust, no mold, no painting or staining necessary, will last through the apocalypse, but expensive as hell. I could see that this place would be after the "big boat" crowd. They had already installed a couple of high-flow fuel pumps.

I walked down onto the dock past the sign marked Private, Registered Guests Only. Well, the gate wasn't closed. Not even any lock on the thing yet, so I walked right on through like I owned the place, plus, unlike a lot of times when I do this, I had every right to be here now. I was heading toward those two sailboats at the end.

Sea Chanty was a nice mid-range Canadian boat, a C&C 34, comfortable to sail and live aboard. The boat beside it was *On Our Way*, the Irwin 37. Both of these boats were sturdy enough to get you where you wanted to go. And down in these warmer climes, who cares about staying down inside of a boat anyway?

In my particular line of work, I get to sail on all types and makes of vessels, from the hugely rich Swans and Hinckleys, considered the Rolls Royces of the sailing world to the equivalent of the Nissans and everything in between. I've been on old boats, new boats — red boats, blue boats, I finished the poem in my head.

Both boats were locked up tight, padlocks securely fastened to their companionways. I could climb aboard them and peer inside, but I wouldn't. Climbing aboard any boat without permission just isn't done. You can lie to the customs guy, you can smuggle more alcohol than you're allowed, you can speed through No Wake zones on your dinghy, you can wander down private docks, but you can't climb aboard a boat that's not yours. Sailors' Code.

"Hey!" I turned. Approaching me was a stocky guy in sunglasses and golf shirt so white it glinted in the sun. "This here's a private dock." The contrast between a white shirt and his dark skin was almost blinding.

"Then I'm glad I found you," I said. There was a small insignia on the right pocket of his shirt, Eleuthera Private Yacht Club.

"This gate was supposed to be locked."

"Well, good thing it wasn't, then." I smiled. "Captain Em Ridge." I extended my hand. "I've been hired to take *Sea Chanty* and *On Our Way* across to Florida.

"You have some ID?"

"Certainly." I reached into my backpack for my captain's license.

He examined my ID, then handed it back to me. "This is arranged with the owners?"

"All set up." I put the card back in my wallet. "Talked to them just this morning. Just need to check her out, get the keys from you and get it provisioned."

He seemed to consider me for a few seconds before he said, "We were under the impression that the person taking the boats was not a captain, but a family friend."

"That's right." I grinned. "That would be Janice. She decided that the job was a bit too much for her, so she called me." His khaki shorts were so unwrinkled they were like two boards down each leg.

"Talk to Ramona. Up in the office. She's got the keys."

"Thanks." He was still eyeing me warily. "What a great place you have here," I said. "I was here way before this place was anything. Wow." I added, "Your name was?"

"Neil. Dock manager."

"Great to meet you, Neil Dock Manager." I finally got him to smile. "I'm hoping to maybe even get going as early as tomorrow. I figure I can mostly provision in Nassau. Want to beat that storm that we're not supposed to get."

"Yeah. Well, if there's anything you need."

"You got fuel?"

"Yeah. Now we do."

I thanked him and made my way up to the marina office. Inside, the AC was doing a fine job of turning the place into a beer cooler, which, in my opinion, was a good thing. To the right, a blonde, ponytailed woman in bike shorts, was walking leisurely on a treadmill, correct that — treadmill desk. A laptop was perched open on a stand in front of her. She hadn't immediately turned to me when I opened the door. Closer, I saw why. A set of earbuds trailed from her ears to an iPhone which lay beside the laptop. I could even hear the tinny music coming from it.

The place smelled of clean, fresh paint. Artwork featuring sailboats and lighthouses brightened up the walls. Leather couches and lounge furniture were already grouped in comfy, conversation circles. Yep, they were aiming for a rich clientele. On the wall in front of her, a flat-screen TV was turned off. I imagined there wasn't anything to connect it to yet. I walked toward her.

"Excuse me?" I said.

No response.

It wasn't until I went and stood right in front of her that she looked up, pulled out the earbuds and said, "Oh! Sorry! Didn't see you there." She wound her earbuds around her wrist. "Something I can help you with? So sorry."

"You're Ramona?" I asked.

"That's me." She stopped the treadmill.

"Neil down on the dock told me that you have the keys to those two sailboats down there. I'll be taking them to Florida as soon as I can. Maybe even tomorrow. I'm thinking it might take me four days just to get to the Gulf Stream."

She climbed down and went to her desk. "Seriously? Tomorrow?"

"That's what I'm thinking, yeah."

"Well, good luck then." She opened a desk drawer. "Here are the keys. You meet the people who own those boats? I heard they left."

"They did. I never met them. All set up by phone." I put the keys in my backpack.

"Have you met Audra?" She asked me.

"The widow?"

She nodded.

"I haven't met any of them."

"I got to know her a little bit."

"Yeah?"

"Not the others. Just her."

"Okay." She seemed eager to talk. I let her.

"She's nice."

"That's nice," I said.

"She was the only one of them who was nice."

"So sad about her husband," I said.

"Wait a minute. Don't go anywhere. I need to get something for you."

I raised my eyebrows, said nothing.

While I admired the paintings on the wall, she went into another room and emerged a few seconds later with a blue file folder from which she pulled out a pencil drawing. I recognized the water and the spit of land to the right. She laid it in front of me. "Audra did this," she told me. "She used to sit at that table out there when the others went out sailing sometimes."

"It's pretty," I said. "You two must've been real close if she gave you something like this."

"Yeah, maybe. I feel bad for her."

"I don't blame you."

"We used to talk." She said, "I hope she's okay. I'm worried about her. Do you have her email?"

"I'm sorry I don't."

"At one time, she confided in me that she'd simply had enough."

"Enough of what?" I asked. "Sailing?"

"She's the only one who seemed normal. They were a kind of a strange bunch."

"So I've been told."

"The other wives..." She rolled her eyes. "They complained a lot. I don't think they realized we're not set up here yet. No laundry or showers or anything." She gave an exaggerated sigh. "Just the bare essentials. They were furious that our internet wasn't fast enough. That sort of thing."

I was finding this rather curious. "Well, if you're not up and running, how did they find this marina in the first place then?"

She shrugged. "We're on Facebook. That's maybe where they saw us, but I think they got the wrong impression when they reserved. And then maybe by the time they got here, the other marinas were full. I told them we'd drive them anywhere they wanted to go to provision. We were totally at their disposal, but they were all unhappy from the get-go. I told them, 'Come to my house and you can even have a shower.' They wanted to go diving and were upset that our dive shop wasn't set up yet. We told them about Sunny."

"Good choice," I said.

"I don't know him well."

"Well, you need to get to know him. He's a great guy."

"Audra told me she really didn't like sailing all that much. She and her husband have a powerboat. Even showed me pictures of it."

"So sad."

"Yeah, sad."

I pulled out my phone. "Can I have the password to your Wi-Fi?"

She gave it to me, and I also gave her my business card, "If you need to get in touch with me, email or texting is probably the best way," I said. "I only text when I'm on Wi-Fi. Costs the sky, otherwise."

There wasn't a whole lot for sale yet in this place, but before I left, I bought a bottle of water from her. It was ice cold and hit the spot.

I headed outside and sat at the picnic table under the palm tree, where Audra had sat with her sketchbook. I decided to send another email to Ben before I headed down to the boats to have a look inside and see what was needed in terms of provisioning.

Ben,

I see that you called. I can't answer because I'm in the Bahamas. Right! I know! But it was a job that came up quite suddenly. Sorry I didn't say goodbye properly. I should have. You can email me, but don't phone because I can't use my phone while I'm in the Bahamas. I can get texts and emails if I'm on Wi-Fi, though.

Em

What kind of a stupid, non-personal email was that? Nevertheless, I pressed SEND. I had barely put my phone in my pocket when Ramona was out the door and calling my name.

"Yeah?" I turned back.

"I just put the weather on. You might want to rethink your sailing plans."

I stopped.

"You're not going anywhere."

To you, dear Mother,

When I was seven, the thought never occurred to me that the reason we tented beside the lake was that we had no place else to live. It was summer. It was fun. It was a grand adventure. I hadn't even noticed that all the stuff we owned in the world was packed tightly in the trunk of that old clunker car. You'd lost your job at the bakery—something about seniority, and so we had to leave the tiny, damp, cinderblock basement apartment we'd stayed in for as far back as I can remember. But, the camping was so much better than that crappy apartment, anyway. And the lake, how cool was that?

I think about that as I sit here at the beach. I don't have much memory before that summer, just bits of things here and there, but nothing solid. It was like my life began during that summer when I was seven.

In school, I told Mrs. Nose about this. I told her I couldn't remember much before that summer. She said that considering what I'd been through, that was entirely understandable. Oh, I should mention that her name wasn't really Mrs. Nose. Everyone just called her that because of—well—if you saw her, you wouldn't end up calling her anything else!

Mrs. Nose was one of the first ones to be nice to me. She was one counsellor at the high school who actually listened when I talked rather than just try to tell me what to do. Mrs. Nose was the one who had given me the blank journal book the first time we met. Even though I gave her a look when I threw it away right in front of her, she kept being nice. She kept not giving up.

She never once mentioned "writing down my anger" again. Once, she told me, "You had some really good times with your mother. Some wonderful times. Why don't you think about those times?"

Now, almost ten years later, I'm finally doing what she urged me to do at the very beginning. I'm getting it all down, the good things and the bad. The camping, the cuddles, all four of us, me and you and Francine and Marilou, sharing a

big bowl of popcorn and watching videos we rented from Blockbuster—*Toy Story, Harry Potter* and more.
A long time ago and a whole world away.

Janice

CHAPTER 6

"That storm? It's coming directly toward us. It'll be here in four days. Maybe five. I got it up on the TV now."

"That has to be wrong. I checked the weather this morning. They said it was nowhere near us."

"Well, I guess the storm had a change of plans. Come back in. See for yourself."

I followed her inside and looked long and hard at the swirling mass on the TV. It was indeed moving toward us. I looked at the proposed track. I studied it for quite a while, calculating. Maybe I could get one boat across before the worst of it hit. If I left today, like right now, I might be able to make it to Florida. Might. That was the operative word. But that meant not stopping anywhere, and I'd have to provision the entire boat, fuel up, check all the systems in about an hour.

"Maybe I could leave this afternoon. Get started anyway."

"You want to chance it? Go ahead. I wouldn't. The last thing you want to be is somewhere between the Bahamas and Florida when a storm hits, and you're in a boat you don't know."

Of course she was right. Back at the dive shop, I'd call the owners again. I'd tell Janice to get the earliest flight out. And what about me? Do I stay on Eleuthera or try to get out myself, and then what? Fly back? I was quite sure the owners would not want to pay for an extra plane ticket.

All around me, workers were up on scaffolding, piling bricks and cement, laughing and talking, oblivious to the oncoming storm. Out on the dock, the boats rocked gently on the serene blue water.

I checked my email one more time—nothing from Ben—

and headed back to Sunny's Dive Shop on the bicycle. I'd check on the boats later. I wouldn't leave today. It was foolhardy to think of heading out today. I'd have to come up with some alternate plan.

The cycle back seemed to take less time than coming, probably because I had so much on my mind. My thoughts raced as I sped across the Glass Window Bridge.

When I got back, I pounded on Janice's door. No answer. I hightailed it to the Tiki Bar. Tina told me that Janice had gone for a walk on the beach.

"You know which direction?" My voice was too loud.

"You okay?"

"Tina, check the weather. That hurricane that everyone said was going to stay way offshore. Like way offshore? Like 'don't worry about it' offshore? Well, the newest forecast has it landing right here in less than a week."

"You shittin' me?" She wiped her greasy hands on her chef's apron.

"Turn on the TV."

I headed back to the beach, and my phone buzzed in my pocket. Maybe it was Ben getting back to me finally.

I pulled it out of my pocket. Not Ben. The Private Eleuthera Marina.

Captain Ridge,

If you're available tomorrow morning, we're going to be moving all the boats to Hatchett Bay. We've got a few moorings there. If you're able to help move them, we could use the help. Be here at 8 am.

Neil
Dockmaster

I emailed back:

I'll be there.

I finally found Janice far down the beach, sitting on a rock, hunched forward and writing in her little book.

"Storm's coming," I called to her.

She looked up at me and shut the book. "What?"

"There's a hurricane coming this way. It'll be here in four days. Less than four days. I'm heading to the marina tomorrow to move the boats to a bay where they'll be protected. If I were you, I'd get online and get the next flight out of here."

She closed her book and put the pen on top of it. "Tomorrow?"

"Tomorrow I'm moving the boats, yes."

"I could stay. I could help. I could at least do that before I go. I don't mind helping out."

"Well." I weighed her words. Maybe she did want to help. "It might be an all-day thing, because while I'm at it I'm going to check out both boats."

"I don't care. What else am I doing here but getting in everyone's way? I might as well help."

"Janice, you should really be thinking about flying home while you have the chance. At least get yourself a ticket."

"No. I'd like to help. I want to stay."

"Well, okay then. You're a fine sailor, and I think the marina could probably use all the help they can get."

"You really think that? That I'm a good sailor?"

"I do."

She jumped down from the rock and joined me on the beach, her eyes glistening.

———◦○◦ ———

Dear Mother,

I've always had this feeling that doom and disaster were waiting for me just around the corner. Like this big storm they're predicting. I never trust things to work out in my favor entirely. My glass isn't half full or half empty. If you open up my cupboard, you will find I don't even own any glasses.

If I get to be too happy, I start looking around the corner for that sure disaster that is about to pounce on me any second. I love sailing and adventures on the water—I really do—but usually only when they're all over. Does that make any sense? Sometimes I'm happier looking back on a good time instead of living in it. Being living in it is too fraught with danger. Like things could go so wrong.

Because I know, I know what it's like to have the very worst happen to you. I remember back to that time. It was only much later after everyone was gone when I realized how much Francine and Marilou sacrificed for us. They gave up a room in their small apartment for you and me, Mother. They took us in when we had nowhere else to go. They made those days the happiest of my life. But it was too good, it seems. The "happy gods" looked down and decided we were too happy, and to each other, they said, "We can't have that!"

And then all of you were gone, just like that.

Your boyfriend, Russell. I need to think about him. I need to bring him to the surface of my memory. I need to write about him, mention his name in all of this. You were so happy with him that I was sure it was going to be the beginning of something good for the two of us. I remember how I first learned of your friend Russell. Marilou let it slip one evening when I asked where you were.

Marilou looked up from the table where she was hunched over a small watercolor painting she was working on. "She's with Russell."

"Russell?"

She put her brush down and clamped her hand over her mouth. When she didn't answer, I kept talking. "Russell? Who's Russell?"

Francine had heard the whole thing from the kitchen. She came out, wiping her hand on a dishtowel, sat beside me, and took my hands in hers, which were cool and floury. She said, "Your mother has a new friend. But she made us promise not to tell you anything about him until she was sure. You have to promise me you won't tell her that you know. *Promise* us you won't let it slip." And she held my hands even tighter.

I gave them my word. But I knew, Mother, I knew.

I longed to ask you but could not.

And now I'm here, writing all of this down. Am I going crazy? Was it Russell? Was Russell the one who did this to you? Is that where all the sadness began? Did he bring it in with him?

I don't want to think that. I want to believe he loved you.

Janice

CHAPTER 7

The marina was bustling with activity when Janice and I were able to get a ride there the following morning at quarter to eight. The construction workers, who only yesterday were plastering cement in a more or less leisurely fashion, were now taking down the scaffolding board by board, hammering plywood over windows, and dragging and piling sandbags here and there around the buildings with loud voices and hurried movements.

Dragging several mooring balls on lines behind him, Neil strode purposely toward us from the dock. I shifted my backpack onto both shoulders, and we walked down to meet him. I had brought along several Tina-made sandwiches and plenty of bottles of water this time.

"We're ready to go," he said. "They want to move these docks up as soon as we get going."

"Wise," I said. I know what storms can do to a dock. I used to have a dock in front of my place on Chalk Spit in Maine. Just before Jesse died, a hurricane turned it into a pile of kindling. Replacing it is still on my to-do list.

Neil outlined the plan. At four or five knots, it would take us about an hour and a bit to motor to Hatchett Bay. When we got there, we'd secure the boats, remove all the sails and canvas, secure the rigging with triple lines, and then come back to the marina on the fast inflatable he'd be towing along behind.

I turned to Janice. "So, Janice, you ready to crew along with me?"

She looked at me curiously for several seconds before she said, "I can take a boat on my own. It's not far, and I understand we'll be motoring rather than sailing anyway. Should be no problem for me."

"You really want to do that?"

She nodded. "I was all set to take them both across the Gulf Stream, remember? I can surely do this little trip."

"Well, okay then. I'll take the 37 and you can take the 34."

On our way down the wharf, Neil quietly said to me. "If it's up to me, I think you should take the 34 and Janice the 37."

The 34 had an iffy engine, he told me. The throttle needed to be babied. Also, there was considerable slop in the rudder. "If she's newer at this than you, I think Janice would be more comfortable on the 37. It's got all the bells and whistles. I know it's bigger, but it practically helms itself."

I said fine. We untied the lines from the dock and motored away from the wharf. There were five boats in total in our entourage today, us two, plus Neil, who towed the large inflatable, was at the helm of a small sailboat in the twenty-foot range. Another marina worker, an athletic girl named Tegan, was on a thirty something foot powerboat, and bringing up the rear was a British couple who'd been living aboard their 45-foot steel sailboat for the past eight years.

The ocean was so placid, so calm, and the sun so hot, it was hard to imagine that in just three or four days, these seas would be churning themselves into six-foot waves and drowning anything in sight. Far out to the horizon, though, I thought I could see it—an ominous, darker shade of blue. Or was I imagining it?

Occasionally, I glanced over at Janice. She looked tiny behind the wheel of such a behemoth boat, but she was handling it well. I remembered how helpful she was on the trip north on my uncle's boat when my mind was scattered and elsewhere. I knew she would have no problem today. Besides, we were all together.

I could see what Neil meant about the wonky engine. A few times, for no apparent reason, it died. I started it up again with no problem, but this would be worrisome during a long crossing. With the boat as hinky as this one was being, I decided to wait until I was safely moored and securely tied before I took a look down below. There would be things I would have to secure down there anyway. What little I could glimpse down through the companionway looked functional and comfortable. The boat did seem to have all the requisite equipment; GPS, chart plotter, VHF, RADAR, AIS.

Neil told me the sails on this boat were fairly new. When I took them down to stow them for the storm, I'd have a better look.

In just over an hour, we were motoring down the channel and into the bay. Ahead were a few sizable orange mooring balls clearly marked with the name of the marina and the words PRIVATE in big capitals. Not that that would keep too many boaters from tying up for a night, or a week, or a month. But today, all were empty. Neil directed me to the furthest red mooring ball. I secured the boat with three lines and plenty of chafing gear.

I knew this was only part of the work. I would have to remove all of the canvas from the boat exterior, which included the Bimini and dodger. It would be long, hot work in the sun. The idea is to remove as much windage as possible — to get the vessel as low to the ground as you can.

I knew this was a secure hurricane hole. I'd been here before. Still, if a storm surge hit on a wrong tide, this whole place could flood, or it could empty out, which would be worse when the waters blew in again. I have sailed the Bahamian islands a lot, and I always think of them as mere sandbars in an unrelenting ocean. You can already see the devastation climate change and the rising sea levels are having on this beautiful and pristine environment, and don't even get me started on coral bleaching. I thanked God that at least the storm wasn't coming on the heels of a full moon tide.

The boat set, I went down below to have a look around. The quarter berth was filled with junk, boxes of paper towels, cereal, toilet paper, and other non-perishables. I checked the refrigerator unit. It was switched off, and at the bottom of the deep container were cans of beer and bottles of water. I was pleased to see the water. Even warm beer would be great.

I opened all of the cupboards and was surprised to see them well stocked with canned and dried foods. I guess they left in such haste they didn't take anything with them. As well, the sheets and blankets in the vee-berth looked slept in and the bed unmade. Fortunately, I always bring a sleeping bag, not that you need one in these islands.

The head was also stocked with their toothbrushes, combs, soap and half-squeezed toothpaste tubes. They really had left in a hurry. There were several bookshelves along one side, and I could see that their taste in literature ran to mystery and thriller. The nav desk was rudimentary but workable. Something bright and yellow on the floor stuck onto my sandal, and I reached down—a sticky note.

Explain it all to Terrance. Keep it simple for Audra. Remember, they're power boaters.

I folded up that particular note and put it back in the nav table.

Out on the deck, I got to work. Around me, the others were doing the same. Even Janice was working hard.

I yelled over to her, "Hey, Janice! Do what you can, and Neil and I will help as soon as we're finished. You got the biggest sails."

"I think I can manage," she called.

While we worked, three more boats came in and grabbed the remaining mooring balls while a few others followed in and anchored. In a couple of days, this anchorage could be so loaded with boats, that you could practically walk across them from one side to the other. And that would bring its own set of problems. If one boat's anchor wasn't secure, that boat could collide with the next boat, and the next, until they all went down like dominoes.

I'd seen it happen. It's a little like driving on my snowy Maine roads. You can be the most careful of drivers out there, but if everyone else is sliding sideways right into you, you don't stand a chance.

In my line of work, accidents and deaths are no strangers. By my own count, I have had three good friends who have vanished off the face of the earth. They went out on their boats to make a passage and were never heard from again. One was on his way to Bermuda, another across the Atlantic, and the third was lost somewhere down off South America where the waters can be decidedly unfriendly.

The work mostly done, I grabbed a bottle of water and drank it down. Usually, I would strip down to absolutely nothing and go for a quick swim to cool off, but this being a fairly public place, I just dove off the side of the boat, clothes and all. I determined to stay in the water until my body temperature lowered to somewhat normal levels and all the sweat had rinsed off.

By the time we had secured the boats and helped Janice, the sun was low in the afternoon sky. On the way back in the fast inflatable, I thanked her, told her what a great job she'd done with all that canvas. I also asked her if she'd booked a ticket home yet.

She shrugged and said no.

"You better soon."

"I'm not worried," she said.

The dinghy ride back in the hot sun had completely dried my shirt and shorts. Back at the marina, I told Neil to email me if there was anything else he needed. I'd be sticking around through the storm, I told him.

It was dusk by the time Janice and I were able to hitch a ride back to the dive shop with the British couple. The sandwiches eaten long ago, both Janice and I were famished. Fortunately, Tina was still cooking, and I asked her if conch fritters were out of the question. She grinned and said of course not. While she worked her magic on the cookstove, I went and showered and changed into something not salty.

Later on—much later—I grabbed another beer and sat

alone on the top step of the Tiki Bar and looked out at the calm ocean. I still hadn't heard from Ben. Lost in my thoughts, I didn't immediately notice the woman who was making her way toward me on the beach. Barefoot, she held a pair of strappy sandals in one hand. A long, filmy beach dress fell to her ankles. As she got closer, I could tell her eyes were fixed on me.

"You're the captain, I'm told?" Her voice was soft and had a lilting quality about it.

"Captain Ridge. Yes."

"My name is Audra. My husband is the one who died. I'm told you might be able to help me."

CHAPTER 8

There was an almost ghostly quality about the woman who stood there. Her hair was cut in a strange kind of craggy way that made me want to lean my head to one side. The hair on the right side of her head reached her shoulders while the hair on her left barely touched the middle of her ear—obviously, some sort of a geometric haircut left too long in the Caribbean sun.

She had that kind of pale skin that sunburns easily, and even though it was evening, I could see the chapped tops of her shoulders by the lights from the Tiki Bar. A woven bag was slung over her right arm.

I looked at her. "You're Audra?"

"Janice mentioned that you might be able to help me."

"Well, I'm not sure about that."

She shifted her bare feet on the sand. The sandals she held had extraordinarily high heels, not the kind that you could make any headway in sand.

She said, "I know you're a friend of the guy who owns the dive shop."

My back was immediately up. She was the one who was planning on suing, right? That's what Sunny had told me. Was she here to pump me for information she could use? That was not going to happen.

I frowned slightly. "I'm sorry about your husband, I truly am, but I don't have any information that could help you. I just got here. I don't know what Janice could have told you." I looked up toward Janice's room, but her door was firmly closed against the night.

A sudden bit of wind lifted the long side of her hair, and

she wrangled it behind her ear with her free hand. I looked out to the dark sea beyond her. Was the storm starting already? I added, "I thought you would be home by now. I was told you all had left."

"The rest of them did. I didn't. I need to stay to figure out what happened to Terrance. I won't go home until I know for sure what happened."

"It was an accident."

She shook her head slowly and deliberately. "That's what the police say, but accidents just don't happen out of nowhere, do they? Especially accidents like this one. Something happened to him, maybe something deliberate. Someone is at fault."

"I don't know how I can help you." I started to rise.

She reached and touched my shoulder. "Wait." Her eyes were wet. "Please." She looked so incredibly sad. Even though this woman may be gunning for Sunny, she seemed lost, fearful. I knew what it was like to be a young widow.

I softened my voice. "I'm so sorry about what happened, but I don't know what's going on any more than you do."

When she reached up for her errant hair again, I could see her wedding ring, a thick band of gold that looked almost too big on those delicate fingers—artist's hands. I thought about the picture she had drawn for Ramona.

"You're the one taking the boats back, right?" she asked.

I told her yes that I was taking over from Janice. "Janice knew your husband," I said.

She nodded. "Yes. Terrance often spoke of Janice, but I'd not met her before a few days ago. Terrance had her contact information in his phone. And when no one could figure out what to do, I remembered that Terrance had this young friend who was a sailor. I thought she could help, or maybe even offer suggestions of what we should do. No one wanted to take the boats back. No one even wanted to get on those boats again. Me, especially. That's why we called her when...when this happened. I gave Marcus her number. He and Wes took it from there, I guess. But…"

After a while I said, "But what…?"

"Terrance had only been with their company for a couple of years. So, we weren't exactly close. The other two were."

"Company?"

"Financial advisers. Wealth management. Wes and Marcus and their wives. They all work together."

I listened.

"Terrance is an accountant, and he was hired to manage their books. Can you imagine that? Financial advisers need someone to manage their books."

Since I doubted there would ever come a time when I would need the services of something called "wealth management," I simply nodded.

"That's why they hired Terrance…"

"I didn't know this—about you all working together."

"I think he was killed because of something at his work."

"Why are you telling me all this?" I asked. "Do the police know this?"

She ignored my question and said, "I understand you dove at the spot where Terrance died."

She was regarding me very intently. *Careful, careful*, I told myself. "Who told you that?"

She shrugged. "Kenny. The one who works with Sunny. Did you find anything? Or anything wrong with the dive equipment?"

"I think you need to talk with the police." I made to get up again. "You need to go to the police. Not to me."

She looked directly at me in the darkness and said, "Well, *something* happened. Nothing makes sense. Maybe it was the equipment. It had to be that, right?"

"In case you want to know, Sunny keeps his equipment in perfect working order. I've never known anyone so meticulous. I'd dive with his gear any time."

She looked at me intently. "Well, someone's at fault."

"Please don't sue him. He is a good, good person."

Her mouth opened. Then closed. "What?"

"I said, please don't sue him."

She backed away slightly "You think I'm going to sue him?"

"Aren't you?"

"Please," she said and touched my forearm. "The police here didn't do anything. They weren't helpful."

"I understand," I said. "And I'm sorry. And I know how frustrating it is to feel like you want to do something, and you don't know which direction to turn. I've been there. I know. But suing isn't the answer. "

"Captain Ridge, I've no intention of suing anyone. It was one of the other wives' suggestions. I think it was Beth's idea. She thought maybe the police would do more if there was the threat of a lawsuit in the air."

"That's not how things work down here. Even the threat of a lawsuit is very serious down here. People don't say they're going to sue and then don't. Keep that in mind."

"But what if there *was* something wrong with the equipment?"

"There was nothing wrong with anything," I said, but did I absolutely know this? What other explanation could there be for Terrance's death?

She wiped her forehead with the back of her hand. "It was such a mistake coming here. Terrance and I should never have come. We, or at least me, were never a part of their little group to begin with. I wasn't close to Michelle and Beth. I don't even know why Terrance and I were even invited other than Terrance works with them. I mean, we don't hang around with them, not socially. There was even a part of me that wondered if they really even *liked* Terrance and me. Especially me." She paused before continuing, "I was thinking of hiring a private investigator just to maybe get to the bottom of all of this. But then Janice said I should talk to you first."

Curiosity kept me there. It was full dark now, and I

couldn't clearly see her face. A lush, warm breeze was coming in from the water.

"Janice told me all about you, how you solved this big murder case a year ago. You and your boyfriend, who's in the police."

Oh, brother, I thought.

"She was impressed with you and your friend."

"He's a cop. In Maine. He can't do a darn thing down here. This is a totally different country. I know him. He would not interfere."

She leaned forward, "Could you just maybe ask his advice? That's all I want. Advice. Like if there's something I should be doing now that I'm not. I don't know any police at home. I don't even know if there's something I should be doing."

"I know that totally helpless feeling, Audra, but, if you really want to, hiring a private detective might be your best bet at this point. I don't know any, but even then, you have to make sure their license extends to this country."

She said, "But could you just ask?"

I said nothing. I was conscious then of how tired I was after the long day.

She was still talking. "Terrance thought this trip would be a good chance for all of us to get to know each other better. For the other wives and me to bond. I have no idea why he wanted us to bond, but those were his words. Terrance was so giddy on the trip. It was…"

Giddy? It seemed an odd adjective.

"He was so excited and happy that we were all together. Most of the time he was higher than a kite. Terrance and I have been together for only four years, but I've never seen him like this. He was so happy to be invited, but then after he died, I've been thinking, what if it was something else?"

"What else?"

She shook her head, shifted her sandals to her other hand. "I don't even know what I mean. Maybe I should go home. I don't know." She looked frightened and, suddenly, so very vulnerable.

"Where are you staying here?" I asked.

"At the hotel in Governor's Harbor."

"And you're all alone?"

She looked at me, then away. "I know. I shouldn't be here alone when my husband's dead, but here I am. My sister was going to come. She's having trouble getting a flight. I just…I think…do you want to know what I think? Why I didn't go back? Why I didn't go back with them? I keep going over this in my mind. I think he must've found some irregularities in the books, maybe with a client or something. And someone wanted to kill him. Maybe whoever it was wanted to kill all of them but got to Terrance first. My mind goes all over the place with this. I'm not sleeping, either."

I knew the feeling.

It was now full night, and we had moved onto the deck. Tina was about ready to lock up the bar. I knew I would regret it, but I said, "Okay. I can't promise anything, but give me your contact information, and I'll see what I can do. Meanwhile, you need to go home. Go to your sister's. Just don't be alone. You shouldn't be alone."

Her smile was broad. "Oh, thank you so much. Thank you so, so much!"

She reached in her bag for a piece of paper and a pen, jotted down her information, and handed it to me. With a sinking feeling, I pocketed it.

CHAPTER 9

Really? You're in the Bahamas? I heard there's a hurricane headed your way. It's all over the news. Are you okay?

Ben's message greeted me on my iPad as soon as I got back to my room. A few short sentences, but I could read between the lines—*Why did you go? Why did you run away without at least saying goodbye? Are you really in the Bahamas? Are you crazy?*

I wrote back telling him that I was fine. We would all be okay. You stay inside during a storm, and you're fine. People who die are the ones who go outside to take pictures for Instagram. I wrote all of that, trying to keep it light. I'll be fine. I'll be okay.

I decided I'd wait a while before I pounced on him with Audra's and Janice's questions.

He wrote right back:

Can we Skype? Do you have a strong enough Wi-Fi signal for that? I need to talk to you about something.

The scared part of me wanted to say, "Nope, not nearly a strong enough Wi-Fi signal." Because I would have to explain, wouldn't I, about why I fled? Why I ran so far away after he kissed me. Yet there was this other part of me that desperately wanted to see his face, wanted to hear his voice, wanted to know that he was okay.

"Okay," I said. "We can Skype."

I opened the Skype signal. It beeped at me, and I pressed the ACCEPT button.

"Em. You're there."

"I'm here."

"Nice to see you."

"You, too."

And there we were, facing each other, thousands of miles apart, and yet, through the miracle of technology, closer than a touch.

He said, "I've been watching the news about the storm. I'm worried about you. When I called, and you weren't there. I drove out to your place. EJ told me where you were."

He drove out all that way?

"I sent you an email," I said.

"I didn't get it until later. For some reason, it didn't come through right away."

"I'm sorry," I said. "The Wi-Fi down here can be kind of iffy."

"Can you get out of there before the storm, Em? Can you fly home? I'm worried about you."

How badly was I screwing things up? "I really need to stay," I said. "I've taken the job of returning two boats to Florida, and if I fly home, it would be on my dime, and then I'd have to just turn around and go right back down again on my own dime. I pretty much have to stay for the duration."

He was looking down at something in his lap. His phone? "Ben...?"

"Sorry." He looked up at me as he put whatever he was working on away, but he didn't explain. It looked like a sheaf of papers. Then he gave me a bit of a half-smile.

I took a breath. "I owe you a big apology, Ben. I came down here without even saying goodbye. That's inexcusable."

Quietness and then. "That's okay. I understand. A job is a job."

"Yeah." I coughed, my voice suddenly hoarse. "A job is a job. It was one of those things that came up quite suddenly. One of the boaters died in a scuba accident, and they needed someone to take their boats back to Florida right away." I didn't need to go into all of the Janice or Audra details now. All of that could wait. Outside Sunny was calling my name and knocking at my door. "Ben?" I put up a finger. "I'll be right back. I got someone at my door here. Don't go anywhere."

"I'm not going anywhere, Em. Not where you're concerned."

Sunny was at my door telling me that they would be boarding up the windows tomorrow morning and could use my help.

"Great," I told Sunny. "You know I'll help with whatever."

"We can use all the help we can get."

"Get Janice to help, too. I'm sure she's able to."

"Already done."

"Just Sunny, the owner," I told Ben when I got back to my computer screen. "We're going to start getting ready for the hurricane. So, yeah, that's what we'll be doing all day. And yesterday—"

"Look," he said. "I've got something I wanted to tell you. I wanted you to know that my wife finally agreed to sign the divorce papers."

"Ben."

He wasn't smiling. "I never thought she would. She sent me an email about it…"

I swallowed. "This must be confusing for you."

"It's harder than I thought it would be. We had this big church wedding. I never thought it would end like this. I wish you were here. I want to talk to you about it in person."

"I'll be home as soon as I can." But I wondered. When would that be? A month? Two months? Who knew how long it would be before the Gulf was calm enough to cross again?

We didn't say anything for a moment and sat there stupidly looking at each other over the wires.

"I tried to get a flight down there to see you," he said finally.

"Really? You were going to come here?"

"As a surprise, yes. But I couldn't get a flight."

"The hurricane," I said.

Our connection faded in and out a bit, and I realized that

he had said an entire sentence that I hadn't heard. "Ben?"

"Em? We're losing each other."

Losing each other. Right.

"Keep in touch," he said.

"We'll probably lose power when the storm hits," I said.

"I'll email tomorrow anyway."

"Good."

"Stay safe. You stay safe."

CHAPTER 10

Stay safe.

It's what people say to each other before a storm, before a long trip, before getting on an airplane. As if you have a choice. As if you can decide not to stay safe, as if you wouldn't do the very best in any circumstance to be safe. So why even say it? If it is so out of our control anyway, why even say it at all? It's like we're tempting fate at the very least. I've come to believe that everything is pretty much random anyway. If there is a God, if there even is a God—and despite my childhood upbringing, I don't know what I believe anymore about that one—He or She isn't too heavily involved in the people of this earth. Otherwise, Jesse, my good and honest husband Jesse, wouldn't have died. No. It's all pretty much random.

My thoughts were going every which way as I lay under the mosquito netting in my room the night before the storm was supposed to hit. We had spent the past day and a half gathering food and boarding up windows and tying down anything that could blow around—beach furniture, tables, chairs, umbrellas. Sunny decided that the safest place for all of us would be in the kitchen of the Tiki Bar. It was big enough, made of cinderblocks and cement, and there was plenty of bottled water there, and food. Lots of food.

Even though I was truly exhausted by it all, I lay there in my hot bed, unable to sleep. There was barely a breeze. The windows in my room were boarded up, along with the windows in Janice's room, along with all the windows in every room in the complex.

Janice hadn't been able to get a flight home, she told me,

but would be leaving just as soon as the storm was over. That's what she told me. I didn't have time to argue.

As I tossed and turned in the hot bed with only the lazy ceiling fan offering any respite, I thought that we could have waited until the morning to do up these rooms. Sunny, however, ever the efficient manager, had wanted to get them up early. "You never know," he said. I suppose he was right. Storms are fickle.

It was dead quiet outside. This happens before a storm. It's as if the animals and insects somehow know it's coming, and they have this sixth sense to flee or hunker down and cover their mouths. Maybe then, the storm wouldn't hear them, wouldn't find them.

I had propped the door open to catch what little breeze there might be, even though this might mean getting a stray chicken or two inside.

Stay safe.

That was it, wasn't it? That was the whole thing, the *real* reason I couldn't be with Ben, could never be with Ben, why I kept running every time we got close. Of course, there was the problem of his marriage. Yes, there was the elephant-in-the-room question of his son. Yes, there were times when I wondered if he still loved his wife. There were times when I still missed Jesse. Still loved him. I probably always would.

Stay safe.

That's the problem with life, isn't it? Nobody can really stay safe. Especially cops. Which brought me around full circle to the entire point. What if I gave my heart to Ben and the same thing happened to him as happened to Jesse? Everyone knows that cops die all the time in the line of duty.

Stay safe.

But will you? Will you, Ben? Can you absolutely guarantee to me, Ben, that you will not go out there and get yourself killed?

No, he could not.

I must've slept because at 7:23 in the morning, I woke

wound up in my sheet and covered in a sheen of sweat.

I pulled the mosquito netting away. The overhead fan was turning. Good. The power was still on.

On my nightstand, my phone and iPad were plugged in. I'd leave them that way until the storm hit. I also have two external battery packs for my devices, plus a little solar power phone charger. I checked to make sure they were charged to their fullest as well. Since you never know what you're getting into on a boat delivery, I'm never without these extra batteries.

I knew at some point during the day, the power would go out. Around here the power goes out at the best of times, and this wasn't going to be one of the best of times.

I cold-showered the nighttime sweat off me, washed my hair, towel dried it and pulled it up and off my head in an elastic. I found a pair of relatively clean shorts and a clean T-shirt, one that I hadn't already sweat in for two days.

The air outside was oppressive and had this funny electric smell to it, like before it rains. Janice's door was shut, and I didn't see her anywhere. Out on the deck of the Tiki Bar, Sunny's wife Delia was sitting on a rattan chair, one of the few not yet brought inside. On the deck beside her, her little girl sat on a blanket and played with a small pile of colorful plastic toys. She had tiny curls and the hugest brown eyes I had ever seen.

I poured myself a coffee from a pot Tina had set out and sat down across from her.

"You must be Delia," I said. "I'm Em Ridge."

"Sunny talks about you."

"Sunny's great. We've known each other a long time."

"That's what he says."

"And this must be Marybelle." I put down a finger for the baby to grasp. She did so.

Delia and I sat and drank coffee and chatted as if nothing was wrong, as if nothing was going to happen later in the day. She told me that Marybelle was nineteen months old and quite a handful. Sunny had brought the two of them here for the day. The way she said it was as if it were simply an outing to the beach.

Eventually, her expression darkened. "Sunny's not so sure about our house. The way it's out on a point and all."

"You'll be safe here. That kitchen is like a fort, all cement blocks. It's the one thing on the island that will live through the apocalypse."

"I hope so." She looked around her at the sky and the ocean. Then she turned back to me. "Do you think it will be a bad one?"

I put both hands around my coffee cup. "I really don't know. Hard to tell."

"Sunny says it doesn't look like it'll be as bad as some we've had."

I could picture Sunny telling her this to ease her mind.

"All we can do is hope."

"And pray."

"Yeah." *Really? You think praying is going to actually help?*

A pink ribbon around the baby's head had fallen off, and Delia picked it up and fingered it in her lap while she talked. "Em, you know that guy who died…I know you're taking his boat back, but you don't think Sunny was involved, do you? In all of that? He's so afraid his business is going to suffer."

I shook my head. "I don't think he'll be sued. I spoke with his widow. I got the feeling she was being pressured to sue by her friends, but that she really didn't want to. I think she's confused by the whole thing. And grieving."

Delia let out a breath and looked past me out toward the dark sea. "I don't know what I'd do if something happened to Sunny."

"Nothing will happen to Sunny."

"He's so worried for his business," she said.

"I know."

Tina called over, asked if we wanted eggs.

"You cooking in this?" I asked.

She looked around her. "In what? It's calm now. Plenty of time."

"Have you and the baby had something to eat?" I asked Delia.

She nodded. "I think Marybelle and I might go down to the beach for a while after I finish my coffee. Be nice to get some air while we can."

"Yeah. Just don't go in the water," I cautioned. "Don't even let her wade in."

She looked out at the calm sea.

"There could be currents," I said. "Even now. I wouldn't trust it."

"I'm worried about my family." She made no move to get up. "My parents over in Nassau. My mother called me yesterday. She wanted me and the baby to come. I decided Sunny needed me here."

Her father wasn't well, she told me, and their house had lots of trees around it. "There's this big, old palm. It should have been cut down a long time ago. But my father keeps putting it off. I'm afraid in a good wind it'll come right down on top of the house."

"I'm sure they'll be okay."

"A couple of my brothers are there."

"Good, they'll watch out for the tree."

"I just wish we could all be together."

"I know."

I have learned in my jaunts down here that family is of supreme importance to Bahamians. I have to compare that to my own family who I hardly even see at all anymore. How did we come to this? In that instant, even with the hurricane brewing out there, I was suddenly and inexplicably envious of her.

Tina brought my eggs over, and I ate while Delia and Marybelle made their way down toward the beach. I glanced up to see Janice sitting out on her chair writing.

A breeze was coming up now, but no rain. Far out on the

horizon, there was darkness.

We spent the morning moving even more furniture to sheds where it would be securely tied. Beach furniture, garbage cans, anything the wind could lift, needed to be tied down. Even though we were doing this, we knew it might not be enough. Sometimes, whatever you do, it's not enough.

I wondered if the deck would be here when the storm was over. Still, we had to try. You always have to try.

By early afternoon, Janice and I found ourselves collecting debris along the beach.

She said, "I'm sort of scared."

"We all are, Janice."

"I mean you see these things on television."

"I know, but Janice, people down here are used to storms. They know how to secure places. Sunny knows what to do. We'll all be together with plenty of food and water."

"Still…"

"The kitchen is cement block construction with good fitting shutters on all the windows."

"Yeah."

"And they're downplaying the storm now. It'll be bad, but it won't be a disaster. That's what they're saying now. Maybe a cat three."

"Good."

At two in the afternoon, we felt the first drops of rain, softly at first. The wind was ever so slightly picking up. In my younger rowdier youth, this is the kind of wind I would head out in a small sailing dinghy, knowing I had maybe an hour before it built to unmanageable levels. Those were the stupid people who died. I used to be like that.

Back in my room, I unplugged my phone and iPad and all my devices. I didn't want a sudden power surge to scorch their insides. Maybe it was time to head over to the kitchen. Before I shut down everything to conserve power, I noticed a couple of new emails.

What? My Uncle Ferd?

I sat down on my bed, my iPad in my lap.

Em,

I heard you were in the Bahamas. I hope you're okay. I'm on another boat now, but it's only temporary. When I'm able to, I'll head to Maine and pick up Wandering Soul. *Meantime, use it all you want. Thanks for taking care of Bear for me. I also plan on heading inland to see Ocean and the baby.*

Ferd

I smiled at this. Ocean was the daughter he had recently discovered, and the baby was his granddaughter. Bear was his cat. I had sailing friends all over the world keeping an eye out for him.

I wrote a quick answer and clicked reply immediately, but I knew he would be long gone from the place where he had sent this email.

I debated whether to email my mother with the news that her errant brother had finally surfaced but decided against it. She had no good words to say about him. Ever. This would only make it worse. Plus, I knew every bad adjective she would use to describe Ferd would be meant for me.

Outside the rain was coming down in earnest. Huge fat drops splatted here and there on the deck of the Tiki Bar where we all stood and watched. Everything was done. All we had to do now was wait. By three fifteen, the seven of us were inside the kitchen of the Tiki Bar, the door closed shut and windows locked and barred. By five the storm was upon us in full force.

Nothing can prepare you for the sound of the wind. It has its own voice, and if you have ever been caught out at sea, you will know what I'm talking about. All other sounds on the planet from the loudest animal shrieks to an active volcano are mere whispers by comparison.

By quarter after six, the power flickered and went out. So that was it. It meant a lot of things, but most noticeably for us, no air conditioning. I knew the heat would become oppressive soon, inside with no breeze, no open windows, no fans. I'd done this before, been huddled up in a small hot room during a blow.

Outside, the wind was growing to be a physical thing, a monster, with tentacles seeking entrance under every window, door and crack in the building. Every once in a while, we heard a bang or a crash, and all of us wondered — what had we forgotten to lash down? Yet we couldn't check. We dared not open the door even a crack. We would stay in this cave like the ark dwellers until all was safe. I could picture the boats out on Hatchett Bay rocking fore and aft on their triple lines. I hoped we'd made everything secure enough.

We had brought a few deck chairs into the kitchen, and Marybelle's playpen was set against the far wall. Despite the loud wind, the baby slept soundly. Delia sat beside her trying to text on her phone. Probably worried about her family in Nassau. From the expression on her face, it didn't look like she was having much luck getting a connection. If the power was out here, the power to the cell tower was probably out as well. You were just wasting good battery power to keep trying.

In one corner, Sunny, Kenny, Janice, and Tina were playing cards by flashlight. I sat against a wall next to Delia flipping through a years' old *Cruising World Magazine*.

I heard several more crashes outside and wondered about the very structure of the deck itself. Would it still be here when the storm finally ended? Were we safe in here? Did we have enough foundation underneath us? We drank bottled water, ate crackers and bread spread with peanut butter and jam while the wind increased.

Around ten at night, we heard a rhythmic banging against the door and a sound like a human voice.

"Sunny!" I said getting up. "Someone's out there. Someone's outside!"

"Nobody could be out there," Sunny said. "Maybe more

palms falling."

"No!" I yelled. "Listen! I hear someone. Someone's there. A voice." I made for the door.

"Don't open it," Sunny called.

"But someone's there! We have to!"

"I hear it, too," Janice said.

"Wait. Kenny. Let's all get that door. All of you. On the count of three. And don't let go."

Janice, Sunny, Kenny, and I stood next to the door. We waited for a slight lull in the wind, and then, two on either side, we pushed the door open with all of our might.

A woman fell forward, stumbling inside. She was drenched, hair plastered on her face, blood running down her cheek. I ran toward the wet figure. She rose up from the floor gasping for air.

"Audra!"

CHAPTER 11

There was a look of terror in her eyes, and she was barely able to speak, shaking, quivering, and completely soaked through. Behind her, she pulled a small airline carry-on piece of luggage, which was battered, torn, wet, and coated with sand.

I grabbed her, pulling her into safety. "Audra!" I said. I helped her to the closest chair, a metal folding one. The suitcase fell to the floor beside her.

Tina grabbed a towel from a hook next to the sink and placed it on her shoulders like a mother, while the rest of the group just stared mouths open. She brushed her wet hair away from her face. How had a person come out in this weather? Where had she even come from?

The cut, we saw, was a scratch on her cheek, and she dabbed at it with the kitchen towel.

"How did you get here?" we all asked at once. "What are you doing here?"

"I drove," she finally managed.

The storm picked up again, the door rattling like an unseen thing.

"You drove?" I asked. "You *drove*?"

"Part way." Her hands were shaking, and despite the warmth of the room, her entire body was shivering. "And then a tree fell on the back of the car, and so I had to get out and walk the rest of the way here."

"You serious?" Tina asked. "You were walking out there in a category four hurricane? In those shoes?"

I looked down at the spike-heeled sandals, still on her feet.

She said, "I tried to keep to places where nothing would blow on me. So I walked, sort of, on the beach. Crawled. Sort of. But I made it. And now I'm here."

"On the beach?" Kenny said. "You were on the beach?"

"Crawled more like."

"That's like the worst place ever," he said. "You're lucky you're alive."

"You could have been swept out to sea," Sunny added.

I'm not a particularly huggy person, but she looked so frail and wet and scared that I put my hand on her shoulder and kept it there.

"I wasn't, though," she said. "I'm here."

"Why did you leave the hotel?" I asked. "I'm sure it had a safe room."

"I had to get here. If something happened, I knew I had to get here. I tried calling." She looked at me. "But we were without power at the hotel. So I made the decision and left. I just walked out. No one saw me. When I left, the power had just gone out, and it wasn't too bad. It really wasn't. I thought I could get here, no problem. Then it just got worse and worse by the minute. I thought I was going to die. But I had to come. I needed to get here. Em…" She looked directly at me. "I needed to find you. I need to tell you something before, before, and if, *if* I was killed in the storm. If I died, I need you to know… There's something you need to know."

I said, "Go on."

"In private."

"Look around you. Not much privacy around here."

In the end, the two of us went into the tiny bathroom and closed the door behind us. The ferocious sound of the wind would give us all the conversational privacy we needed.

"It's about my husband," she told me, breathless as we stood face to face in the small bathroom. I leaned against the mini-sink, and she sat down on the closed toilet lid. "I need you to know something about him."

"Okay."

"You promised you'd ask your cop friend for advice."

"I haven't had a chance yet."

She went on. "When we talked before, I debated whether to tell you this part or not, and then, when I didn't, I thought better of it, and I kept kicking myself because someone needs to know this. Because what if I died in the hurricane and no one knew?" Her voice shook.

I looked at her.

"Remember when I told you my husband was antsy before the trip?"

"Yes. You used the word giddy."

"Giddy." She paused. "Yes. Um. Giddy. Antsy. Worried. Out of his mind with worry. Before the trip when we were packing at home, he kept saying he was going to 'blow the lid off' something. When I would ask what it was, he said he would know for certain once we were down here and sailing. And he never got the chance to blow the lid off anything. I never found out what it was. And then he died."

"'Blow the lid off'…" I thought about those words. "Blow the lid off what?"

"That's what I don't know. That's what has me so worried."

"Did you tell the police what he said?"

"No."

Even though it was ninety-five degrees and counting in the bathroom, she hugged her arms around her as if for warmth. "Plus, something else. That's not all. Earlier, before we even left on the trip, I overheard Marcus talking to my husband. I remember him saying something like, 'Don't you dare tell anyone about that.' I don't think I had ever heard Marcus that angry. I asked Terrance about it, whether there was some sort of argument between Marcus and Wes, and Terrance just looked at me weird for a minute before he said it was nothing. And not to worry about Marcus. It's so weird. Marcus and Wes. Well, the four of them, their wives, too. They have this strange bond. It's like they all hate each other but — and this is the only way I can describe it — like they hate each other but are too afraid to break up with each other. On the trip, it was like, sort of like they were all trying to play the part of happy couples on vacation together, but everyone had been miscast."

I thought about that.

"Marcus," she went on. "Marcus can be a bit of a hothead. I was always slightly afraid of him. But what I've been thinking about a lot and what I wanted to tell you is that I think Wes and Marcus are protecting someone, someone who may have followed us here. And then killed Terrance."

Something crashed against the building. We paused for a moment and looked up at the high boarded window as if that would tell us anything. Finally, I said, "Do you have any idea what your husband might have known?"

"Probably something about the business. His work computer is home, and the first thing I'm going to do when I get home is to check through it. I don't know what I'm looking for, but that's what I think. Maybe something he found out. I have his iPad here, but I can't find anything on it. It's in my suitcase. I hope it's okay. Everything got so drenched when I came here."

Her wet clothes, the cotton dress she wore clung to her, and she picked pieces of it away from her body. She said, "I know I sound crazy, but if you could have seen Terrance, the way he was. The nervous energy he had." She wiped a wet strand of hair from her face. "He knew something. And it got him killed." Her words trailed off. She reached up and wiped her eyes with her fingers. "Michelle and Marcus were on their boat, and Terrance and me were on Wes's boat, the bigger one, with him and Beth."

"Close quarters," I said. "How did that work for you?"

"Strange. The whole thing was strange. I just...I just want justice for his death."

I nodded. I knew how she felt.

CHAPTER 12

By early morning, the storm had pretty much blown itself out. Throughout the night, we all had found places to sleep. Sunny, Delia, and Marybelle claimed the back corner next to the bathroom. Delia had been smart and pre-planned with blankets and even two small blow-up air mattresses. I hadn't thought to bring anything like that with me.

Neither had any of the others. I spread out my jacket and curled up on it in the corner. Near the door, Janice leaned against the wall, bent over her writing. I wondered how long the batteries in her phone would last since she was using it as a flashlight. She probably didn't realize that once the storm was over, it would be several days, if not weeks, before power was restored. Sunny had a generator, sure, but that would be reserved for critical items like food.

Audra had changed out of her wet clothes and had put on another cotton dress, this one was covered in large blue flowers. It looked like the sort of dress you could buy at an open market in Nassau. She sat against the wall near the bathroom, her knees tucked up, her dress covering them. She stared straight ahead, eyes open. She needed to be home, I thought, in the embracing arms of family and friends, instead of grieving here in the middle of a storm in the company of strangers.

The first thing Sunny did in the morning was to open the windows to let in some air. A welcome relief.

The entire earth was lit with a sun so bright that it hurt my eyes. The sea glinted. It was almost as if the planet was apologizing for the storm. "See, I can be nice. I can be pretty. I'm not always like I was last night."

The beach was littered with debris of all shapes, sizes, and colors as if it were flecked with precious stones instead of plastic bits and garbage. Large swells broke onto the shore. The gentle breeze and bright sunshine seemed to mock the uprooted palms. Their scattered branches littered the deck. Part of the deck looked as if a giant hand had scooped down, picked it up, then changing its mind, threw all the boards back down again, letting them scatter where they may.

The winds would also have blown in tub fulls of man o' war jellyfish, whose stings are excruciating. (Been there. Done that. Don't ask.) Portuguese man o' war jellyfish have no natural means of propulsion, thus they rely on tides, winds, and currents. After a storm like this one, they would be strewn all over the beach. I knew that Sunny would be putting the red flag up on the beach to signify that swimming was dangerous. Then with gloves, shovels, and pails, he and Kenny would gather all the jellyfish. I looked with sadness at a favorite shade palm of mine that lay face down on the sand.

One by one, we ventured out onto the deck. The first thing Sunny did after clearing a walkway was to dig out the generator and fire it up. I had lots of reserve battery power for my iPad and phone, but since there was no Wi-Fi anyway, I left everything turned off.

Sunny and Kenny examined the deck and decided it could be repaired using the boards that had blown off. A lot of it hadn't been damaged. Sunny was right. The storm, though bad, was not as bad as it could have been. We dodged the bullet this time.

Gradually, up and down the beach, people emerged from their homes, and like people everywhere after a catastrophe, they hung together in groups, talked, compared notes, pitched in, cleaned up, worked together. It would take some time to get everything back to normal, but that's what people do here.

By evening, a lot of things on the beach and at the Tiki Bar and environs had been put right. I pulled the plywood down from my own windows, and Janice did the same.

It wasn't until late evening that I noticed Audra seemed to be gone. She'd been here in the morning, and then I'd lost track of her.

"Do you know where Audra went?" I asked Tina.

"She said she was going back to the hotel to try to get a plane out."

I thought about that. "How did she get there?"

"She said she had to walk to her rental car. She was worried it was wrecked. She has to take care of all that."

"She walked?" I was again incredulous.

Tina shrugged. "I guess so. I didn't see her leave, so maybe someone from the hotel came for her."

"She's one spunky lady."

"I would say so."

When I got to my room, I saw that an envelope had been pushed under my door.

If you find out anything about Terrance, can you call me? I'm heading home as soon as I can. Thank you all for you did for me last night. I'm glad I got to tell you what I did.

It was from Audra.

I refolded the note and put it into my bag, along with the piece of paper she had handed me earlier with her contact information.

Not until the following day was I able to head out on Sunny's bike to see the boats. It took me that long to unearth his bike from behind the chairs and tables and beach umbrellas we had lined up in the shed.

It was good that I was biking rather than driving because there were numerous places where the debris and tree branches were still piled so high that they covered the road. On the Caribbean side, I noticed a group of sea kayakers out there barreling across the water. The sight made me sad, and I stopped for a while and watched. It was while I stood there that I heard a sound behind me. I turned to see Janice pedaling along.

"Hey!" she called.

"Janice! What are you doing here?"

"Tina said you were coming out to look at the boats. I thought I'd come help."

"Did you get a flight out yet?"

"No service yet. As soon as my phone works, I will."

"Where'd you get the bike?"

"It's Kenny's."

The bike ride over the debris-strewn road was gorgeous as it often is after a storm, and when we got to the bay, the water sparkled.

There were about a dozen boats out there, and boat owners milled about. The two we had secured were fine and bobbed gently on their moorings. I knew the mooring lines would be chafed, but that's why you put on extras when preparing for a storm and, of course, a whole lot of chafing gear.

A few of the boats weren't as lucky. A boat pulled into the anchorage after we did, had obviously not taken down any of its fabric, and shreds of sail and canvas hung off like ghostly fingers. Another boat whose anchor had not held had blown too close to the shore and now lay on its side.

They could have avoided all of that damage if the owner had taken proper precautions. Fortunately, none of these errant boats had come near our two. The live-aboard couple from Britain were out on their boat, putting up sails and securing canvas. I waved to them, and they waved back. He cupped his hands around his mouth and yelled, "You need a dinghy ride to your boats?"

"Sure!" I called back. "Thanks." It would be far better than rowing out there on the iffy, leaky rowboat that was tied to the dock and filled now with water.

We checked both boats, one at a time, and all seemed well. I decided we'd wait until we talked to the owners before we put the canvas and sails back on. I'd have to check if there were any change of plans since the storm.

All I had to do now was stay here on Eleuthera, take one

day at a time, and wait for a weather window. I knew I might be in for a long wait. It could be several weeks before there were no dancing elephants out on the water, as the locals called them. I'd been on many deliveries in my life, however. Waiting was part of the game. An engine breaks down in a remote locale and you might wait weeks for parts. A ripped sail and you might wait a month to get it repaired. Waiting was just part of the nature of the beast.

Finally, when I got back to Maine, maybe with the money I earned on this job, I could make some repairs to my house. I'd build myself that new dock I wanted. Perhaps I'd even dig out my old kayak and have a look at it. And I could show it to Ben. *Ben!*

CHAPTER 13

It was a good ten days before the Gulf Stream settled down enough to begin the sail. And yes, the owners said they would reimburse me for the time I spent on Eleuthera. I suppose there are less beautiful places to be stranded.

When Wi-Fi was restored, there were two short emails from Ben waiting for me. I carried my tablet around with me and Skyped him live pictures of the devastation. I guess the two of us were back to being the way we were. Light and cheery. Maybe it was better this way.

I was surprised that Janice wanted to stay, but she said she had nothing at home right now, and why not stay and help with the boats. She said she was already learning a lot from me. Okay, fine.

During the days, I could forget about Audra and her request. I hadn't mentioned anything to Ben, and it seemed that soon, the accident was forgotten. No more threats of lawsuits. I was merely getting two boats ready and provisioned like any normal delivery.

Janice was a great help and seemed to be a different person now, capable and strong and talkative and eager, the way I remembered her from a year ago. We moved the boats from Hatchett Bay to the Marina, she on *On Our Way* and me on *Sea Chanty*.

And then the day came that I was going to start taking the first boat across. I was all provisioned and ready to go when Janice came to the door of my room behind the Tiki Bar carrying her duffle bag.

"I'm all packed," she told me. "I'm all ready."

"When's your flight?"

"I'm not flying anywhere. I'm coming with you."

I stared at her. "Janice?"

"I can do this," she said. "I can take *On Our Way,* and you can take *Sea Chanty.* I'm already used to her. It's the least I can do. Then you'll be home that much quicker."

She had proved that she could handle *On Our Way* when we'd moved them to and from the anchorage. But could she manage all the way to Florida?

Her hands shook a little as she grabbed a handful of hair and shoved it behind one ear.

"I can do it," she said. "Please let me. I need to do this. I don't want any money. I already said you could have it, but this would be good on my résumé. I can do it."

"I know you can."

I'd be with her. I'd never let her out of my sight.

Okay. We'd go together. And, as she said, I'd be home that much sooner.

Dear Mother,

The hurricane is over, and nothing is the same. It's like looking at a different postcard of the same scene. There used to be this little thatch-roofed shed on the beach where Sunny and Kenny stored stuff. It's demolished and parts of it strewn everywhere. Before the storm came, I remember Kenny looking at it and saying, "Maybe we should take that thing down."

"No," I'd said. "It'll be all right. Don't you think?"

"Hard to say."

In the end, it was gone. I don't know why the destruction of that little shed has affected me so much. Maybe it makes me think of something—I shouldn't latch onto anything too much in this life. Things can be taken away at a moment's notice.

In light of the storm, because of everything, I've made a decision—I'm going to stay. Despite how much I want—need—to get away from here and from everything that reminds me of Terrance's friends, I'm going to stay. I'm going to help Em take the boats across. I owe it to Terrance. I owe it to you and Francine and Marilou. I even owe it to myself.

All this might be because of what Audra told me. She came to see me the day after the hurricane and asked if I was going to go with Em on the boat delivery. I told her no, that I was trying to get the next flight home, but that I was having trouble. Everything seemed to be booked. At the time, I wanted to get off the island as quickly as I could.

She said, "Good! That would be the safest thing. If you value your safety you should head home. Don't spend any time on that boat. No time. Do you hear me? *Not that boat.*"

What did she mean by "not that boat"? Does it have something to do with Terrance? Why would she tell me all that? When I pressed her on it, she turned and walked away. I have not seen her since.

The police report is settled—Terrance's death was an accident. I'm not sure I believe it, but some days I fear my paranoia is getting the better of me. Like all the stuff I collected on the murders. That's got to be insane, right? To keep all those articles, like, I'm going to make some sort of ghoulish scrapbook? Most people would think I was nuts! But if Em is in danger, I need to be here for her. I'm responsible for her being here. I got her into this mess. I can't leave her.

Russell. All of this is about your friend Russell. I never spoke to him. All that happened and I never did get to meet him, talk to him. I saw him by mistake one evening. You continued to be so secretive about him. But I understand that now. I was young, and you wanted to protect me. There would be no inviting the boyfriend for overnight with the daughter in the house. Well, we shared a room, you and me, so that would have been *totally* inappropriate. Ha-ha. Plus, you had told me that everything would be made right in time.

I remember that one time. There were never a lot of people over. I don't remember parties. No, we four—you, me, Francine and Marilou—were mostly enough for each other. I was well looked after. I was never alone. If you were working, Francine or Marilou was there for me. Marilou would make popcorn, and the two of us would watch a movie. Or if it were Francine, she and I would bake something, usually brownies, which were my favorite, or she would bring something home from the restaurant where she cooked. We were a family.

Every once in a while, people would come over, friends from work, a few apartment neighbors. I remember people in and out occasionally. Not a lot.

On the day I saw Russell, I wasn't supposed to be there. I was going to be at my friend Tam's house, but Tam's mother drove me home early because Tam was sick.

You and Russell were sitting on the couch, close together. His arm was along the back of the couch, and you were leaning into him. Both of you were laughing. When you saw me in the doorway, you were instantly alert. You whispered something to him, and you both got up. He turned, looked at me for a scant moment and went into the kitchen. I am trying to remember what he looked like. He wore a Red Sox T-shirt. I don't know why I remember that particular detail. I just do. I barely remember anything else.

I followed you both, waiting for an introduction, but by the time I got there, he was out the door and walking sadly, slowly

91

away, shoulders slouched.

"Who was that?" I asked you.

But you turned and were back in the living room before the question was even out of my mouth.

I wish I could remember more. Was his hair light or dark? Glasses? I think not, but I can't be sure. I can't be sure about much. It was so long ago.

Francine once told me that Russell carried a lot of "baggage." I didn't know what she meant, and I pictured him dragging bunches of old suitcases behind him whipping up dirt and dust as he did so. When I asked Marilou if this is what it meant, she said that was "about right." Francine warned that if you stayed with him, there would certainly be trouble.

And that's exactly how it happened.

Janice

CHAPTER 14

Maybe this would be a good thing – Janice on one boat and me on the other. Being home sooner might be nice – a plus as far as I was concerned. I was missing my house and my animals. And Ben.

Janice seemed nervous, which was understandable, even though I kept assuring her she'd be fine. The weather was looking good, the boats were working well, and we had supplied them with all the safety gear known to humankind.

At one point, I said, "Janice, you can change your mind. You don't have to do this."

To which she replied, "Yes I do. I want to. I need to. For Terrance. For my friend Terrance."

"I understand."

It was time to leave.

I hugged Sunny and Tina and told Sunny to hug his wife and kiss his baby daughter for me. I also asked him to keep me informed about the case. If there were any new developments, I would like to know. He promised. Tina gave us two bags of food. "Conch fritters," she told me. "Just heat them up lightly in your frying pan."

Kenny drove us to the marina in Sonny's recently repaired car, which rumbled and hissed over the uneven pavement, worse now since the hurricane.

It took us a full day to sail to Nassau where we did our final provisioning. Even though we were on separate boats my "no drinking on delivery" rule still held. I thought Janice would take one look at the party scene in Nassau and be gone, but she wasn't. She mostly stayed aboard *On Our Way* and wrote in her journal. When I asked her once if she was keeping a sailing journal of this trip, she shook her head, closed the book quickly, and said, "It's something for my mother."

"Nice," I said.

Before we left, I'd gone over with Janice on how to sail alone. Had we crewed together, we would have taken turns at the helm. This trip would be much like driving all night to a destination. Only on a boat, you can catch little cat naps. And with two boats with auto-helm, we could shadow each other.

I told her how to sail all night solo. You sit out on the deck and set your iPhone for twenty minutes. You're allowed to doze for around twenty minutes because when you're sailing, it takes about twenty minutes for something on the horizon to get to you. Every twenty minutes, you scan the horizon. And scan it well. I told her to keep the radio on and loud. "It's easy to fall asleep," I told her. "So make sure you set your phone timer to wake up."

She said, "I won't sleep at all."

"You say that now, but nighttime can get very hypnotic on a boat. Long about three o'clock, that's the worse time. That's when your body craves sleep."

"I'll be okay."

"I'm just a radio call away."

"I know."

"I'm right with you."

"I know."

We had left Nassau early and made it to the NW Channel Light around suppertime. We crossed the Bahamas Banks and passed just south of the Mackie Shoal light late at night. Even with all the electronics, it is wonderful to see that little group of two white flashes, just twenty feet above the water. Next along the way was that beautiful red "dash dot dot dot" on North Bimini to our starboard. Exiting the banks just south of Turtle Rocks, we locked in the course of about 275 degrees west. The calculations all worked out, and we got a nice push north from the Stream. Port Everglades Inlet, here we come.

Fort Lauderdale in just under thirty hours.

When we got to Florida, Marcus and Wes would be meeting us, putting us up in a hotel room, and driving us to the airport the following morning. And the trip would be over.

Early in the trip, Janice and I talked by radio a few times, but close to the land, there was lots of radio chatter. Out on the ocean, there was less, none actually. She would call me sometimes just to "talk." She was anxious to get home, she told me. She wanted to go up north and visit her Mama. I found the term endearing.

"I'm sure she'll be happy to see you again."

"I hope so. I hope she remembers me."

Odd. But there was so much about Janice that was odd, including her ubiquitous name badges, so I let it go. The closer we got to Fort Lauderdale, the more I detected something else in her voice, a kind of trepidation.

Mom,

It was Uncle Clifford who taught me how to sail, Uncle Clifford with his big grey beard and his big flannel shirts. After I'd been on the farm for a month, I found myself wandering around to the back. I found a shed door open, and I ventured inside. I think I was looking for a place to be alone, a place to hide. Since you died, since you all had died, I'd been flitted from here to there. No one wanted me, a girl with "extreme anger issues," which is a nice way of saying that I was spitting-nails-mad at the world most of the time.

The Cliffords took on kids that nobody else wanted. I'd heard the stories. They would make you toe the line. There would be no getting away with anything at the Cliffords. I didn't find them to be that way.

Instead, I found a boat. And a whole new world.

Way in the back, up against a far wall and near a bunch of old tools and junk, was a sailboat just like the one I'd seen that little boy sailing on so many years ago. Or, at least it looked like the same kind. I moved some of the stuff and boards away to get a better look. I heard a noise. I turned.

Uncle Clifford in the doorway.

I backed away, put my hand to my mouth, sure I was "in for it."

"Janice? It's okay. You're allowed to be in here."

I swallowed.

"It's okay."

I pointed to the boat. "Is that a real boat?"

"Sure is."

"Does it work?"

"Last time I had it out on the water it did."

"So that's a real sailboat? It works for real?"

"Yep. Really works."

"Wow. I can't believe you have a real boat."

"You want to try it, maybe?"

"Do you think I could?"

He told me he'd sailed when he was younger, and if I wanted, we could take the boat out. We could even look into a few sailing lessons. Would I like that?

Yes!

We pulled it out from behind all the piled-up boards. We hosed off the spiders. I scrubbed dust and dirt and got rid of the accumulated mouse droppings. I cleaned it until it shone. It became my after-school project. Mama Clifford helped as well. We patched the rips in the sail, and Uncle Clifford brought home new line from the hardware store.

Three weeks from the day we found it, we were ready to take it out onto the lake.

A one-person boat, Uncle Clifford was only able to instruct me from the shore, but soon, I was off. It felt natural. I felt like I'd been doing this all my life. I know it's hard to believe, Mom, but I had watched that boy and had memorized his moves. I knew what to do. Instinctively, I knew what to do.

Sailing was the start of me not being so angry.

Janice

CHAPTER 15

Fort Lauderdale is a huge city with thousands of sailboats, powerboats, inflatables, ski boats, and cabin cruisers coming and going at all hours of the day and night. In the waning light, we zigzagged our way past dinghies, kids on little powerboats, sailboards, kayaks, stand up paddle boards and some sort of bicycle on a paddle board contraption that I'd never seen before. There was always something new. Janice was following me turn for turn as I maneuvered through the busy harbor.

She seemed nervous but in control. The Port Everglades Inlet was clear. The half knot current was nothing after crossing the Stream. I called the 17th Street Bridge on channel 9, and they answered right away. The bridge opened up to allow high-mast boats through on the hour and half hour. We'd be through shortly. I slowed down and glanced over at Janice. She seemed fine if a little nervous. Boat traffic such as this can make even the most seasoned of captains nervous. She was doing quite well.

Once we got through the bridge, I could see the space on the dock Wes had radioed me about. I headed toward it with Janice close behind. I slowed a bit and radioed her and told her to head in first, and then when she was secure, I'd tie it behind her.

"But I'm behind you."

"You're a bigger boat. It'll give you more space to dock. Go slow past me, and I'll follow you in."

"I can't." Her voice sounded strange and muted like she was speaking to me through water.

"Sure you can. There's plenty of room. Just come ahead.

I'll watch you. I'll guide you in. You can do it. Just go slow."
I flipped my boat into neutral.

"It's not that. I can't…I can't meet them."

"What are you talking about?"

She didn't answer me. A few moments later, she motored up alongside me. I could see the set of her mouth, the stiffness of her shoulders. I called over to her, "Janice?"

She frowned and kept going. Even though I could tell she was nervous, her boat skills were fine.

"You're doing fine, Janice."

"It's not that…"

A couple of dockhands wearing the marina insignia on their white cotton shirts grabbed our lines and tied us up, first Janice and then me. By now, all of my possessions were packed up into my duffel bag, backpack, and computer case. One leftover food box was out in the cockpit. I had left the entire cabin in pristine condition. It's what I always do.

Even though I had never met them, I knew that the two men standing back and watching us had to be Wes and Marcus. Ahead of me, Janice was placing her bags onto the dock. Her back was turned away from the men. The taller of the two was looking at her, an inscrutable expression on his face.

Hefting my bags, I made my way toward the two. "I take it you two are Wes and Marcus? I'm Captain Ridge." I kept my smile bright despite the scowl I saw on the taller one's face. That's what it was, a scowl—not even a frown. I kept my best boat delivery captain's smile on my face and grinned even more broadly.

The scowler was the first to speak, "I'm Marcus Downey."

"Wes Rhorson," said the other.

"Nice to meet you. I'm Captain Em Ridge."

"M, like the letter?" This came from Wes.

"No, Em as in short for Emmeline. Emmeline Ridge."

Wes was shorter, stockier, and wore his fair hair military-style short. He nodded at my explanation.

"Well, we're here," I said. "The boats are in good shape. They survived our little hurricane quite well, thanks to some really good people at the marina on Eleuthera."

"Good," said Wes.

"We followed that on the news," Marcus said.

Janice was already up on the grass verge, her bags around her, ready to leave. She looked anxious. It was plain to me that she had no intention of coming over and talking with them. I knew she was nervous, but before our departure, I had talked to Marcus and explained that Janice would be taking one of the boats. They were fine with that.

I ventured, "I'm sorry about your friend, about Terrance."

They avoided my eyes, and Marcus looked down, shook his head and mumbled something that sounded like "tragedy."

Even though the moon had risen, the Florida heat surrounded us like a steam bath. I wiped my forehead with the back of my hand. This is so unlike the islands where there's always a breeze.

Marcus said, "We've got us all booked in a motel just up the road. In the morning, we'll drive you to the airport to catch flights. Not any flights out this late."

"Fine," I said. "We're ready. Boats are locked up. Can they stay here?"

"Yep. We're all set."

On the way to the motel, Janice and I sat in the back seat of the car. Her hands were tightly fisted in her lap, and her ubiquitous name pin hung limp and vertical from the spaghetti strap of her tank top.

The motel they drove to was probably less than a mile from the marina. We could have walked it, but I was grateful for the drive. I was feeling a kind of weariness that went beyond the physical exhaustion of being up the past thirty hours. I was hungry as well.

They gave us separate rooms, which sort of surprised me. I'm used to people being as stingy and cheap with their money as can be. I've been piled four deep with a boat crew in one room, guys and girls together. It doesn't matter. Even though this was a 1.5-star motel, having my own room with air conditioning would be a luxury.

I raised my eyebrows when I saw that our two rooms were on opposite sides of the second floor of the motel, about as far away from each other as was physically possible. The two of them took rooms side by side between us. Maybe it was just exhaustion with a side order of paranoia, but I was beginning to get the feeling they wanted to keep us apart. As well, there had been no mention of eating. Even though I was tired, I was thinking that a nice Guinness and a plate of wings from that pub just down the road with the outdoor music would go down nicely right about now.

When we got our keys, Wes said, "We'll be ready to pick you up at seven tomorrow morning."

"Fine," I said.

"If you're hungry, there's delivery pizza. Just call down to the desk and add it to our tab."

"Fine."

There was a strange energy between the two of them, something I couldn't define. It was like I was being challenged or threatened. I couldn't tell which. Were they hinting that we shouldn't be leaving our rooms? Delivery pizza? No way.

Once in my room, I texted Janice.

How about we meet in ten minutes for drinks and supper over at that outdoor bar just up from where we docked? I don't know about you, but I'm famished.

Surprisingly, she was right on top of her text.

Sure. Getting this weird vibe from those two. Maybe we should go down the back stairs.

Really? I texted back. *The back stairs?*

Trust me. I know those guys. Well, I sort of know them.

Okay. See you in 10.

I unpacked what little I had, and then took a quick hot shower. It doesn't take me long to shower and change—I guess I'm simply not that fussy — or maybe I'm used to the kind of short lather-up showers you get to take on boats. Dive in the water, wash up, including your hair, in the salt water with dish soap, then back on deck to rinse off with about a coffee cup full of fresh water. Hey, it works.

Half an hour later, we were sitting across from each other at an outside table. A bluesy sort of live band was playing way over on the other side of the deck. I had a Guinness in front of me, and she had a light something-or-other beer. Two orders of BBQ wings were on their way — the hotter, the better with ranch dressing. And some deep-fried dill pickle spears.

After I'd taken a good long sip of my beer, I put it back on the table and said, "Okay Janice, what's up? You haven't said a word to those guys. Talk about weird vibes."

Quietly, she said, "I found something on the boat. It spooked me. Really spooked me."

I leaned forward. "What did you find?"

She looked around her furtively before pulling a newspaper out of her backpack. She flattened it with her hands on the table in front of me. It looked to be the whole second section of the *Boston Globe*. I looked at the date across the top. Eleven years ago. The paper was yellowed and dampish.

"What is this?" I asked.

"I found it." Her voice was triumphant. "On the boat. I pulled open the nav station for maybe a chart, and there it was, right on top. Well, it was sort of stuffed near the back. But it was there."

I put my finger to the edge of it. "So?"

"Turn to page two."

I did so.

She pointed to an article. *Police Not Looking at a Link Between Murders.* I looked at her quizzically.

"Read it," she demanded.

I did so. The police were still looking for a suspect who had killed a woman in the Boston area and whose body was discovered in a quarry by two hikers. Less than a week later, two women she shared an apartment with were found bludgeoned to death in their home. The police were not speculating that the deaths were linked. They also had no suspect but had interviewed several persons of interest. I kept reading. The names of the victims were unfamiliar to me. All of the women were in their early thirties. All worked at the same café in downtown Boston. Staff at the café had been questioned, but no one had yet been charged.

I stared at it, not totally understanding. "Why is this important to you?"

She tapped her finger on the newspaper. "That's my mother. She was the first one killed."

"Your *mother*?" I stared at her. "You were writing a journal for your mother..." Her eyes were too bright, and not for the first time, I wondered if everything was all right with her. "Your mother lives up north, I thought..."

"My foster mother. My real mother was killed. And yes, strange as it seems, I'm writing for her. After she died, they moved me around a lot."

"I'm so sorry, Janice. I had no idea."

"It happened when I was thirteen."

I glanced down at the article. "Which of those pictures is your mother?"

"That one." She pointed to the woman in the middle, a pretty woman with a wide smile, long brown hair. Virginia Strong. She had the same lean features as her daughter. I kept reading. The other two were Francine Hinson and Marilou Robertson.

She shrugged. "Kind of strange, don't you think? This article about my mother on a boat that I'm hired to deliver? It's like they wanted me to find it. Taunting me with it."

I picked up the paper and turned it over.

"Terrance was on the boat," she said. "Him and Audra. Maybe he brought it."

"Why would he?"

"Because of her, Francine…" She pointed to the paper. "That's Terrance's sister."

My eyes went wide, but before I could read any more, she had grabbed the paper, closed it quickly, and shoved it down the inside of her bag. Across the parking lot, Wes and Marcus were moving through the tables and people toward us.

"We've got company," she said.

"I see."

"Can we join you?" Wes asked.

"Sure," I said as if this were just four friends getting together. "We've got wings coming. We can get a few more orders. They're on special tonight."

Marcus said, "We thought you girls would be tucked away for the night by now. Tomorrow is an early morning."

"I can sleep on the plane," I said. "And when I get home."

"Same here," said Janice. She held her satchel close to her chest. Even when our wings arrived, she would not put it down.

We ordered more. More beers. More pickles. Another plate of wings. From a distance, we looked, I am sure, like four friends eating wings and drinking beer at an outdoor bar and listening to some half-decent acoustic blues. But, if you got up close, you would notice the difference. One of us—Janice— was not talking at all, and her motions were stiff, robotic. Marcus talked very little. Most of the conversation was between Wes and me, and we talked insignificant things, sailing, restaurants, beer. But it was almost like we were trying too hard to have a conversation, like we were miscast actors playing our parts.

CHAPTER 16

At ten to seven the following morning, I grabbed a Danish and a Styrofoam cup of bad coffee from the "free breakfast buffet," which was basically a pot of weak coffee and a plate of plastic-wrapped grocery store pastries. I was the first one there.

A few minutes later, Wes and Marcus showed up and poured themselves coffees to go. No sign of Janice. I texted her. Quarter after, and she still wasn't there. I texted again. No answer. This went on. At seven-thirty, I was banging on her door.

"Janice! Wake up! We're all set to go. We've got to go. I've got a flight at ten!"

I tried to peer in and around the curtain in her room but could see nothing.

"We're just going to have to leave without her," Wes said.

"No." I kept texting and calling. Her room phone rang and rang. Her cell phone rang and rang.

"Something's wrong," I said. "Something's wrong. I'm going to see if we can get into her room."

"Let's just go," Marcus said as he nervously shifted from foot to foot. There was something pent-up about him like if you stuck a pin in him, he would explode.

When I explained the situation to the front desk, the skinny blonde behind the desk said, "You mean the girl in the last room?"

I nodded.

She flipped through some paperwork. "She checked out."

"What? When?"

"About an hour ago. Maybe earlier."

"Really?"

"Really."

"Where did she go?"

"Our guests don't normally tell us their travel plans. Oh, wait. I almost forgot. She left something." The woman reached into her desk and pulled out a small white envelope, the kind you would put a greeting card in. "You're Em Ridge?"

"Right."

"She asked me to give you this."

CHAPTER 17

I turned my back on the two of them and tore open the envelope. Inside was a small note that was written on a torn piece of newspaper, perhaps the only paper she could find.

Em,
I had to leave early. Family emergency. I found my own way home.
Janice

That was all. "She's gone," I told them. *Family emergency?*

Wes grabbed the note from my hand. It took him much longer to read than the scant words on the paper required. He handed the note to Marcus.

"What's the matter with that girl?" Marcus said.

"Idiot," Wes added.

I looked from one to the other. Their over-the-top reactions puzzled me.

"Looks like it's just us three, then," Wes said.

"Looks like it," I responded.

"We should get a move on, then."

"Yes." I reached for the note.

"You want it back?" Wes asked.

"Yeah. Thanks." I don't know why, but it suddenly felt very important that I keep it. "It's addressed to me."

Reluctantly—too reluctantly, I thought—and with an enormous furrowing of brow, Marcus made a show of handing the note to me. Along with the note, I saw that he was pressing something else into my hand. I looked down at it. His business card. I looked up at him, surprised. In a low voice, he said, "In case you ever need to talk." I looked over at Wes who was loading his duffle into the trunk of the rental car. I was quite sure he hadn't heard this exchange. I also got the impression that he didn't want Wes to hear this exchange. I had no idea what was going on. I stuffed the card deep into my pack and got into the back seat.

The drive to the airport was quick and uneventful—not a lot of traffic, which was good. I was tired, anxious to be home. Did Janice really have a family emergency? Or had something else—worse—happened to her? I thought about Terrance. I thought about the connection between his sister and Janice's mother.

Two minutes into the trip, I leaned forward in my seat, took a breath and said, "I talked with Audra. She seems to think her husband was murdered."

Even though he was the one driving, Wes turned slightly in his seat to face me. "When the hell did you talk to Audra?"

"On the island," I answered. "She stayed. She was with us during the hurricane."

"Don't believe anything she says," Wes said.

"What do you mean?"

"She's crazy," Marcus said.

"Audra thinks Terrance was killed by a client. From your business. Do you think that might be the case? And that you may be all targeted?"

Marcus shook his head. "If someone was unhappy with our work, we would have been aware, not Terrance so much."

"He's not been with us long, and he mostly worked from home as it was," Wes added.

About a mile from the airport he looked at me through the rear-view mirror and said, "What were you two girls talking about so intently last night?"

"What do you mean?"

"When we came upon you in the bar, you two were in deep conversation. It looked serious. Like you were looking at something."

"We were."

"You were looking at a newspaper? We saw you put it away."

"Yes, a newspaper." I suddenly didn't want them to know. "Janice wants to buy a boat. She was showing me an ad in the paper." I wondered if they could tell this was a spur of the moment story.

"That makes sense, I guess," Marcus said.

"Yep. We've sailed together before. Before this, I mean. That's why she called me in the first place."

"What kind of a boat does she want?" Wes asked.

"Something in the small range. Maybe under twenty feet. She wanted my take on an ad she saw."

"What was the ad for?"

"Boat. Smaller sized sailboat." Why did I get the idea I was being grilled?

"You don't remember the kind of sailboat it was?"

I sighed theatrically. "Okay, it was a West Wight Potter."

"And what did you say?"

"That it's a great little boat." What was going on here? "You guys came over, and she put the paper away, and that was that."

"That was all?" Marcus asked.

"Of course. Why all the questions?"

"We're just interested," he said.

Marcus turned the radio to a classic rock station.

"Just don't," I heard Marcus say. "Just don't."

"What? You don't like the music?"

I watched between the two of them.

"Not that," he said. "You know what I'm talking about."

The scant conversation which passed between them seemed strained and awkward.

They drove me to my gate and stopped. There remained one thing, however. At least for me. They hadn't paid me. Before I got out, I said, "I understood from Janice that you would be paying me directly? Will you be sending me a check, or do you have one now?" I sure could use that money now, I wanted to add.

The two looked at each other for a few minutes. Wes said, "If you made any arrangement about money, that would have been between Janice and you."

I looked from one to the other.

"We gave Janice the money last night," Wes said.

"Cash. In an envelope," Marcus added.

My world seemed to turn on a hinge. "Seriously? You paid her? You gave her money in an envelope? Why didn't you give that to me?"

"She was the one we originally hired," Marcus said.

"If she made any arrangements with you, that was between you two."

I slammed the car door, furious. It wasn't their fault. Not really.

As soon as I was through security, I called Janice's cell. No longer in service. Why was I not surprised?

CHAPTER 18

So, she stiffed me. Janice stiffed me. After all I did for her, after all this time, and she turns around and rips me off. I was angry as I sat at the crowded gate waiting for my flight to be called. How long had she been planning this con? And why me? Had I done something to her the last time we were together on the delivery of my uncle's boat to set this in motion? Is that when she decided to enact her revenge? But why? As much as I thought and racked my brain, I could not think of why she would do this, take me down this garden path and then drop me off the cliff at the end.

I tried her email again. Almost immediately, it bounced back. I sent her another text. Undeliverable. I checked her Facebook page. She had taken it down? What the hell? What the hell, Janice?

What was that newspaper article about? Was her mother really murdered? Was that all a lie, too? I sighed. At last, I was boarding the plane—the ticket I'd bought and paid for on my nearly maxed-out credit card.

Things didn't improve once I was seated on the plane. I had a middle seat between a big guy in the aisle and a skinny, nervous woman who kept crossing and uncrossing her legs and pushing the window shade up and down while she tried to find the best place for her knobby knees.

I shut my eyes, triumphantly claiming the left armrest as my own. Fight me for it, buddy. I'm in the middle seat, and I'm in no mood.

I was so worked up. I almost missed the flight attendant coming by with drinks. I asked for a ginger ale. I really wanted a beer, but I don't have any money, remember?

There's not a lot of cash in boat captaining if you must know. I tend to rely on odd jobs, moving random boats from Point A to Point B for example, or cleaning boats. I do a lot of cleaning and scrubbing barnacles and general scum off the bottoms of boats. I also get to scrub out a lot of heads and holding tanks. Lucky me. Sometimes I think about the other captain friends I have, some who have cushy jobs on private multi-million-dollar yachts with their fancy ascot-wearing billionaire owners. So far, that little job opportunity hadn't manifested itself to me. Too hard, I slammed my ginger ale cup down on the tray table in front of me. Drops spilled on the table. I mopped them up with the postage-stamp sized napkin.

"Bad day?" It was the guy beside me.

"You might say that."

"Family?"

I wanted to say none of your friggin' business, but instead, I said, "Work. Stupid job."

He nodded. "Yeah. I get you. Bad economy."

"Yeah." I put my earbuds in, effectively putting an end to further conversation. I was still too mad, too upset, and I didn't want to add "sobbing uncontrollably in front of complete strangers" to my list of humiliations.

I didn't call anyone when we finally touched down in Portland. I simply dragged my bags with me and made my way to long-term parking. After I paid the ransom to get my car, hoping my Visa wasn't overextended into the "you-stupid-shit-you-can't-charge-any-more-to-this-account" range, I headed for home. At least I had that. At least I had a roof over my head. If I didn't outright own my little piece of real estate at the end of Chalk Spit Island — left to me by my late husband and given to him by his family who didn't want it — I'd be living under a bridge somewhere.

Before I reached my island, I checked the tides on my cell and was gratified that it was low tide. I could drive the tidal road home instead of having to call Geoff who ran an ad hoc ferry for the locals. I live at the very end of a gorgeous, windswept and wild island near Portland, Maine. It's a tidal island, and at low tide, there's a fairly passable road. A ferry used to run until the government cancelled it during a flurry of cost-saving measures. Thirty years ago, my little island was a thriving fishing community, with stores and shops, even. Those were the days when the ferry ran all the time. Now, there are a lot of tumbledown shacks only vaguely reminiscent of earlier more prosperous times. I can name all of the people who live on the island full time.

The tidal road was better maintained then, too. I've lived here for seven years, but already, I can see the havoc that climate change is wreaking. A good full moon tide and the road might be passable for less than twenty minutes.

I wondered how long it would be before the waters of the Atlantic crept into my little house. Would it happen little by little or all at once? Sometimes I dream that water is seeping its fingers right under the doors into my bedroom at night. I can see the day when this little once-thriving island will end up being a destination for eco-adventure campers and sea kayakers only.

But now, I wanted to be home. All I wanted was to be home. When I got there, I'd go over to EJ's with the pretext of picking up my animals, but really, I wanted to talk. He would make me a cup of tea, and we'd sit in his little kitchen, and I'd rant all about my trip. He was just about the only person I wanted to see this afternoon. He would listen. That's something about EJ. He always listens. He is an elderly man of indeterminate age who has lived in his little house on the island forever. He knew my husband's family from way back.

Late afternoon and it was gloomy and windy on the tail end of my drive home. There are stories about this whole island being haunted and cursed. Next to me, the sea roiled. I could even feel my car shudder a little in the wind. A freakish fear crept into my thinking, and it felt less about what I might encounter on the road and more about dead scuba divers and bludgeoned young women.

EJ invited me in for tea, as I knew he would. I gratefully accepted. My animals seemed pleased to see me. We sat on metal chairs at the plastic covered table in his old linoleum kitchen, and he listened to my rant, pursing his lips every so often at my telling and re-telling of it. I told him about the diving accident and Sunny's concern about Janice and how she had this whole "scared to death" act going so that she could get me down there to do her work for her. And then keep the money.

EJ said, "Maybe she still intends to pay you."

"Oh. Yeah. Right. That's why she disconnects her cell phone and entirely removes her online presence."

"She must really be afraid of them," EJ said.

I paused for a moment before I said, "Or on to her next con job with her next new name by now. EJ, you are so trusting. That's what I like about you. You always believe the best in people."

"Well," he folded his weathered hands on the table, "I wouldn't give up on her. Oh, wait..." He got up and, from his fridge, produced a plate of meat slices and some sugar cookies. "From my niece. Take them with you. I'm sure you could use some nourishment. Plane food isn't the best."

"And I didn't even get any plane food. No money. All I got was half a glass of ginger ale."

"Didn't they give you a meal on the plane in those cute little boxes?"

"EJ, how long has it been since you flew anywhere?"

He shrugged. I helped myself to cookies and some of the meat slices. I was hungry. I was ravenous.

EJ never eats things like bread or cookies. Therefore, I'm often the happy recipient of all of the sugar carbs his family brings him. EJ has very odd eating habits. He only eats meat and potatoes. He shuns sugar in all forms, hence these cookies. But he also doesn't even eat fruit. He might down a few veggies, like things you can cook in a pot roast, carrots and potatoes, just so long as they all taste like meat. So when his relatives come and visit, they always leave food for him, hoping he'll expand his diet. He never does.

"What've you been cooking?" I asked him. "Smells good in here."

A deep-fried whole chicken, he told me.

"You should open a restaurant on the island here, EJ."

"Right. That's all I need." And he laughed. "People think I'm too much of an old coot as it is, living way out here. People think I'm out trapping raccoons to roast."

I laughed.

"Someone asked me that once. Do I trap animals? As if I even own traps."

We chatted a bit more. This time, I let him talk. He gave me all the neighborhood gossip. Dot had been by herself for the past number of weeks as Isabelle was off getting her knee replaced and was still away, recuperating on the mainland with another of their sisters.

Little Liam — EJ always called Jeff and Valerie's son Little Liam, even though the fifteen-year-old was as tall as me now — was away at science camp, and the summer renters in the house next to mine seemed like "nice people."

He was in the middle of telling me about Jeff's new dinghy when my cell phone dinged. I looked down. A text from Audra. *Audra?*

"Trouble?" he asked.

I looked down at it: *I've looked all through Terrance's computer. I don't know what I should be looking for. Did you get to talk to your police friend yet?*

I turned my phone over. "Nothing I can't get to later." I put my phone away and picked up a third cookie. And a fourth, which got EJ on his feet and doling out pieces of chicken from his fridge for me to take home.

Which I finally did. At home, I unpacked. All my wet and soggy sailing clothes got piled up next to my washing machine. I emailed Skip and Sue. They were my friends from

Florida who had introduced me to Janice in the first place. Maybe they would know where she was. Maybe she'd even conned them.

I texted Audra. *Sorry. Audra, I just got home.*

She must have been right there because she wrote: *I'm really scared. I don't know what to do.*

I wrote *I'm sorry. I really don't know what to say. Hey, do you have any other phone numbers or emails for Janice? I'm having trouble getting a hold of her.*

She gave me the numbers I already had, and I sighed.

It was after ten before I finally got everything unpacked and my food put away, the dog walked and the cat fed. But not before I glanced out into my bay.

I checked the marine weather on my phone. Force of habit, I guess. Even when I've got no trips planned, I'm there at the marine weather app, checking daily.

Strong winds were headed up the coast of Maine. The Eleuthera hurricane wasn't finished with me yet.

CHAPTER 19

At night, there was the wind. It wrapped its tentacles around my little house, underneath me and on top of me, held me on both sides, choking me, making it hard to breathe. It was as if the wind would pick me up whole and lay me down in the middle of the cold sea. I shuddered and curled myself into a ball under my blankets. I could not get warm.

I awoke sometime later to my dog whimpering and pawing at my face. I got up and let him out briefly. He wouldn't go far. He would run out, do his business, and be back inside before I even turned around. I went and stood beside my big picture window. I heard the wind high in the pines and on the sea. Through the trees, I caught a glimpse of my uncle's boat rocking up and down on her mooring.

I didn't feel like running after an errant sailboat in the middle of the night, but if it had to be done, it had to be done. I'd done it before. I stepped into my boots, wrapped a jacket around me, grabbed a super-duper flashlight, and stepped outside in the wind and rain. Rusty was already whining by the door, and I let him in. It wasn't until I was close to the water that I was able to glimpse the boat still secure on her mooring. Everything was fine. I didn't need to be out here.

Good. I went back inside and fell back into a fitful sleep.

In the morning, the wind was still strong, but somehow, in the full light of day, it didn't seem quite so bad. I took my coffee out onto my porch and stood there for a while. Tree branches lay across what I like to call my front lawn, which is really just a sloped area that leads down to the water. Some of the stuff that I keep stored underneath my house had blown loose. I saw boards and debris and buckets. The rain had ended, but the ground was wet. I checked my roof and found all intact. I headed down toward the water across the mushy ground, stepping over tree branches. A couple of small pines had been blown down. I'd get to them when things dried out a bit. The work here never ends. *Wandering Soul* looked okay out there, and my own boat, *Wanderer,* tied up against Jeff and Valerie's strong, wide dock was okay, too. What I really should have done before I went to bed was to take *Wanderer* out to my second mooring. In strong winds, boats fare better out on moorings than they do bashing up and down the sides of docks.

I spent the windy day inside, doing laundry, cleaning up my little place, checking my phone at intervals, and listening to music. Thankfully, we still had power and Wi-Fi. I got out a garbage bag and got rid of all of the composting veggies and fruit in my fridge. I had not expected to be gone so long. I hate wasting food, but what do you do?

As soon as it wasn't crack of dawn morning, I called Ben. He needed to know I was back. There were a whole lot of things I needed to tell him, all of the Janice and Audra crap notwithstanding.

"Why didn't you call me?" he asked when I told him where I was and what had transpired. "I would have picked you up from the airport."

"My car was already there."

"Well, I could've taken you to the airport, too, you know?"

"I know."

"How was your trip?"

"Oh, it was…well, not the best…But, whatever. I'm home now. And…"

"Em…" he interrupted. "Can I see you? Can we get together today? Can you come to town?"

"Why don't you come here?" I suggested. "EJ gave me lots of food. He even cooked a chicken. Plus, I have beer."

"Beer. How can I refuse beer?"

While we talked, I checked the tides on my phone. "The

tide is good in about an hour if you can make it."

"I'll make it."

An hour and a half, I thought as I hung up. An hour and a half to get this place and me presentable. I'm lucky. The floor of my house is old hardwood—stained, dented, and shiny from so many years of living. All it requires is a quick sweep and it's done. Plus, I needed to quickly get my yard in shape. I have this big crawl space under my house, and this is where I store junk—2 by 4s that might come in handy someday, grunge encrusted mooring balls, and dozens of lobster floats that have come to shore, and for whom I can't find the owners. The unwritten rule is that you're never supposed to touch a lobster float in the water, but if it comes ashore on the high tide and sits on my property for months on end? Well, that's another matter. Most of these were so old that all identifying information had long washed clean, anyway. A lot of this stuff had blown out onto my lawn. I'd get it cleaned up before Ben arrived.

My Jesse-built kayak was under there, too. I looked over at Rusty, who was curled up on his well-worn blanket by the fireplace, and I let my thoughts go back to my husband. Rusty was Jesse's dog and always went with him on the kayak, sitting proudly up in the front while Jesse paddled.

Two hours later, Ben called. He wasn't going to make it. When he got to the tidal road, there were signs up that it was closed. High winds were forcing water across the road, even at low tide. He'd called Geoff, who told him he couldn't run the ferry. Not with these winds and high water.

"Okay, then. Don't chance it." I could barely fathom how let down I felt at the thought of not seeing him. Water across the road? This was happening more and more frequently.

"Maybe tomorrow then, Em?" His voice crackled. "I'm losing you on this cell phone."

"Talk to you tomorrow."

"Em…Eh…Em… G…bye." Even cell phone signals were sometimes precarious out here.

It rained all afternoon, hard rain, and I groused around my house.

Late evening, Ben called again. "Em?"

"Hey."

"I just got a call from this person you know, Janice. Well, a message, actually. She left a message."

"What!" I was instantly aware.

"She wants to see me tomorrow. Eleven thirty at the rest area out on 95. That's what the message said."

"I'm coming, too."

"That's why I'm calling."

"I'll be there. If I have to get in my neighbor's dinghy and motor all the way in through rough water, I will be there."

———◦○◦○◦——

To you, my sweet mother,

I've been driving. All day, I've been on the highway. It feels like I've never been doing anything else in my life but this. My body, my mind—so weary. I am off the road now. I have pulled into a rest area. Maybe I'll get a wink of sleep before I meet with that police officer tomorrow. I can't afford a motel, or I would be going there instead of here. Well, yes, I do have that envelope of cash that Wes and Marcus gave to me, but I can't use that, of course.

Wes handed it to me after our wings that night in Florida. I could have gone over to Em's room right then to give it to her, but I know she would have seen the look on my face, that I was planning to leave, and she would have made me talk. I couldn't risk that. I can't put her life in danger, too.

I hope the police officer shows up. I only left the one message. Couldn't risk sending more. I swear if I get there and he's not there, I WILL keep the money and run. If I get there and a million police cars are waiting for me, I won't even stop. I'll just drive on. No one will recognize this car. No one will know it's me.

I feel lost without Terrance in all of this. How am I to carry on with the investigation? Even though Terrance and I never met in person, I feel like I've lost a great part of myself. He was a rock in my storm.

I want to write about how Terrance and I met. I need for you to know this, Mother. I don't think you ever met Francine's brother. Did you?

Four years after you died, Terrance emailed me. Because I was so young—seventeen is so young—I really didn't know the family members of the victims. I knew that Marilou had a couple of sisters and that Francine had a brother. Those aren't the things you pay attention to when you're thirteen and three of the dearest people in your life are gone.

I almost missed his first email, but with a subject line like "Your Mother," I fetched it out of my spam folder and opened it up. He wrote that he was Francine's brother and that he had devoted his life to finding her killer and bringing that person to justice. He had spent the years since she died collecting evidence and news articles, emails—anything he could get his hands on. He knew who my mother was and was asking me if I had more information.

I didn't answer right away. I'd been on my own (and living in foster homes is sort of like being on your own) long enough to be wary of anyone who emails me. So I deleted it. He kept writing. "I'm sorry if I scared you. I'm really who I say I am."

With the help of an online geek friend from school, I checked him out. He seemed legit. At least his ISP wasn't from some weird Russian country or something. And if he was spamming me for money? Well, good luck with that one, fella. I finally wrote back, tentatively at first. We developed a kind of online friendship. Gradually, I began to trust him. I know, I know—he could have been anyone! And didn't I know that online predators appear all nice with scrubbed ISPs and everything? But you have to understand me. I don't trust a lot of people. I can smell a liar a mile away. Some might say I was lucky, and maybe I was.

He was the first to mention Russell to me and how he had disappeared right after the investigation.

He wrote: *No one disappears. It's impossible to just disappear.*

He said the police were confident that your murder and the murders of your two friends were not related. That's what I believed at first, too. But not Terrance. He connected them right away. The crimes and murders bore no resemblance to each other. That's what the police said. You were killed when someone smashed something hard against your head. Your body was moved after that. Marilou and Francine were killed in their apartment. You would not believe how hard it is for me to write these things down, to actually get them down as words on paper. You. Murdered. Francine and Marilou. Murdered. Even after all this time, it doesn't seem possible.

There was no sexual assault in either crime. For some reason, that he never fully said, he thought that was significant. The second was the timing of it. Terrance felt it was just a bit too coincidental, all three friends dying within weeks of each other.

We kept corresponding. Whenever there was new information, he sent a copy on to me. I printed everything out, all that he sent. Everything. He would send me a link, and I would go there and print it, sometimes without even reading it all the way through.

He once contacted a TV station about doing a documentary on the crime. He had found a reporter who was interested in taking this on. I wasn't so sure I wanted to be involved. I'm a private person. I've had to be, plus I didn't want some television crew trampling all over my memories and possibly destroying the few photos I have of you. Because I only have a few. I admit that I was relieved when nothing came of this documentary.

Every three or four months, I'd get an email from him wanting to know how I was doing and had I heard anything? I told him I was sailing and had decided to go for my captain's license. He said that was a good idea. We used to chat about a lot of things. He became a friend.

About two years ago, he said he had a new and promising lead. When I asked him what, he wouldn't tell me but said he would keep me informed if anything came of it. He was keeping it pretty close to the chest for the time being. That's what he said.

I didn't hear from him for a year. I thought maybe something had happened to him, so I emailed on his birthday, and he apologized for taking so long to get back to me. He said he was closer; he was definitely closer.

He wrote: *Something's going to break. Something's going to break wide open!*

A couple of months ago, he emailed that he had some breakthrough information about who killed his sister and her partner and my mother, but he had to be absolutely sure before he went to the police. Absolutely sure, he told me. Rock solid sure. He wasn't quite sure yet. But soon. Soon.

And then, out of the blue a month ago, I get this call from Audra. I couldn't believe that after him being so close to the truth, he goes and gets killed in some stupid scuba accident on vacation!

Audra said they needed someone to deliver the boats and

that she'd found my name in Terrance's address book and would I do it?

Really? Terrance mentioned me?

I said yes. Of course, I said yes. Terrance had given me so much information and help.

After that is when I panicked.

Janice

CHAPTER 20

Half an hour later, I was pacing up and down the hallway at the police station waiting for Ben. Earlier, I had called Geoff and begged him to take me across. Emergency, I told him, and so despite the dangerously high water and the current rushing through the channel like gangbusters, the ferry was waiting for me. I was nervous about seeing Janice—how should I approach her about my money? Demand it? But as I drove over here, I also realized that I was more anxious about being with Ben.

"Hey, Em," he said to me as I got out of my car at the police station.

"Hey yourself," I retorted. "You got your hair cut." Call it nervousness, but I have no idea why that popped out of my mouth.

"Got 'em all cut." That old saw. He opened the patrol car door and I slid into the passenger seat.

"Did you talk to Janice again?" I asked as we pulled into the line of traffic.

"I tried. It was just that one message. The number wasn't working."

"Yeah, same here. I tried, too. She owes me a pack of money." I spent the next few moments telling him about that.

"Did I ever meet her?" he asked me. "I know she was on the boat you brought up. I can't remember."

"I don't think so. I think she was gone before you and Joan arrived."

While Janice had been with me when I delivered my uncle's boat north, she got off in the Chesapeake, and then Ben and my friend Joan joined me for the rest of the trip home to Maine.

On the way to the rest stop, I told Ben all about the hurricane, my trip, Janice, and her news article and Audra. I kept glancing at his short, short hair. He looked so obviously like a cop today that I smiled in spite of myself. His clean-shaven face, his neatly pressed shirt—the guys I mostly hang with are sailor types who end up going months between haircuts, have beards, chapped red faces, rough tans, and muscled shoulders. The guys I hang with usually skirt the rough edges of the law. How could it be that I was falling for a cop?

"Sounds like you were right in the thick of it," he said.

"Yeah. Not by my own choice."

About a mile from the rest area Ben looked over at me, "After we meet with Janice, you want to get coffee somewhere? You and me?"

"That would be nice."

This wasn't one of those rest areas replete with food courts, coffee, shelves of flavored bottled waters, Wi-Fi, maps, and hotel guides. All this place had was a wooden building with restrooms and a few picnic tables. There was a space under the trees where people could take their dogs, and next to that was a watery area—either a legitimate pond or the overflow from the rain. Two ducks swam around on it.

We didn't see Janice in any of the cars. I got out and went inside and called her name in the ladies' room. An elderly woman was washing her hands. I asked her if she'd seen a small, thin, blonde woman. "Her name is Janice, and you can't miss her. She would probably be wearing a name tag."

The woman shook her head and left.

Outside, Ben and I sat at a picnic table watching our phones. Time was edging on. Already, she was twenty minutes late.

I asked Ben, "Do you have her original message on your phone? I think I could tell if it came from her. Her voice, I mean."

He shook his head. "It was left on the police station phone."

I nodded. Of course. She wouldn't have had his private cell phone number.

Five minutes later, a white car with a smashed front bumper arrived. It was Janice. I could see her worried face in the windshield. She parked beside Ben's car and got out. From the back seat, she pulled out a shopping bag. Her eyes widened when she saw me.

"You came," she said.

"Did you think I wouldn't?" She reached into her bag, and handed me a thick envelope. "I was going to give this to Ben to give to you, but since you're here…" I took it. "Payment. I didn't mean to run off with it, but I was afraid that if I left it at the front desk, it wouldn't get to you. That someone might take it. I didn't want to chance that."

"Thank you," I said, shoving the envelope deep in my shoulder bag.

Her pale hair pulled back tightly into a ponytail. Her too-big T-shirt hung on her bony shoulders. She looked tired. But that ubiquitous name tag brooch was pinned to her shirt.

We three sat at one of the picnic tables, she on one side, and Ben and me on the other. Janice reached into her bag and pulled out two boxes. They were the kind of rectangular boxes that reams of paper sometimes come in.

She said to me, "Did you tell Ben what I found on the boat?"

I nodded.

"I've been collecting news articles about my mother for a long time. And here is all of it. I made photocopies of everything I had. I kept the originals. Everything is in order. Two-sided to get everything to fit in the boxes. I was mostly up all night doing this."

A dry leaf blew across the table and landed at a space right in front of her.

She went on. "It's stuff about the murder of my mother and

her friends. I printed off links from the web, whatever I could find. Some police reports."

Ben took the lid off one of the boxes.

"I kept everything," she said. "I bought every paper that had anything about it, and I still look on the web to see if there's any new information. We even had a Facebook page made up, but we took it down. I took it down."

"We?" Ben looked up at her.

"Terrance and me. I took it down after Terrance died."

"Terrance?" I asked. "You and Terrance did this?"

She nodded. "We worked together." She pointed at a picture of one of the roommates who'd been shot. "That's Terrance's sister, Francine. She was like an aunt to me. Or even kind of a second mother. Both of them. I had two 'second' mothers and one 'first' mother."

"And you kept all of these," Ben said.

"Terrance is…was…just as interested in all of this as I am. A lot of these are duplicates of what he had. The Facebook page was his idea. Terrance was getting close to the truth. He told me that. And then…"

Ben put down the piece of paper and looked across at her.

"I didn't agree with him," she was saying. "Not one hundred percent. But he thought the murderer was my mother's boyfriend, Russell. After they were all killed. Russell disappeared. It's all in there. I even printed off some of the Facebook posts before I took down the site. Some of the comments."

"So, all the Facebook page stuff is in here?" He tapped his finger on the pile of papers.

She said yes.

"Did the police find this Russell person?" I asked.

She shook her head. "They talked to him after my mom died. He had an alibi. He was at work when my mom was killed. Francine and Marilou thought it was Russell. They were sure of it, but I just don't know. My mom was so happy when she was with him."

Ben leaned toward her and asked gently, "Did Russell actually disappear? What happened to him, do you know?"

She shrugged. "All I know is that the police questioned him, and then let him go. And then, after Francine and Marilou died, they questioned him and again let him go. And then after that, he was just gone. He just moved away, I guess."

"And no one's been able to find him?" I asked.

"Not that I know of."

Ben said quietly, "I'll take down his information. This might be worth a second look."

"And now Terrance!"

Even more quietly, Ben said, "Why do you think Terrance was a target?" I've been with Ben when he's questioning people, and I'm always amazed at his gentleness. It's as if his voice moves down a register with every question so that those he's questioning have to lean in to hear. If their voices get louder, his gets softer. I've seen him do this more than once.

"Because of the newspaper I found on the boat!" she said. "I'm trying to figure it out. I've been trying to figure it out all these years, and then I get a call that Terrance is dead, and they want me to take these boats back to Florida. I thought it was fate. And then, when I got there, to the Bahamas, something clicked. It was like this weird déjà vu from a nightmare when I saw the four of them. I can't explain it. Whoever killed Terrance—what if—maybe after all this time, they're killing off anyone related to my mother and her friends. I saw them and just started freaking out." She turned to me. "That's when I called you. It was like everything started coming back to me."

Ben said, "The newspaper you found on the boat, where did you find it?"

"In the nav table. Right on top. Like they wanted me to see it. Like they put it there specifically for me to see it."

This wasn't exactly what she had told me, but I didn't say anything.

"The police always told me that the crimes weren't related. That my mother was killed for whatever reason. And then Francine and Marilou were killed in some sort of hate crime, not related to my mother's death. But Terrance reached out to me. He contacted me. He doesn't believe that theory for a second."

In his quiet way, Ben asked her more questions. I learned about her life. I learned what happened to her after her mother died. I learned how she met my friends Skip and Sue in Florida and how she ended up staying with them for a while. I wasn't quite sure why Ben wanted to know all of this, but I found it interesting.

I asked, "Where did you go after you left Wes and Marcus in Florida?"

"I took the bus and first went up to Skip and Sue's. I didn't tell them what was going on. The fewer people who know, the better. That's their car. Or one of their cars. They loaned it to me." She pointed at it. "Right now, I'm staying in Boston."

"And you drove all the way up here?"

She nodded.

"From Florida?"

"Yes."

"Where are you staying?" Ben asked.

She shook her head. "I can't tell you that. A motel. That's all I can say. It's not safe."

"Janice," Ben said, "we can keep you safe."

"No! No."

"I can't force you to, Janice. But if you came with us, we could keep you safe."

"No! You don't understand!"

At that moment, a small car pulled in right next to our two cars. Janice glanced at it briefly, and a look of horror crossed her face. "I have to get out of here." Her hands shook as she fumbled for her keys. "Keep those articles. I have the originals. I'm afraid of being followed. Look through them. Terrance said he was close to the truth, and I think it's all in there. Somewhere, somewhere it's there. Maybe you can find it."

Ben said, "Janice. Come with us!"

"No!"

"What is your number then?" Ben asked. "How can we contact you if we find something?"

"I'll call you. I'm heading north."

"Wait!" But she was already making her fast way to the car.

We watched her go.

CHAPTER 21

"If I could've kept her on any pretence I would have," Ben said. "You just can't force people."

"I guess not."

We were quiet as we went through the papers in the box page by page. I was astounded at all the photocopying she had done. She must've been up all night. Smaller articles were grouped on one page and photocopied with larger ones, and all in a kind of chronological order. To save space, she had used both sides and small margins. There were news articles from numerous papers, printouts from the web, copies of emails, police reports, and items from that famous Facebook page.

The very first article in the massive pile was the one that was on the boat, the initial report of a woman's body found by two hikers. I studied the picture of Janice's mother. The resemblance to Janice was stunning — the same feather blonde hair skimming the shoulders, the same hint of a smile, the same large eyes which always gave Janice a "deer in the headlights" look. I wondered idly if she too wore a name tag, Virginia Strong.

The police had no one in custody and reading between the lines, no leads.

Three weeks later to the day, her roommates were found bludgeoned to death in their apartment. No leads. No weapon found. Now, years later, the case was long cold with no suspects. I read a few emails from a Toronto production company who wanted to turn the works into a crime documentary, and then finally, their email saying that budget constraints were forcing them to cancel on the project.

"Ben, do you think it's weird that there was an article about this on the boat that Janice was on? Do you think there *is* some sort of connection?"

"I don't know. That would have been the boat Terrance was on, right?"

"Yes."

"Maybe he was working on something. She said Terrance was close to the truth. Maybe he had the article with him."

"She seemed so afraid," I said.

"Maybe she has every reason to be afraid."

He regarded me over the top of his skinny glasses. "How well did you get to know the victim's wife? You said she stayed with you during the hurricane?"

"I sort of got to know her. A bit. She wants your help, too. That's why she came to me initially. And that's why she hiked through the storm. I've told you everything she told me."

He said, "You trust her?"

"I think so. She seems okay. Genuine. She's an artist, apparently."

"I wonder," he said placing another article back in the box. "It's family we look at first when it comes to these kinds of crimes."

"You think Audra could have killed her husband?" I watched him intently.

"I'm not sure what I'm saying, Em, or even thinking. These things could be two different crimes. The initial police report could be right."

"So now we're talking three different crimes and not connected. Virginia was killed by the missing boyfriend, Russell, Francine and Marilou killed in some sort of hate crime because they were a gay couple, and Terrance because of something he found out at work."

"It does seem a bit coincidental, doesn't it?"

"I'll say. Just because the police couldn't find anything doesn't mean there wasn't anything to find."

After a few minutes of studying more of the printouts and

casting theories back and forth, he turned to me. "Em, why was Janice wearing a name tag?"

"I have no idea. She always does. I've never asked her. I've never thought it was quite appropriate to ask."

"Maybe she's got more problems than we know."

"Maybe." Does wearing a name tag mean you have problems?

After a while, we packed up the papers, both realizing that this would take hours and hours. We headed out onto I-95. A few blocks from the police station, he said, "About our coffee…"

I knew what he was going to say. He didn't have time. He changed his mind. There was a pressing case. He wanted to go through all these papers. We'd have to postpone. His wife. His marriage. We'd have to reschedule. Maybe he'd changed his mind about me completely. Now that I'd run off and left him for a month, he'd found someone else.

I waited.

"How about lunch instead of coffee. I know a good place…."

"Sounds fine."

The place he took me was a restaurant which featured huge gourmet hamburgers with elephant-sized pictures of burgers plastered all over the walls.

After we ordered, I said, "I need to apologize for running off to the Bahamas like I did. I should have let you know. I…"

"It's okay, Em." He covered my hand with his. I didn't move away. "I'm still working through a whole bunch of trash, too. That's why I want to talk to you."

The place was crowded and noisy. A bad thing because more people might hear what we were talking about, and a good thing, because the noise might cover up any private words we shared.

"I told you my wife has agreed to a divorce?"

"You told me that, yes."

The look in his eyes was so endearing, so soft. And

yet…and yet…

Our cheerful and talkative waitress took our orders, smiling all the time and making typical waitress small talk. I just kept wanting her to be gone.

When she left, I said, "And, I have something I need to tell you."

He looked at me.

"I need to tell you why I can't be…um…with a cop."

"Go on."

I took a breath. "Cops die. I already lost someone I loved. I can't…can't do that. Not again." I paused a moment. "You remember my Uncle Ferd?"

He said yes.

"I'm like him. I'm too much of a free spirit. I have this job that takes me away for months at a time. You…you wouldn't want that. You would want someone to settle with you in Portland and stay home waiting for a cop who may or may not even get home. I'm not that person. I can't be that person."

The more I talked, the more I realized just how much my heart was breaking and falling apart around me like confetti. Why couldn't I fall for a sailor? Someone who was rough and tumble like me? Someone who understood my life?

There was a loud birthday going on at the table next to us, and in a minute, all the waitresses and waiters came out carrying a lit birthday cake and all singing loudly. Some stupid song. Too loud. Too long. I wished they would stop. Miss Chatterbox brought our hamburgers, but I suddenly wasn't hungry. Of course, we had to wait for the requisite song to be over before we could hear ourselves talk.

When it was over, and the song and music had settled down, he looked at me and said, "Do you think that's what I'm asking you? If you think that, then you don't know me at all. You can trust me. Em, you can trust me. I know what you do. I know who you are. If I can accept your life, you need to accept mine."

"There's something else though. Something that I'm

having trouble trusting you about."

Those eyes of his pierced my soul.

"There is something you've never told me," I managed.

"What's that?"

"Your son."

CHAPTER 22

For a long time, neither one of us said anything. The longer the silence went on, the more I wanted to grab all of my words out of the air and shove them all back inside. I was on the edge of a cliff. The birthday table became suddenly quiet as well, as if they, too, were waiting. I stared down at my colossal burger, at the "special sauce" which dripped out of the sides of the bun, the little seeds on the top, the mountain of fries beside it.

Ben folded his hands and looked away from me, past me, not meeting my eyes. And then, "You saw the picture." A statement.

"Yes."

"On the internet."

I thought about that photo—Ben, and next to him, his much tinier wife, the top of her head barely reaching his shoulders. And their baby, a little boy by the looks of it. Everything blue on him, from blue shorts to a white T-shirt with blue piping and little blue slippers. One of them looked half on, half off. Probably, a minute after the picture was taken, both mother and father were on the ground looking for the errant shoe.

The article had mentioned a son. No name, however. Curious, though, because when I'd re-Googled it some months later, the picture was gone, and all mention of the son was gone. It was simply not there. Still, I had seen it. I had seen it.

He owed me an explanation, didn't he? If what we had was a *relationship*, he owed me this. Maybe the picture was put in erroneously. Perhaps it wasn't even his wife. But if that were the case, surely by now, he would have said something like, "Oh, you saw that picture? That was me and my sister and her baby. The paper needed a picture, and they grabbed that one from my sister's Facebook page and thought it was Cindy and me and ran with it. Stupid mistake, but it was made right. You mean all this time you've been worried about *that*?"

But he said nothing of the kind. Instead, he folded his hands on the table and looked down. I tried to read the atmosphere, tried to decide if I needed to say something. Maybe something like, "I'm sorry, Ben. I should never have brought it up. I saw this picture, and I thought…" But I didn't. I felt like if I opened my mouth, all the wrong things would come spilling out.

"My son died, Em."

"Wha…?" The room shifted.

"He died…"

"Ben, I'm so, so sorry. I didn't know. I didn't, um… I shouldn't have…"

"It's okay."

I said, "It's not okay. I'm so sorry. If I had known…"

"I should have told you. I was just…um…guarding a confidence. Still, I should have told you." He took a deep breath. "That's all a part of what happened. That's part of it all. I wanted to tell you. But my wife. I needed, um, to protect her privacy."

"I understand. It's not necessary to tell me anything."

"Cindy wanted — demanded — that all pictures of him be taken down from the web. The paper complied. It was like it never happened."

I felt my eyes well. "Ben…"

"My son…" He paused. "My son Will. He just got sick one day. One ordinary day, he was just sick like all kids get. And he just…died. It was the flu. That's what they told us at the hospital. Just something so stupid…" He rubbed at the side of one eye. "Kids get sick all the time… How can a baby die of the flu?"

"I'm so sorry." His hands were on the table. I reached over, touched one. It was an instinctive gesture, and in the next moment, he was holding my hands, and there were tears in his eyes.

"Maybe if we'd taken him in earlier. To the hospital, I mean. Maybe if we'd noticed…"

"Ben…"

"It's just. They tried everything. They don't know why. He just had one of those virulent strains of the flu. The church people came. Our minister prayed over him. Lots of people prayed. Fasted and prayed. There was even a Facebook group. A prayer chain. What kind of an effing god needs more baby boy angels in heaven?"

"Oh, Ben."

"That's what some people told us. That God needed another angel in heaven."

"No one should have said that."

"Yet they did. That God had a reason for this. I don't care about the reason. There is never a fucking reason to kill a child. Never a reason. Will's death took me away from the church. But it drew Cindy in closer."

"Ben…I…" I had never heard him use language like this. I sometimes do. I hang with sailors, and without much compunction, I can go right into the language of my peers, but never Ben. Not him.

"We were fast becoming a statistic, Cindy and me — couples who don't stay together after the death of a child. Em, I should have told you this a long time ago. I shouldn't have kept this part secret. But it was too painful. Cindy and I had counselling. Lots of it. I actually thought we were going to make it. She was even putting together a memory book about Will. I took some time off work. I was ready to go back. Or I thought I was. I wasn't. That's when the drug bust fiasco happened. I blame myself. I should have taken more time off. All of it was too much for my wife. She had lost so much. First a son, and then a maligned husband…"

I looked into his face.

"After I shot that boy, that's when she wanted to forget about Will. That's when she wanted all the pictures destroyed and every mention removed. 'Two boys dead!'" she said. 'Two boys dead. You killed both of them.' That's the first she blamed me for Will's death. If I'd taken more notice. If I'd come home from work earlier. There were a million reasons to blame me. I realize now that she had to blame me. If she hadn't blamed me, she would be blaming God."

I couldn't imagine what he had gone through.

Surprisingly, he gave me a bit of a smile then, a small hint of one. "Six years ago. Will died six years ago."

I thought about this. At about the same time Jesse died, Ben was going through his own particular kind of hell.

"That's why I'm…" He paused. "It's taken me so long to finally decide to move on. Maybe with you. But you have to know what kind of damaged goods I am."

"No more than I am."

"But maybe we should…" He didn't finish the sentence.

"Should what? Take some time?" I offered.

"No." He regarded me. "Unless that is what you want. And, um…maybe you're right. Maybe you shouldn't be with a cop. Maybe nobody should. Cindy couldn't cope. You do know the divorce rate for cops, don't you?"

I started to say something but didn't.

Neither of us finished our meal. He drove me back to my car in silence, and when I said "goodbye," there was no kiss, no taking of my hand, no "I'll call you soon."

Were we over? Is that what this was?

At home, I took a blanket outside and wrapped myself in it and stayed that way for a long time on my front porch couch until EJ came over with a plate of food.

"Thanks, EJ, But I just came from lunch."

"I'll put it in your fridge, shall I?"

"Yeah. Fine."

"You okay. Em? You look sort of…"

"Yeah, I guess I look sort of like a lot of things…"

I told him everything, all about Cindy and Will and Ben. He sat with me for a long time, offering platitudes and words of wisdom, which coming from another person, would be eye-roll-worthy, but coming from EJ, I knew he meant them. I knew he cared. But the one thing he never said was, "God has a reason." Because sometimes God doesn't have a reason. Sometimes things just happen because the world is so truly and completely screwed up. I wanted to thank him for not saying that.

After he went home, I stayed on my porch. I read somewhere that for each person there is one soul mate. I had that in Jesse. Ben probably had that in Cindy. Maybe there are no second chances for anybody in this whole sad earth.

Maybe tomorrow, maybe the next day or the day after, I'll get another delivery call. Perhaps soon, I'll be wending my way to the Caribbean or South America or even the Mediterranean. They would solve Terrance's murder, or not, but I would not be a part of it because I would be running. I would run and continue to run and run and run. I gazed out at my uncle's boat, still there, while no one knew where my uncle was. My mother is right. Ferd and I are peas in a pod.

When I went back inside, I opened up my Facebook business page, where I often get job enquiries, hoping, hoping I could leave again. Soon.

And received the shock of my life.

CHAPTER 23

It was a message from Sunny, a private message to me, but right there on the very public front page of his Facebook business profile, right between tourists' underwater photos of fish and reefs and happy customers praising Tina's conch fritters. Because he had "tagged" me, the whole thing was posted on my page, as well. He had set the message to go out to every person on the planet, and probably the solar system if they have Wi-Fi in space.

Em,

Terrance was murdered. I'm pretty sure about that now. The police have been on my case about my equipment. It's the police now and not a lawsuit. They don't think I did it, though. They are telling me that they think someone else might've come to the island and done something to the equipment. They have all these questions for me. Where do I store my gear? Is the equipment locked up? That sort of stuff. Here's another thing — the day before they went out on that dive? I saw Marcus and Wes arguing. I don't exactly remember what they said, but I think I heard Marcus saying, "You're pretty sure of yourself, aren't you?" That's what I think I heard. Then Terrance showed up, and they both stopped talking. It was like they didn't want him to hear what they were saying.

The police brought back my gear, so I had another look at the regulator. Here's what I think — someone came up behind Terrance when he was swimming and maybe pulled off his mask and yanked out his mouthpiece. I had Kenny stand in front of me, and I stood behind him and tried to pull out his mouthpiece. The strap on his mask wasn't ripped, but the mouthpiece had been bitten pretty hard. One thing they never found were the cable tie that would've held the mouthpiece to the regulator. I don't know what that means, but in looking over all of the equipment, I never found that. I ended up having a long talk with Marcus. He agrees with me. I'll explain what he told me as soon as I have worked it out. Maybe you should call Marcus, too.

Sunny

A plastic cable tie! I tried to remember. I had picked up a cable tie from the bottom when Sunny and I were diving. I had just thrown it away thinking it was just so much ocean garbage. Was it important? I wasn't sure. I'd have to ask Sunny, but the first and foremost priority was to call Sunny and get him to take this private message off his Facebook page immediately. I quickly took it off my own profile, but not before I'd copied and pasted it as a note to myself. I looked at the timestamp. It had already been up for almost six hours. I printed it just for safekeeping.

I tried calling Sunny on my cell. No answer. I sent him a private Facebook message, wondering how private it really was. Probably not very in his case.

I found his wife Delia's page and sent her a message. *Please get Sunny to call me as soon as he can, and if you can, get him to take down his Facebook post right away.*

Despite everything, Ben and I were tied together on this, and Ben needed to know. Instead of calling his private cell phone—I didn't think I could deal with that—I called his number at the police station since this was a police matter. I knew he seldom answered that phone, so I could simply leave a message without having to talk with him in person.

"Please call me," I said. "It's important. Sunny left me a weird message."

I opened up my laptop. There was nothing new about the scuba death on Eleuthera. A bit about the hurricane with photos, I saw, but nothing about what Sunny had just written.

I got up feeling jittery and went into my kitchen. I looked around for something to drink and decided on an espresso. Good choice, Em. Nothing like a late afternoon espresso when you're already restless and can barely sit still.

Marcus? A fight between Marcus and Wes? What could that have been about? And call Marcus? About what?

I remembered the way Marcus had pressed his business card into my hand. "Call me," he had said. Why? Why had he suggested I call him? I dug the card out of my bag and then looked up their money management website. Terrance's name was there, too, yet there was no mention of his death. Should there have been by now? Maybe. Maybe not.

I meandered link by link back to the murders of the three women. So far, the only connection was the news article Janice found on the boat, which could easily be explained by Terrance bringing it with him to do further study.

I didn't have the printouts. Ben had them — so I looked up and read stuff I could legitimately find online. I learned all about the three women who had died — their stories, their lives. There were photos — the three of them sitting together at a table, sitting together on their couch and smiling at the camera. Better times. The news was clinical, factual, but as I read through and followed the links, I thought about the child, Janice, who had lived through all of this.

I kept reading and checking my phone for Sunny. Or even Ben, until I looked up and saw Dot waving at me through my kitchen window. I was so not in the mood to be sociable, but before I could say I was too busy, she was inside my kitchen and rooting through my cupboards for wine glasses, all the while chatting on and on about Ferd and his boat and how she had some news to tell me. But wine first. Wine first. Wine is always first with Dot.

She poured two full glasses. And I do mean full. Right up to the rims. This woman, this neighbor of mine, also happens to be a one-time lover of my uncle's from a long, long time ago. I think she still holds out hope that he will someday come back to her.

She told me she got an email from Ferd just this morning. Right when she got up, there was this email from him, first in her inbox, and had I heard from him? Because she'll go months and months without hearing from him then all of a sudden, *poof,* five emails in a row well, not five more like three, and what was anyone to make of that, but had I heard from him? And then there's her sister who thinks she should quit holding out a candle for him, and maybe Isabelle is right, and should she get on with things, but at seventy-one, how much "on with my life" was there to be got and there was this one nurse in the hospital where Isabelle had her knee replacement that she'd like to throttle with her bare hands…

I barely got a word in. I'd heard all this from Dot before, plus I kept thinking and worrying about Sunny and Terrance. And Marcus and Wes. And Janice. I remembered the way her hands shook, the way her whole body trembled when she opened the cardboard box of printouts.

Meanwhile, Dot was pouring herself a second full glass, again to the rim. "You just don't know about people, do you?" she was saying. "You just never can tell about people. The nicest ones can end up being the meanest, and the meanest looking ones, the ones you least expect, can end up being the nicest. Like that nurse I was just telling you about. And Ferd. When we were together back in the dark ages, I thought we'd be going on forever. Ha-ha to that one. Yep, you can never tell about people, can you?"

EJ had told me something similar. Was the universe trying to tell me something? Marcus had seemed so droll and angry. He would, I was sure, turn into one of those stooped-shouldered old men, who continually frowned and chased kids off his lawn with his cane while Wes would end up being the affable grandfather. And the grieving widow Audra? Was she really grieving? Or was she melodramatically over-playing everything?

After the third full glass of wine, Dot left for home and thanked me for listening to her and helping her solve all her problems with her sister.

I said, "Give my love to her."

"I will, kiddo."

Later, half a glass of wine still to consume, I went back to my laptop and stumbled upon Terrance's obituary and read it all the way through. And then again. There was something off about it. Something definitely off about this whole thing.

CHAPTER 24

How was it that Audra's name was not mentioned in the obituary? Not even once. I read that Terrance Hinson was predeceased by his parents and one sister, Francine Hinson. No other siblings. No other relatives. No children. No other names. The obituary gave the places and dates of his schooling and a rundown of his work history. It read like a résumé, a curriculum vitae—factual and barebones. The funeral home website had a place where people could post memories and pictures. I checked. No one had.

Who was Audra, then, if not his wife? I thought back to the times when Audra seemed to be almost overacting. The way she fell into my arms when she came through the door during the hurricane. Had she really been wandering around in a category four storm? Was her car really stranded? Were all those crocodile tears of hers real?

I wondered if I should call Marcus and ask him why Audra's name was not in the obituary. Maybe that would be a place to start. Or how was this my business anyway?

In the morning, I took Rusty outside. Maybe all I needed was to get my mind off everything, by doing a whole bunch of mind-numbing but much needed physical tasks around my place. I pulled debris off my lawn, clearing a path down to the water. I cut down overgrown shrubs until my place looked half decent again. I piled the debris to be burned.

A few hours later, I walked around to the back and crouched down and looked under my house. There it was—like a giant corpse wrapped round and round in a blue tarp. My kayak. Jesse and I used to love kayaking. It was one of our things—that and sailing.

After Jesse died, some of his friends took care of it for me. Since my husband was killed on one of our two identical kayaks he had built, they had the foresight to understand that I probably wouldn't want to use it for a long time. They were right. They'd wrapped it all up with rope and bungees and had shoved it as far underneath my house as it would go. For six years this beautiful handmade wooden kayak had been wrapped up in plastic and was probably, by now, home to mice and spiders and all manner of rot, mildew, and mold. For a long time, I simply didn't care. I just wanted it gone, yet somehow, I couldn't bring myself to give it away or sell it. So there it sat.

I crawled under as far as I could, swatting away the multitudes of spiders. I shoved and pulled. At one point, the tarp snagged on a nail as I wriggled it left and right to free it. Finally, the entire massive wrapped-up hulk was lying in my backyard.

I undid the lines and cords with my pocketknife until the boat was completely uncovered. Something caught in my throat. Beautiful still. After all this time.

I went inside and filled a bucket with warm water and mild soap and grabbed a bunch of rags. I also found some wood oil that didn't look too much past its prime. Outside in the sunshine, I scrubbed my boat clean until it shone almost to its former glory.

All the while I worked, I kept checking my phone. Still nothing from Sunny. Or Delia. Or Ben. A whole day had passed.

In the late afternoon, I got a call from the Bahamas.

Dearest Mother,

This isn't going to be a Mrs. Nose post. This isn't going to be a happy memory. This isn't going to be anything like that. I need to write about that day. That horrible, horrible day. I want to finally get it all down on paper. I've put off writing about it—thinking about it really—and I need to go back and remember everything about that day.

I am writing it down here not so that I can find forgiveness. There will be no forgiveness. I don't think you need to forgive every bad thing that has ever happened to you. But I need to let go of it for my own sake. And, perhaps, for your sake too, Mother.

The first thing different about that day was that you weren't there to pick me up after school. I waited and waited. Finally, Marilou came, and there she sat, frowning behind the wheel of her car and waiting for me. Probably you had to work late. It had happened before. And when that happened, either Francine or Marilou came to get me. But they usually didn't look this mad.

"Where's my mom?" I said as I slid into the passenger side.

Her eyebrows were scrunched together behind her glasses, and her hands shook slightly as she put the car into drive. There were lines on her face, too. Lines I'd never noticed before. She looked old. I realized then that she wasn't mad so much as scared.

"We're not sure where she is," is what she finally said.

"But where *is* she?" If I talked louder, maybe I'd get an answer.

She turned toward me. "Did you see your mother before you left for school this morning?"

"No," I said, stretching out the word NO for several paragraphs and ending with a raised inflection like a question mark. I hadn't. I'd assumed you'd worked late and got into bed without waking me. This had happened before. You had recently put a pretty room divider between our beds so I could decorate my own side how I wanted. You told me I could do that.

"I thought she was sleeping," I said.

"You didn't see her before you left this morning?"

We still hadn't moved out of the parking lot.

I said no and shook my head. I hadn't looked over the divider to your side of the room. If you hadn't stirred, you were probably tired. I'd let you sleep then. I got up by myself since both Francine and Marilou were at work by then. I made my own breakfast. I was really noisy too, but still, you didn't waken. I'd assumed you were very tired.

"Did you see her last night, then?"

"She was working. Francine was at home. We watched TV. Me and Francine."

Marilou looked away from me and out the window. I followed her gaze. Something was very wrong.

"She wasn't working," Marilou said. "No one has seen her since yesterday afternoon."

"Oh…I thought…"

"She didn't show up for work. They called. We thought she was out with Russell." Marilou spat out the name. "And she never came home."

"Maybe she's still at Russell's." You had never stayed overnight at Russell's before, but there was always a first time, wasn't there?

Marilou said, "Francine and I went there earlier. He told us he hasn't seen her." Carefully, she drove out of the parking lot. "But he could be lying."

"Why would he lie?"

She didn't answer that.

It was strange to think that the whole time I'd been at school, your two friends had been out looking for you, worrying for you, wondering where you'd gone.

"We called the police," Marilou said, "but they can't do anything until she's been missing a bit more."

"Why not?"

"It's the law or something."

I stared at her.

"I tried to tell the police that she would never take off and leave you. Ginny would never do that."

I nodded. You wouldn't. "Where's Francine, then?" My

mouth was becoming drier and drier.

"She's still out looking. She took your mom's car. And that's another thing..." She held the steering wheel tight with both hands. "Her car's there. We told the police that."

"What did they say?"

"They still can't do anything."

As we made the last turn toward home, I wasn't immediately worried. When you're thirteen, the world is still a good place, a good and safe place—and an honest place. I was sure you'd be there when we got back. You'd be full of crazy excuses about traffic and busyness and not knowing where the time went. That would have been so like you. Scatterbrained. Scatterbrained but caring. Always finding the good in people.

You weren't there.

After a sleepless night, the police finally came to our house that morning and talked with Marilou and Francine. No one took much notice of me. I think they assumed either Francine or Marilou was my mother. Even though the two of them had banished me to my room with the door shut, I overheard snatches of conversation. You couldn't have been with Russell because Russell had been at work. His workmates at the bank plus his girlfriend could vouch that he was there. *Girlfriend*? This was the first I'd heard that he had a girlfriend. I thought you were his girlfriend. Did you guys break up? Could you have been so heartbroken that you had gone off by yourself? The police asked that.

Francine said, "No," and Marilou said, "Never," both at the same time.

Francine added, "He wasn't good for her. There were a whole lot of reasons why, but he would never do that. Not now. Especially not now."

At the time, I didn't understand what Francine meant by that.

A week later, when they found your body in the quarry, they asked about me. Marilou said I was her daughter. I was so happy she said that, and when a police lady asked me the same question, I lied and said yes, and that Francine was my aunt.

"So you're sisters?" The police looked at the two of them.

"No," I piped up. "I just call her my aunt."

I was already learning how you hedge and dodge questions. It would serve me well in life.

Now, so many years later as I write this, I think that I can't believe they didn't check this out more thoroughly, but they didn't. Would they today? A quick call to the school would have confirmed it.

But I was glad I was with Francine and Marilou. We three stayed in the apartment. We sat on the couch and alternately cried, and hugged each other, and ate hamburger casseroles and pizzas and lasagnas and plates of homemade muffins that friends and neighbors brought over. I didn't go back to school for a week.

Even though he had a new girlfriend, Francine and Marilou kept going to Russell's house. They didn't tell me, but I was sure they thought Russell was to blame. They just needed proof. More proof. They would get it. They would find it.

"He's guilty as sin!" Francine said loudly one night. "He did it. He knows he did it and yet he sits smugly at that house with that woman. The two of them." Francine and Marilou had all sorts of theories they were working on.

I wasn't the one who found their bodies. I think I would never have gotten over that particular horror if it had been me. Three weeks after you died, no one came to pick me up after school. I waited and waited. Instead of going back inside and telling a teacher or going to the office to call, I decided to walk the mile or so home on my own. I'd done it before. It wasn't far. I would be okay. Even at thirteen, I was already getting good at being on my own.

Closer to home, I saw the police cars parked outside of our apartment. I brushed past to get inside, but a woman, a police officer, held me back, and then taking me aside, she told me that someone had broken into our apartment and that Francine and Marilou were both dead.

Shortly after that, I was taken into the system and placed in foster care homes.

That's when all my fear and anger began.

Janice

CHAPTER 25

"Sunny? Sunny? Is that you?" I didn't recognize the caller ID, and the connection fizzled in and out. "Sunny? If this is you and you can hear me, you need to take down your Facebook post right away. I tried calling you yesterday!"

Static. After the call died completely, I called the number back. It rang and rang. As soon as I ended that call, my cell phone buzzed.

"Yes!"

"Em? Em Ridge?" It wasn't Sunny. Female voice.

"Delia?"

"This is Tina."

"Tina!"

"Sunny's dead!" There was a loud cry after she said this.

"What? What!" The connection squawked. I was frantic. "Tina! What did you say?"

"Sunny. They found him last night."

"What do you mean Sunny's dead?"

"Kenny found him. In his dive shop. He was stabbed."

"What? Stabbed? How?" *Sunny*?

"Em?"

"Yeah. Tina. Go on."

"Em, I'm walking down to the beach to try to get a better signal. Wait. I think this is better."

It was.

"What happened?" I demanded.

"No one had seen him since the morning. He was supposed to take some divers out, and no one could find him, so Kenny took them out. And then, finally, in the evening, Kenny found him behind some of the wetsuits and underneath a whole bunch of junk in the back of the dive shop. The police think that whoever killed him didn't want him found right away,"

"I can't believe it!"

"And do you know what the police are saying? They're saying that he probably got into a fight and ended up getting the worst of it! Sunny? A fight? They don't know the same Sunny we know."

This was true. Fighting was so not a part of his nature as to be laughable. "I can't believe it, Tina! I can't believe what you're saying to me. This just can't be. There has to be some mistake."

"Em, listen, I gotta go in a minute. I'll call you back. I got a bunch of people up at the Tiki Bar. Believe it or not, we've got tourists here now, so everyone's trying to do double time. And the police are all over the place, too. I might need to call you right back. Wait, I have your email, right?"

I gave it to her. "Tina, keep me in the loop. Promise?"

"I promise," she said. "The police were here all last night. Oh man. This is so hard. Everyone's in shock. All that time Delia thought he was here, and all that time, we thought he was home with her. We thought he must've been sick or something, and that's why he wasn't answering his cell, but that's not unusual for him, so no one thought to go over to his house and check, and meanwhile, Delia's trying to call him because he's not home and won't answer his cell."

I felt a sob rise in my throat as I thought about his young wife, his baby. I remembered the way he held his daughter on his lap and read comforting stories about puppies and kittens and rabbits to her while the winds howled outside. His voice, as he read, even calmed me as I had been sitting there on the floor of the kitchen, leaning against the wall, knees drawn up, while outside trees were being shaken to their roots.

She went on. "Nassau came again. Useless pieces of shits don't understand our way of life out here. They're the ones think Sunny got in a fight. Maybe they fight like that in

Nassau, but not here."

I agreed.

"They keep checking the guest registry. And who would have Sunny got in this supposed fight with? Kenny and I have been checking through all the guest records, but it's not like a murderer is going to sign the guest book before he comes and stabs the owner."

"How is Delia? And Kenny?"

"Pretty broken up, as you can imagine. Delia's parents just got here. Her brother, too, I think."

"Good. She's going to need support."

"Oh, Em, here I am in the Tiki Bar cooking up fish and chips and making coffee and serving beer all the while, right next door, Sunny is lying there dead." Her voice broke. "If I had just heard him, but we had the music so loud. If I had heard him call out. Maybe we could have gotten to him in time."

"Do you want me to come? I'll come."

She sighed. "I don't know. I don't know what's going to happen."

After we said goodbye, I sat down on my front porch couch. For several minutes, I wasn't able to move. I just sat there weeping into my clenched fists. I called Ben on his private cell. Despite how we had left things, Ben needed to know this.

He didn't answer, and so with a voice that I couldn't keep from breaking, I left a voice message telling him that Sunny was dead and that I was alone and not handling it well. When I ended the message, there was a part of me that wished I could take it all back. I had probably come across as sniveling and afraid. Well, maybe that was okay.

I went outside and knelt beside my kayak. I pressed my face against the wood and sobbed. I was crying for Sunny and Delia and Terrance, and for Jesse and Ben and his son and Janice and her mother and Francine and Marilou, and broken kayaks and storms, and all the bad and evil people in the world that make things worse.

I was crying because I was also beginning to understand that it was my fault Sunny was dead. My fault. If I hadn't asked him to "keep me informed," he wouldn't have written that letter to me on his open Facebook page, a letter which certainly got him killed. How was non-internet-savvy Sunny to know it was so public? He never goes on Facebook, or the internet even.

I felt a hand on my shoulder. Startled, I looked up. Ben! In the next moment, I was in his arms, and crying.

"Sunny's gone," I mumbled into his shoulder. "Sunny's really gone."

When we broke away from each other — and it was me who did the breaking — I told him about my conversation with Tina. I told him about Sunny's Facebook message. "That's what I called you about yesterday. I left a message at the station. Now…this…happened today."

"Aw, Em, you should have called my cell yesterday."

"I know, but…" And then I was quiet. "Maybe if I had…" I looked at him, "…this whole thing could have been stopped. If I had done that, got a hold of you sooner, maybe Sunny would still be alive. I told him to keep me informed. I told him…" My voice broke. "And he did keep me informed. Right there on a public website."

He took my hands in his. I let him. "This is not your fault. I've read the message. I don't know why someone would kill him for that message."

I backed away, looked at him. "But he wrote…"

"It's not your fault."

The words I had earlier told Tina fell flat with me now.

"Em, there could be lots of reasons. Plenty of reasons. Could just be a disgruntled customer. Could be anything, Em. And maybe it was just a fight like the police are saying. You told me yourself that the last time you saw him before this recent trip was almost ten years ago. How well did you even know him now?"

"I know him. He's one of those people—was one of those people—who you can not see for years, and then, when you're together, it's like you never left. I've known Sunny a long time."

I pulled away from him slightly and sat down on the ground, my back against the kayak. I shaded my eyes with my hand. He sat beside me. Neither of us said anything for a long time.

After a while, he seemed to notice what we were leaning against. He ran his hand over the wood.

"Is this the kayak you were telling me about?"

I nodded and wiped my eyes. "Yes. Jesse made this. This is the one."

He stood up. "Your husband crafted this? By hand?" He walked around it.

I told him yes.

"It's gorgeous, Em," he said running his hands over it.

It made me feel proud. "It is. I know." I stood up beside him.

"It's in good shape, too," Ben said. "You say it was underneath your house all this time?"

"Six years."

"Not a lot of mold or mildew that I can see. Not anywhere."

"Think I just got lucky. I'm thinking of selling it. I don't know what to do with it."

"Do you have a place you can hang it? It would be better if it was up off the ground."

I pointed behind me. "EJ always let us store our kayaks in his shed. I think the wall racks are still there."

"Should we go see?"

I knew what he was doing, trying to engage me in some task so that I wouldn't think about Sunny.

EJ's shed, of course, was not locked. No one locks their stuff around here. Inside, past clutter and junk, two racks were still there on the wall, a bit cobwebby, but sturdy enough, Ben noted.

After we got the boat hanging on the wall, Ben said, "This is quite the shed."

"A junk collector's paradise. This shed could be on that hoarders show." We stepped around an old bicycle, wheels and tires for various wheeled vehicles, junked pots and all manner of tools and implements, as well as piles of newspapers, and three old barbecues. EJ often cooked his meat outside and went through barbecues like people go through paper plates.

I said, "I want to show you something." I climbed over a series of rusted hubcaps on my way to a locked cabinet against the back wall. I knew the combination, and when I keyed it in and opened it up, there it was—EJ's old intricately designed handgun. An antique by anyone's standards, its handgrips were ornately carved, and it was larger than most, heavier, too. I pulled it out and laid it in Ben's hands. "Ever see anything like this?"

He took it and examined it. "Wow," he said. "Heavy, too. I've never seen a gun like this before."

"It should be in a museum. I keep telling that to EJ. To take it to the historical society, but he says, "Well, you never know when you're going to need a gun like this."

"He has shells for this, even? They even make shells for this?" He was examining every part.

"I doubt it."

"It's quite the gun," he said handing it back to me.

I locked it up again in the cabinet, and then we left.

Back at my house, he said, "I brought bagels. You want one?"

I stopped. "You brought bagels?"

"From that favorite place of yours. You were upset. They're a sort of peace offering. They're in the car."

"Well, I have coffee. You want to stay for a bit?" I wanted him to say yes. I really wanted him to say yes.

"Yes."

We were in my kitchen, buttering bagels when he said, "I've had a chance to go through most of what Janice photocopied. She even got a hold of a few police reports and personal emails."

We took our coffees and newly buttered bagels out onto my front porch and sat down on the couch.

"What do you make of it all?" I asked.

"I've been doing a bit of my own research. Remember when Janice mentioned her mother's boyfriend, someone named Russell? I found very little about him in any of the information. He was briefly a suspect but then discarded. That was in one of the police reports."

"Where is he now?"

"Gone. Moved. Left no forwarding information. I also did some calling. It's been thirteen years, but a few tenants in the apartment where he lived remember him. No one has heard from him in a long, long time. I'm also trying to find Janice. I've been able to contact a few of her former foster parents. They all speak pretty fondly of her. She was described as troubled, but sweet. I had a long talk with a family called Clifford. They have a farm in western Mass and take in a lot of foster kids. Mostly troubled kids. Mr. Clifford had nothing but good to say about her. They haven't heard from her in a long time."

I put my coffee down beside me. Out on the bay in the sunshine, Liam was tearing around in his inflatable.

He turned to me, "Do you still have that message on Facebook that Sunny sent to you?"

"I copied it before I deleted it off my page. You think it's related?"

"Maybe. Can you send it to me?"

I went inside and got my phone, and after a few clicks, I said, "Done. You should have it now."

"I might send this on down to the police in the Bahamas."

"Boy, for someone who doesn't like to get involved in other jurisdictions, you really are this time."

"I think we're involved in this one, we both are, Em, but there's something else I need to tell you. There's another reason I came out here today."

I looked at him expectantly.

"I'm taking some time off starting in a couple of days. Some time away. I've got some final stuff to take care of. If you need to get a hold of me, I might not be in Maine.:

Later, when he drove away, I watched until I could only see the back of his car as he moved away from me down the road.

CHAPTER 26

The call came from an unknown number. *Tina?*

"Em? Is this Em Ridge?" A female voice. A clean line. Not Tina.

"Yes?"

"This is Audra."

"Audra! Hello."

"I have..." She paused as if stumbling over her words. "It's... I have something I need to ask you. A favor."

"Okay."

"Well, a job actually." Ben's warnings and my doubts came zinging at me all at once, yet I couldn't help but be taken in by the sadness in her voice. "I went to your website," she said. "I notice you do boat surveys."

"I do. Yes."

Boat surveying was something I had recently added to my list of nautical things I could do to make money. Surveyors are needed in this insurance-crazy world. So far, it hadn't been all that lucrative, but it was building.

"I'm thinking of selling our boat *Myriad* now that Terrance is gone. Well, I haven't made up my mind. Not entirely. But I do need to get it surveyed, regardless. There was a letter from our insurance when I got home, so I'm wondering if you would be willing to come down and do this, or if you can't, maybe you could recommend someone?"

I asked her a few questions and discovered that *Myriad* was a 32' trawler with a diesel engine. I tried to detect something in her voice, anything, that might lead me to believe she was deceiving me, yet all I heard was a grieving woman who wanted to get rid of a boat that she and Terrance had shared. And I could certainly relate to that, couldn't I?

In the end, my need for employment won out. My need for employment always wins out. "If you need me to come, I can." Then I let my breath out. "But I'll need travel expenses on top of my fee. That's on my website, too."

"Not a problem. And if the surveying takes more than one day, I have plenty of room in my home if you would like to stay here. If not, I will certainly put you up in a motel nearer to where the boat is. I'm about forty minutes away from my boat."

"Fine."

I gave her all my information, and we decided that since my schedule was free, I could just as easily do this as quickly as possible. I'd drive down tomorrow. I also decided to take her up on her offer of staying at her home. Maybe I would learn something valuable.

She said, "When you come, I also need to talk to you about something else."

"Yes?"

"Some things have happened here."

"What things?" I was immediately wary.

"We'll talk when you come."

Even as I started to pack, doubts were forming.

CHAPTER 27

Early the following morning, I was in my car and on my way to Boston. Audra lived just north of the city, and my phone's GPS was telling me that it would take an hour and a half to get there. That's without traffic, and at this time of day, that could be problematic. As I got caught in yet another traffic snarl, I began to wonder what the hell I was doing here, and did I have a reasonably sensible bone in my body? More to the point, was I driving right into the lair of a murderer? Thoughts like these can occupy your mind when you're bumper to bumper, your coffee's gone, the guy in the beat-up old Ford beside you has the drum beat of a song so loud that you can't even hear your own playlists—but that's okay because you're sick and tired of all the songs you own anyway. So you switch to FM, but that's not much better. So, you wait. And ruminate.

What if—what if this Audra was an imposter? She wasn't mentioned in the obituary, right? And really, when you think of it, had I ever really seen her and the two other couples together? On the other hand, she had stayed on the island when the others left. Sunny, Tina and Janice hadn't thought it particularly strange when she stumbled into the cookhouse in the middle of the hurricane.

I followed the friendly voice on my GPS off the highway, down the exit, and turned right. Down this road for a mile and a half and then a sharp right and then a couple of lefts, and I was in a wooded area with big homes. After a couple more right turns, I was driving down a road with lovely older brick and stone homes. Nice area. Not too pretentious. Not the McMansions that you sometimes encounter around the outskirts of Boston. Down this road for a bit until the destination was on my right.

Hers was a three-story brick home set back from the road. When I pulled up the driveway, she came out and waved me in. I was to park on the right side of the driveway. It was only when I got out of the air-conditioned car that I noticed how sauna-like it was here.

"You made good time," she said.

"Traffic was pretty bad, but I was on the road quite early. Had to catch the tide." When I explained where and how I live, she merely mumbled something that sounded like, "Interesting."

I followed her into her blessedly cool home and down a hall to a small guest room on the main floor. She told me to drop my bags and then come further down the hall to the kitchen in the back. She'd be there with coffee ready. "I've got all the boat documents in the kitchen for you to look at."

"Sounds good."

We had decided today she would show me the boat, and we'd take it out for a quick spin. Then tomorrow, I'd head back on my own and do the comprehensive survey, which would probably take me most of the day. I'd drive straight home after that and write it all up and email the report to her.

The guest room was cheerful and inviting, the walls covered in paintings — huge things replete with great swashes of color — wide-leaf flowers, fairy girls in wide skirts, wolves, moons, eerie landscapes with swooping gulls, dragons. Her name Audra was scripted on the bottom right of each one. The paintings could be illustrations in a children's picture book of imaginative stories. Or dreams, maybe.

"Sit down, sit down," she said when I entered the kitchen. She was standing, though, like a statue next to her sink. She looked full of pent-up energy. I wondered if I should tell her about Sunny, but I decided it could wait.

"I have something for you." I pulled out her drawing from the envelope and placed it on the table. "The girl at the marina wanted to make sure you got it."

She glanced at it as if she couldn't quite place it.

"You left it there."

"I guess I did." She paused. "I don't even like to think about those times."

"Why?" I asked.

"I spent a lot of time by myself on that trip…" She turned. "The carafe is filled with coffee. Let me just get the cream. I seem to remember you like coffee, right? I can't live without it. Really, I can't. I'll take this full carafe of coffee up to my studio, and an hour later, I'm down here making more."

"I hear ya."

"The boat papers are there on the table for you to have a look at, and then we can drive out, and I'll show you the boat. We'll take it out. We can take my car. No sense taking both. This boat was Terrance's pride and joy. Well, both of ours, actually."

"Fine." She was talking too fast.

She slid her drawing into a drawer while I sat down and opened up the file. It included the boat registration, a few manuals and several prior surveys, the last one being five years ago. The boat was registered to Terrance Hinson and Audra Black. I commented on this.

"Black is my art name," she said by way of explanation.

I went through more of the documents. It was a registered vessel, rather than a licensed one, which meant it would be easier to take it offshore to foreign ports. She poured me a coffee, and I swirled in the cream.

"Sugar?"

"No thanks."

A few minutes later, she said, "I trust by now you've had the misfortune of meeting Wes and Marcus?"

"They drove me to the airport after Janice and I got the boats back," I said while leafing through the papers.

"And their lovely wives?"

"I haven't met them, no."

"Well, you haven't missed much. Beth, now she really is a piece of work. I know I told you all about them already, but it bears repeating. Don't, if you can help it, get on their bad sides."

"I'll make a note of that," I said while leafing through the papers.

"Don't get on any sides of them. Did you get a chance to talk to your police friend?"

"He's looking into all of it," is what I said. What do I tell her? That Ben might suspect *her*? "He had a question, though. We both did. In Terrance's online obituary, your name isn't there."

For a long time, she looked down at her folded hands and remained quiet. Finally, "They hated me. Wes and Beth and Marcus and Michelle. They all did. Hated me. They wrote the obituary."

"I thought the funeral home would write it. Or his wife."

"I was still in the Bahamas at the time waiting for the hurricane to be over when the obituary was written. I didn't have much say in it."

I found this extremely odd. "He doesn't have other family?" I asked.

She shook her head. "Maybe he has cousins somewhere, I don't know. All of his family are dead. His parents are both dead, and his only sister was murdered. So, it was just him."

"Why would they leave your name out?"

"We weren't legally married. Engaged. But not married. Not yet. Our wedding was all planned."

"I'm sorry. I'm so sorry."

"So that's why."

I nodded.

"Come with me," she said. "I'd like to show you something."

We went up three flights of stairs to a high loft with slanted ceilings and large dormer windows front and back. Her art studio looked to be her place of refuge and creativity.

Paintings were everywhere, large, colorful ones on easels and leaning five and six deep against the walls. The place smelled faintly of an odor that was unfamiliar to me, probably some sort of paint thinner. I am familiar with boat smells, not art studio smells.

"My sanctuary," she said. "I used to think this was a safe place. I told Terrance it was. I thought it would be a safe place for him to hide his obsession. Turned out it wasn't."

"His obsession?"

"Finding out who killed his sister. That was his obsession. Up here is where he kept all of the papers and information about her murder. Thirteen years ago, and they never found who did it. We've been together for five years. I never knew what he was like before this obsession. Still, I love him—loved him." She went on. "When we first met, he didn't talk much about it, but then it became more and more evident. When I think about it, it's been since getting the job with Wes and Marcus that he's been sort of nuts about it. Totally off the rails. I think it's because, with his job, he has the tools to examine some of the dark places on the internet. If you ask me, that's why he wanted this job in the first place, why he was so eager to apply, even though the money wasn't as good as he could get elsewhere. Being with Wes and Marcus allowed him access to all sorts of articles and information about the murder. He faithfully printed every news piece and report. He wanted them printed and filed. He didn't entirely trust the cloud, or whatever that place is. He stored them over there."

She walked over to a file cabinet which was in a shadow and against a far wall.

"He and Janice both had copies of everything. They shared things online. They were working on this together. Terrance was so afraid someone would steal them, and now that's exactly what happened. His files are all missing. Every last one."

"Really?"

She pulled out several empty file drawers.

"Janice has copies though, too," I said. "So, it's probably not a disaster."

She shook her head. "Terrance had things he didn't share with Janice. Personal emails from his sister. The two of them corresponded a lot before her death. He was sure there were clues in those emails. He was afraid that sharing too much with Janice would put her in danger.

"When did you notice everything was gone?"

"When I got back. I came up here, and things didn't seem right."

"What do the police say?"

She sighed. "I didn't tell the police. I know they wouldn't take it seriously. They were just files and look here." She picked up a small decorative box from the top of the file cabinet. In it was cash — twenties, fifties and hundreds — lots of them.

"My art money. Whoever came in here and took the files wasn't interested in money. So what would the police make of that? Oh, and here's another thing — when I got home and got onto Terrance's computer, all of those emails were deleted. I couldn't find anything." She hugged her arms around her to keep her hands from shaking. Her cheeks looked wet with tears.

"Have you been in contact with Janice since Eleuthera?"

"No, I met her for the first time in the Bahamas. She lives in Florida, which is kind of far from here. She and Terrance never even met in person." She looked out the window, bit her lip, and went on, "I knew something was wrong. I just knew it. I thought he had found some discrepancies in the books and that's why he was killed. Now I think it's something more sinister, something he found online, someplace online that normal people can't get to. Something he never got a chance to tell me. Maybe something to do with his sister. And now it's all gone. Em, I'm more scared than I have ever been in my life."

Mama,

I was eighteen when I saw a picture of you dead for the first time. I could have googled it long before that—I know I could have—but something kept me from doing it. When I was thirteen, all they told me was that something "really bad" had happened and that you had died. They never told me how. I didn't ask. It's something you don't think to ask when you're thirteen.

After you died, after it happened, I was shunted from foster home to foster home. I finally ended up with the Cliffords about two years after it happened. I never much thought about how you died. I just knew you were gone.

A man had killed you. When I pictured it, it was somehow more sanitized—as if death can be sanitized. I pictured it as something quick. A gunshot to the head and from behind so you wouldn't even have that one second of recognition. That's how I wanted it to be—not tortured and killed and dragged through the dirt on your belly, tearing out your teeth and wrecking your face. So savage it was. I read all about that later. I didn't know it then.

I wish I didn't know it now.

Your dead face was in the links that Terrance sent. He sent me so many links that he probably didn't realize what he was sharing. Or maybe he did. Maybe he thought I was old enough now to handle this information. I don't know that I was. Are we ever?

Here are the findings as noted in the police report: You had died by blunt force trauma, likely from being hit on the head by something never found or by hitting your head hard from a fall against a hard object. It was determined that the massive trauma to your face and teeth and upper body happened post-mortem. They concluded that your body had been dragged some distance over rocks before being covered up by stones down at the quarry. Your body could have been wrapped in something that fell off. No blanket was ever found, but some fibers were picked from your body and examined. Nothing conclusive.

That's what it said. Nothing conclusive. A murder so savage and nothing conclusive.

When I finally brought myself to do it, I looked at the picture of your face for a long time, studied it. It was unmistakably your face, but not your face, not your alive face, your real face. It was as if someone had taken the basics of your face all apart and then put everything back together again to make a mask for a horror movie. I kept looking at it. I am using the word "it" instead of "you." I notice that I am doing that. Maybe it's my way of making it not so real.

And then there was Russell, your love Russell. He was working at his job at the bank at the time of your disappearance and death, though. Terrance didn't believe this. Terrance was certain that Russell could have slipped out, killed you, and then got back to his work without raising suspicions. Later, he could have done the same with Francine and Marilou, murders he also had a convenient alibi for.

When the police finally went to get a DNA sample from Russell, he had already left. Neighbors said he and his girlfriend had packed up quickly. Why didn't they look for him? Why the hell didn't they go after him?

Jan

CHAPTER 28

After Audra had donned a pair of beat-up boat shoes, we drove to the boat in her brown jeep, a vehicle which seemed out of character for this artsy woman. She increasingly surprised me. We sped on backroads around the city to south Boston. I didn't know half of these roads even existed. She hated driving highways. She did everything she could to avoid highways and toll roads and heavy traffic. She knew all the back roads to everywhere, she told me.

She talked. And when she did, it was like a dam opened up, and everything she had kept bottled up since Terrance's death spilled out. She talked about Terrance, Boston, her art. Maybe she felt safe with me, or trusted me somehow — we two young widows. She told me all about how she met Terrance, how they had set a wedding date for the fall. Even though they were older, it would have been the first marriage for both of them.

"We were planning a small wedding. Just a few close friends. I didn't even want to invite Michelle and Beth and their husbands, but of course, Terrance had insisted. I'd been in a couple of long-term relationships, and I use the word relationship very loosely, but then, when I met Terrance, that was it. He was it for me." She blinked back the tears.

"I'm so sorry," I said and meant it.

"Those four? They ignored me at the funeral. It was like I wasn't even allowed to be there. Like I wasn't welcome at all. They handled all the details, and I'd been in such a state, I just let them. It's a mistake I will always regret."

"How horrible that you had to go through this."

"My sister came with me to the funeral. We left it quickly.

They all seemed to stick together and exclude me. Even my sister noticed and remarked on it later. 'How well did they all know Terrance?' she had asked me. I said they were his bosses from work. I remember she got this weird expression on her face and just said something like, 'that's so strange.'"

"People can be strange at funerals," I said. "Death brings out the worst in people sometimes. It can bring out but best, but it also brings out the worst. You seem close to your sister. That's nice."

"She had to fly back to Washington. That's Washington state. I miss her terribly. I'm even thinking of maybe moving out there. But then again, I might be disappointed. She has her family and her kids." Her voice trailed off. "Do you have brothers and sisters, Em?"

"Two sisters. Twins. Younger than me. My husband's funeral? They didn't even come."

"Really?" She raised her eyebrows.

"In all fairness, one of my sisters was expecting. Her due date was right around my husband's death, so I can't really fault her for that. But my other sister didn't come. My parents came. They barely stayed one day. They had to hurry back to the problem pregnancy. I got this vibe from them like, how dare Jesse die when your sister is pregnant! Like it was me who somehow planned that. Just to upset them."

"That's horrible."

"That's life. I'm over it now." I paused. "Sort of."

We were near the ocean, and she was slowing, so I assumed the marina wasn't too far away. I was unfamiliar with this part of south Boston, and even though I had travelled extensively by boat all up and down the coast, I couldn't place in my mind this particular stretch of water.

"There's a marina or yacht club around here?" I asked.

She shook her head. "Private home. Friends."

Minutes later, we were parked at a gate. She pressed a few numbers into the combination box, the gate opened, and in we drove.

"I don't think anyone's here," she said. "I'll have to check. I usually go in and say hi if they're home. Wonderful people. Patrons of the arts. And she makes the best muffins."

"Nice."

The driveway was long and winding and flanked on either side by professionally manicured trees. Ahead through the foliage, I could see the water, sparkling as if scattered across the surface with gems.

"This place is amazing," I said.

"It is, isn't it?" she said parking near to the dock. "The house still looks all closed up. I'm assuming they're still in France. The people who own it live mostly in South Carolina. This is their summer home. They told us we could put the boat here on their dock. They never use it. They don't have a boat anymore."

The house itself was high and majestic, white with pillars and several decks facing the water as well as a swimming pool, covered now with a blue pool covering, and tennis court. I waited in the car while she went to the door and rang the bell several times. A muffin would have been nice, but alas, no one appeared to be home.

She got in the car and drove closer to the water. At the end of a dock was a gleaming deep blue trawler, in the Maine lobster boat style.

"Your boat?" I asked. "It's beautiful." I saw the boat name *Myriad* written in gold script across the stern.

"We like it. We feel fortunate to have it. It's a lot for one person, though. I may sell it and get something smaller for me. Maybe a little runabout of some sort, a Boston Whaler or a Carolina Skiff. I do love fishing, as it happens. You'll see all the poles onboard. Terrance hates fishing—*hated* fishing. This is so hard."

"I know."

We boarded it, but before she unlocked the cabin door, she stood looking at it for several seconds frowning.

"What's wrong?" I said.

"Strange."

"Huh?" I looked over her shoulder.

"Maybe nothing."

"What?"

"Probably nothing."

"What is it?"

"I never leave the combination like this."

I looked over her shoulder where she held the combination lock in her hand.

"I know it's weird, but when I lock it back up, I always leave the numbers in a certain way. I always move the right-hand number to six and the left-hand number to seven. It makes no sense to the combination, but it's sort of my way. Right now it's all jumbled."

I looked at her. She really left her combination lock a "certain way"?

"Maybe you were in a hurry," I offered.

She looked thoughtful. "No. That's just not me."

"Terrance?" I ventured. "Was he here, do you think?"

"Again, no. He's as fastidious as I am. More so, in fact. Especially with what happened to his sister. It was him that got me doing this to the lock. I don't know." She backed away slightly. "First the papers and now this lock."

"Do you want to call the police?" I said.

She shook her head. "I'll have a real careful look inside."

Inside, the first thing she did was to open the hatches and let the air in. Then she stood in the main cabin and looked around.

"Everything okay?" I asked.

"I think so. It's just. It feels, I don't know, sort of different. Maybe it's just because Terrance is gone now. It just feels weird."

"You've every right to feel weird."

"That has to be it. Maybe it's just me. Me coming onto this boat for the first time since Terrance died. Maybe it's too soon."

I stood looking at her. "Do you want to go back home? I will understand, I truly will."

"No, it's got to be done. The insurance needed this survey like yesterday."

She gave me the grand tour of the boat, the berths, the nav station, the plumbing system, the electricals, the galley, the head, the engine room. She was quite knowledgeable. I did not doubt that she could run the entire thing on her own.

There were fishing rods all over the place, too. Some were attached to the ceiling with hooks, and others were simply laying along the hulls up in the front berth. It looked like this was a well-used boat, which made me happy. I hate it when people buy expensive boats and leave them.

All looked fine, so we fired up the engine and let it idle as I walked around the deck. The walk-around complete, we undid the lines and headed out to sea. The sun was hot on this late fall day, but the breeze out on the water made it almost too cool. I was glad I'd thought to bring my windbreaker.

She stood beside me as we pulled away from the dock and headed out to open water. "I'm quite certain he didn't come here," she said. "And fiddled with the lock, I mean. He would have told me. I think he would have told me. But maybe not. He'd been so distracted that week anyway, so distracted maybe it just slipped his mind. Still, I can't imagine."

"Why was he distracted?"

She said, "He was so excited to be going on that trip. Hyper. Way more than he should have been since he knew how I felt about Beth and Michelle."

"You have no idea why he was so hyper and excited? I know you've mentioned this before"

"I don't know. I still think about it. I keep going over and over in my mind. Around four months ago, he comes home after work and says to me all happy-like, 'They invited us on their cruise to the Bahamas!' I had no idea what he was even talking about. When I found out the grand plan, I told him no way. No way was I going. I was most adamant. Especially sharing living quarters with Wes and Beth of all people."

"What changed your mind?" I asked.

"Terrance finally did. He was so eager about this. He kept telling me that they were turning a corner and that he knew this would be a good time for us all to bond. He said they wouldn't have invited us if they didn't want us to be with them. I had my doubts about that. Plus, his work was going well. He was going to buy into the company and didn't want to jeopardize that. Finally, I broke down and agreed to go."

In the week before the trip, she told me that Terrance had gone from times of elation where he would turn to her and say, "Something big is going to happen" to times when he would retreat to her art studio and spend countless hours going through his files, page by page.

"He would spread all the papers all over the floor and just sit there surrounded by the death of his sister. And then in the next minute, he'd say, 'You watch, Audra, I'm going to blow the lid off this entire thing!'"

"And you have no idea what he meant by that?" I asked.

"He never got the chance to tell me."

During the time leading up to the trip, Terrance spent an increasing amount of time up in the studio and going over the photocopies, his laptop beside him.

I asked, "Is it possible that Terrance moved all of his files himself? Maybe he packed them all up and took them to a more secure location?"

"I don't know. Of course, that's possible. And maybe that's part of the reason I didn't go to the police. Because what if they came, and then two days later, I find them in a plastic tub in the basement marked 'Christmas decorations'?" She sighed deeply. "I just don't know what to think anymore."

"I need to tell you something," I said. "Sunny's been murdered."

"What! You mean the guy from the dive shop? In the Bahamas? The nice one?"

I told her yes.

"Oh, my God!" She put her hand to her mouth.

"The police don't think it was murder, but I think it might be connected with what happened to your husband. Janice came to see Ben and me."

"Janice? Why? What did she want?"

I told her about Janice's collection of photocopied news clippings and police reports. I also told her about Janice finding the newspaper section aboard the boat that she and Terrance had been on. I asked, "Do you think Janice could have taken the papers?"

"I don't know if there would be a reason to. I got the impression that these were duplicates. Terrance and Janice shared information." Then more quietly, she said, "Something happened the night before Terrance died. He told me something."

I looked at her, waited.

"I didn't tell you everything on the day of the hurricane. I remembered something else. He and I were lying close together in bed. It's pretty hard to have much privacy on a boat, much less a private conversation, but he whispered to me, 'Whatever happens tomorrow, just know that I love you.'"

I stared at her. "Really? He said that?"

She nodded.

"Did you ask him what it was about?"

"Yes. Over and over and louder and louder. And then he took my face very close to his and told me to be quiet, be *very* quiet. I remember it was dark, and when I looked into his eyes, I could see he was afraid. I had never seen him that way before. I kept saying, 'What's wrong? What's wrong, Terrance?' and he kept putting his hand over my mouth and telling me to be quiet. He'd tell me in the morning. We'd go off for a dinghy ride. Just the two of us and he'd tell me. Finally, from the other berth, Wes yells in, 'Hey, you guys, keep it down in there. These are thin walls, remember? Keep the marital urges to a minimum.' But Terrance was shaking. I held onto him, I held him really close all night long." Her voice broke. "The next day, he was gone."

"Did you tell the police this?"

"Who? The police in the Bahamas? I tried. But they never questioned us separately. Wes and Marcus, all four of them could hear all my answers, and I had this feeling that Terrance didn't want them knowing what it was. So, I kept quiet. The police, they just wanted us gone and for it to be an accident. They needed it to be an accident. Murder is bad for tourism."

I nodded. We were quiet for a while after that. I took the helm while Audra went down to the galley to make coffee.

Instantly, she was back up. "Em, we got problems down here. Major problems."

—◦◦◦—

Mother,

It's been a few days since I gave Ben (and Em, too, really. She was there!) all of those papers at the rest stop. When I left, I told them I was going away because, when I drove away, I had no clear plans. Only after a couple of miles did I know where I was going. I took the exit. I know the way by heart.

After a long while, I turned up the mile-long driveway to the Clifford farmhouse. Nobody seemed to be around. No one came rushing out of the house. No barking dogs came out to greet me. The truck was there, but all was quiet. I pulled my car next to the truck and got out. I stood there for a minute smelling all the smells I remembered—the farm, the gardens, the overladen late summer flowers in the boxes under the windows, the barns. I walked slowly up the uneven flagstone path to the door. Before I knocked on the door, I fiddled with my name pin, straightened it. It always seems to go sideways on my jackets, no matter how I affix it to what I'm wearing. I wanted to make sure they could read it and maybe save them the embarrassment of not remembering who I was.

For a long time, I stood there on the front porch. Maybe, even with my name tag, they wouldn't remember me. I felt a twinge of something. Fear? And an awful thought—what if the Cliffords didn't welcome me? What if they forgot who I was? What if they only liked me because of the money they got as foster parents? Now that I was gone, they would have no reason to even listen to my story. Or take me back in. I was an adult now. Their responsibility for me ended a long time ago.

I'd been so looking forward to getting here, driving twelve hours straight and sleeping in the car along the side of the road when I got too tired. I wanted the Cliffords' advice. I wanted to tell them what I'd discovered about Terrance and you. I wanted to tell them Terrance was dead. Murdered. I wanted to tell them what I was beginning—maybe—to believe.

The Cliffords knew all about my fixation with your murderer. The Cliffords tried to dissuade me, saying that the police were working on it, but I don't think they believed that any more than I did.

When I was with Captain Em and Ben at the rest area, I didn't fully understand things. It wasn't until driving to the Cliffords that something clicked. Maybe it was because I had the time in the car to think, to remember. I began to understand why it was that I had such a visceral reaction to the couples whose boats I'd been hired to deliver. I began to understand why I had fainted, hung back, felt like throwing up when they were walking toward me on the beach.

I stood there on the Clifford's porch now, my fingers forming into fists to knock on the door. (The doorbell was perpetually broken.) A little girl, a ragamuffin of a skinny little thing in shorts and dirty knees came around the side of the house. She stopped when she saw me. She wore a pink T-shirt and pink flip-flops that were miles too big for her. Maybe they belonged to Mama Clifford. The Cliffords were adamant about shoes on the farm. We were absolutely not allowed to wander through the barns or anywhere in bare feet. "Too many nails," Mama Clifford used to say. "Nails and bad things. Everyone wears shoes. That's the law."

"Hello," I said to the little girl.

She stared at me, eyes wide.

"Is Uncle Clifford around?" I asked.

She pointed out to a far field where I could just make out a figure atop a green tractor. My breath caught in my throat. I wanted to see him. I wanted to run out there like I had done so many times before. More than anything, I wanted Mama Clifford to put her arms around me and tell me everything was going to be okay. I wanted Uncle Clifford to hitch up the trailer and load up the small sailboat and take all of us to the lake.

But as I stared at the girl, at the figure out on the tractor, I knew that I couldn't. It would put them in danger. It might even put this little girl in danger. If someone were looking for me, the Clifford's farm would be the first place they would come.

Without saying goodbye to the little girl, I turned and walked back to my car. I got in and drove back down the driveway and out onto the highway. I did not look back.

Janice

CHAPTER 29

Water was bubbling up through the floorboards. It was already an inch deep in places.

"I can't believe this is happening," she said reaching for towels. She pulled off her shoes to go barefoot in the water.

I poked my head outside and looked around. We were a few miles out from Boston. There were no boats in the vicinity for me to hail. Because the wind was calm, I shut down the engine and headed quickly down below. We needed first to figure out where the water was coming from; then we could seal it. Then we would tentatively limp back to shore.

The logical place for a leak of this magnitude was one of the through-hulls. I checked them all but found them to be intact.

Audra was moving scatter rugs and containers from the floor. I'm always amazed at how quickly a boat can fill with water. Drill a hole in the bottom of a sailboat only an inch in diameter, and you can fill and sink an entire boat within fifteen minutes.

As soon as I opened the half door to the engine room, I realized I should have come here first. Water was burbling up like a fountain from near where the shaft met the bottom of the boat. The stuffing box.

"Should we call a mayday?" she said.

"No need yet. I think I've got it located. If I can stop this, we'll be okay."

Maydays are only called if life is in imminent danger. I plunged my fingers into the water to tighten it, surprised at how loose it was and how much water was making its way into the boat. This was curious. Before taking the boat out, I had finger checked the stuffing box. It was tight then. It had seemed perfectly fine. How had it loosened this much in so short a time? I finger-tightened it, and it lessened the flow but didn't quite stop it. When I brought my fingers away, they seemed to be covered in some kind of a waxy substance or compound, almost pinkish in color. I brought them to my nose. I couldn't figure out what it smelled like. When I had looked at this earlier, all was dry. I decided that this had to be some sort of substance that became liquid under heat. In other words, the boat would be perfectly fine when sitting at the dock. But when the engine heat reached a certain level, it would liquify.

"Found it," I told Audra when I emerged, wet and dirty from the engine room.

"What is it?" She was still mopping.

"The stuffing box."

"What's wrong with it?"

"There's some sort of compound on it. I can't tell what it is, but I'm going to need some tools. A couple of wrenches would do it. I saw a toolbox somewhere?"

"Yes, Terrance's. Over there." She was still mopping, damp hair in her face.

"And some rags?"

"Under the sink in the head. I'll get a bunch for you."

I opened the toolbox to find it—empty. "Audra? Does Terrance have any other tools? There's none in here."

"What?" She came over behind me and peered into the empty box. "This is impossible! There are always tools in here. In fact, it's usually overfilled. You have to lay all the tools a certain way, or you can't even get the lid down. How can this be?"

"Maybe he came back before you guys went on your trip?"

"And took all his tools out of his toolbox? That's crazy."

I said, "Those people whose dock you use? Could they have been on your boat?"

"They would never do that. They're not even here."

"I'm going to need some sort of wrench to properly tighten this stuffing box. I may be able to tighten it enough by hand until we get to shore. We'll need to keep checking."

"I'm baffled. I don't understand," she kept saying. "Who took the tools? They were all here before. They're not at the house."

Meanwhile, I was kicking myself for not bringing my own tools. I always carry a small set with me on a survey, but as I wasn't surveying this until tomorrow, I had conveniently left them in my tool kit in my car back at her place. I wrapped a rag around the stuffing box and turned it until I got it passably tight. I would need to work on it properly when we docked.

I went up top to see where we were. The nearest boat was a speck on the horizon and no hazards in the way.

"Should I call for help?" she asked. "We have towing insurance."

"I've got it dried off and tightened now. At least for the time being. If you can take the helm, I'll keep checking on it and finger tightening it until we get to the dock."

"There are some tools in my jeep," she said.

"Good. We'll get this figured out."

"You said there was something on the stuffing box, and you have no idea what it is?"

"I don't know, but I'm going to find out."

"Could it have been put there purposely?" she asked.

"That's what I'm beginning to think."

"The combination lock." She wiped her brow with her hand. "I knew it. It wasn't Terrance. He wouldn't have come here without telling me. And his missing papers. It's all connected. I don't know how, but it is."

I nodded. I was beginning to agree with her.

"I should probably report this to the police," she mused.

"You should."

"The boat could have sunk."

"It could have."

"But I'm not going to," she said frowning.

I looked at her sharply.

"Because they won't believe me. They won't get the connection. Can you..." She turned to me. "Can you talk to your friend Ben about this, too?"

"I will when I see him next. But I still think maybe you should report this to the police."

"I'll think about it."

"Do more than think about it."

She shrugged, looked away from me.

Once we had docked *Myriad*, I worked on the engine with the tools in Audra's jeep while she mopped the boat out.

"So," I said to her on the way home, "you still want me to survey the boat tomorrow?"

"Of course." She took the same circuitous route home. "And I think I know who did this. I think I know who was there."

I looked over at her. "You do?"

"The four of them. Wes and Beth, Michelle and Marcus. I think they did this."

I stared at her.

"I wouldn't put it past them. Their wives."

"You think Beth and Michelle did this? Why?"

"They hate me," was her answer.

It was the way she said it, almost like a simpering child, her bottom lip puckered out. It was an expression there for just an instant, and then she was back to being her rational self.

When we got to her house, she pulled out a bottle of wine, and while we ate a salad with feta cheese sprinkled on the top, and drank wine, she talked about Michelle and Beth. Maybe it was the wine or everything she had been through over the past month, but I began, again, to see the theatrical Audra, the eccentric Audra, and I wondered if what she was telling me was all entirely true. Was any of it true? Maybe Ben was right. Maybe she did this whole boat thing herself. Because why wouldn't she go to the police? I hadn't seen the level of fear that I would have expected during that situation, did I? Or even the level of mourning.

"It could have been them," she kept saying. "I wouldn't put it past Beth or Michelle to do this."

I nodded, drank my second glass of wine, and ate my salad.

Later in my room, I looked up Michelle's number online.

I called her. No answer. I left a message. "Hello, Michelle? We've never met. I'm Captain Em Ridge. I was the one who took your boats to Florida after the accident. I'm in Boston. I'm here to survey Audra's boat tomorrow. I was just wondering if you'd like to get together for a late coffee or something tomorrow after I complete the survey, and before I head home. Text me or call me."

After I put down my phone, I wondered why the hell I had just called her. What did I hope to find out?

On the way to the boat the following morning I got a text from Michelle.

I'm glad you called. Do you mind if Beth comes along? She wants to meet you, too. There are some things about Audra you ought to know.

CHAPTER 30

The coffee shop was fairly crowded at quarter to five in the afternoon when I got there after a straightforward boat survey where I found nothing more amiss than a few things that needed minor, easy fixes. It was a good boat, a solid boat. I found no more trouble spots like the stuffing box, and when I was finished, I made sure I set the combination lock the way she liked it.

Those two women sitting at that table over there frowning into their frothy coffee drinks had to be Michelle and Beth.

I approached them. "Michelle? Beth?"

The woman to my right nodded and motioned to the empty seat across from her, "You must be Emmeline then. I'm Beth."

"Nice to meet you." I sat down.

"And I'm Michelle," the other said.

The one named Michelle had eyes that darted like she was constantly on the lookout for something or someone. Her hair was expertly highlighted and blow-dried to perfection. She wore a clingy red sleeveless top and white pants. Not many women—certainly not me—could pull off an outfit like that. My neighbor Dot would call her kind of hair, "movie-star-hair." Yet there was something cringing about her, like if you touched those bony shoulders with the end of your finger, she would pull out her claws.

"It's nice to meet you both," I said.

"Go get yourself a coffee if you want one," Beth said with an indication of her hand. "The line's short now. It was long when we got here. Then come back. There's lots to talk about. Lots we need to tell you."

She looked to be a courser, shorter, sturdier version of her friend. Even in this heat, she wore a long-sleeved dark shirt with extra long sleeves, the kind with thumb holes that come down below the wrist. The turtleneck was high on her neck and ended right up under her chin. Bulky, shiny jewelry hung from everywhere—her ears, her wrists, her neck, her fingers, her thumbs. I wondered if she wore all of this on their boat. I decided that she probably did. I've known women who wear all kinds of dangly stuff while sailing. Me? I always worry about catching an errant ear hoop on a moving sail and losing at best, an earring, or at worst, an earlobe.

I wound my way through the maze of tables to the counter to get a coffee and a sandwich. I was suddenly hungry. This was the kind of coffee shop that served lentil sandwiches and soy milk lattes and toxin-ridding teas with exotic names. All I wanted was plain coffee. I'm very boring, very predictable when it comes to coffee. No frothy chai latte soy milk whipped-cream covered drinks for me. I had a bit of a drive ahead of me tonight which warranted an extra large one. And a ham sandwich. I wanted a plain old ham sandwich with mayo and real butter rather than some whole grain sandwich piled high with sprouts and avocados. And that's exactly what I ordered, a ham sandwich on rye and don't go easy on the mayo.

The first thing Beth said when I sat down was, "Tell us that you didn't tell Audra you were meeting with us."

"I didn't, but why would I not tell her?"

"Plenty of reasons," Beth barked. "Why are you here, anyway? I mean down in Boston?"

"I was surveying her boat."

Beth stared at me for several seconds, her mouth opened, until Michelle said, "I told you this, Beth. I told you that's why she was here." Her hands shook a bit as they surrounded her cardboard coffee cup.

"How was it?" Beth asked. "Her boat?"

I've always maintained a certain level of boat

surveyor/client privilege, so all I said was, "Everything checked out."

She eyed me. "Well, that's good then."

"I thought so."

"She's got this thing about us," Beth said. "Audra does."

"What thing?" I picked up my sandwich and took a bite. For a hipster coffee shop, the plain sandwich was surprisingly good.

Neither answered. I waited.

"She just doesn't like us," Beth said. "Just ask her."

Michelle looked at me, "I'm intrigued," she said, "as to why you called me in the first place."

I had no good answer to this. Curiosity? A morbid interest? "Maybe I just wanted to meet the women whose boats I was hired to deliver."

Beth added, "I was with Michelle when she got your email. Of course, I had to come, too. Wes and me," she went on. "We just got back from being with Wes's mother. She's not good." She shook her head. "Really not good. Really bad."

"Sorry to hear that," I said.

"And then the moment we got back, I'm over at Michelle's, and your email comes."

"Good timing," I said.

"Did Audra say anything about us? About me in particular?"

I didn't want to tell her that Audra had called her "a piece of work." I put down my sandwich, looked at them and said, "What do I need to know about Audra? Why did you want to meet me?"

"Basically," Michelle said, "we don't entirely trust her."

"Why not?"

Michelle continued, "Terrance was an asset to the company, but..."

"But what?" I asked.

A look passed between the two of them.

"At the beginning," Beth said. "He was an asset at the

beginning."

I said, "Okay. I'm not following. You said Terrance was an asset to your company, but not to trust Audra — who doesn't even work for you?"

Beth said, "He was an asset at the beginning of his time with us. The operative word being 'was,'" she added. "He worked out fine initially."

Michelle said, "We liked Audra at the beginning, too."

"She seemed nice."

"We really tried."

"With both of them. We really tried."

"So did Marcus and Wes."

Back and forth. Good friends finishing each other's sentences. They had known each other for a long time. Friends from childhood, I'd been told.

I asked, "How is it that you came to hire Terrance in the first place?"

Michelle pursed her lips. "He applied, what was it, Beth, mere hours after we posted the job online?"

"Something like that. Yeah."

"It was sort of weird."

"What was weird about it?" I asked.

"It was almost too perfect. He was almost too perfect for the job."

"Had all the qualifications we were looking for."

"Every single one."

"We hired him almost immediately. It seemed perfect."

"He left a better paying job to come work for us. That was curious."

"Why was that so curious?" I asked.

Michelle peered down into her coffee and kept her eyes away from me.

"What about Audra?" I asked.

The women were quiet for a moment, and then they looked at each other. Beth said, "The two of them seemed to have one goal, and that was to sabotage our company."

I put my sandwich down.

"Wes and Marcus couldn't even see it," Beth said.

"Not at first."

"Some money's gone missing," Beth said.

"Money?" I wasn't expecting this.

Michelle put both hands flat on the table. "Beth, we don't know any of this for sure. We shouldn't even be talking about this. You remember how Marcus warned us..."

I looked from one to the other.

"It's what Wes said. He's the one who figured it out, Michelle."

"What did the police say?" I asked. I didn't remember hearing or reading about any money being gone.

"We didn't call the police," Michelle said. "It was such an insignificant amount."

"We decided to deal with it internally."

"Just a couple thousand dollars."

"Just over a thousand, and I, for one, find it coincidental that it started just at the time when we hired Terrance. It was almost like they targeted our company," Beth said.

"We don't know that, Beth. Please..."

I noticed a twitch in Beth's right eye, and she was playing with those long sleeves of hers, pulling her thumbs out and putting them back in again. She pulled the sleeve up over the wrist of her right hand. A line of raised welts surrounded her wrist like a red-jeweled bracelet. When she saw where I was looking she quickly pulled her sleeves back down over her wrists, her thumbs through the thumb holes, her hands in her lap.

"How did the two of you meet?" I asked in an effort to shift the conversation. "I know you've known each other a long time."

"Since school," Michelle said.

"Childhood friends."

"We grew up like sisters."

"Like sisters."

"Beth lived with us for a while. In middle school."

"So you lived together?" I asked.

Beth sighed. "Okay, here's the story since you're so interested. I had a pretty crappy childhood."

"My parents took in kids," Michelle said.

Beth's voice softened. She smiled, even. "I went there. And everything changed after that."

"We became instant sisters."

"Instant best friends."

"Shared a room, even."

"And we've been together the whole time since."

Michelle looked at her friend. "Except when you went away."

"Except for that one time."

"We were going to go to the same college..." Michelle explained.

"But I didn't get in," Beth said. "I went away for a while. Hitchhiked around for a year."

"I wondered if we would even see each other again."

Michelle looked at me and the awkward nervousness she had displayed before turned into a cheery grin. "And she came back married! I've never forgiven her that, that I wasn't in her wedding party."

"Really?" I said. "You came back *married*?"

Beth grinned. Michelle said, "But I quickly forgave her because that's how I met Marcus. Marcus and Wes were friends forever. Just like Beth and me."

"And you married Marcus," I said.

"They were college buddies," Beth said. "And I credit Michelle's beautiful family and Wes for saving me. Wes has been my salvation."

I nodded and drank more of my coffee.

"The four of us have been pretty inseparable since."

"He swept me off my feet." Her voice was monotone, and she pulled at her shirt sleeves.

"After you stole him from his old girlfriend," Michelle said with a smirk.

"Oh, that story," Beth said. "I don't even know if it's true or not. It's been told a million times by the guys." She made a dismissive gesture with her hand. "And so, I guess yes." She nodded. "Apparently, he had a girlfriend. The story goes that when I came on the scene, they broke up over me."

"Well," I said, and then, "if you four were so close, and you thought that Terrance and Audra were stealing from you, why would you invite them on a sailing trip with you? Isn't that just asking for trouble?"

"It was Marcus's idea," Michelle said. "Wes didn't want them to come." She looked at Beth, and the woman nodded, all that jewelry clanging. "Marcus thought all we had to do was to get to know Audra and Terrance better. We were able to leave our kids with my mother, and we went."

"You have children?" I asked.

"We have two daughters," Michelle said. "Twelve and fourteen..." The way she said it, I expected any minute for her to whip out her phone and start showing me pictures.

"Nice," I said.

"Wes and I were never able to have children," Beth said.

"Oh."

"We wanted them." There was a sound like sadness when she said this. "We tried and tried, but it didn't happen. But I love Michelle's daughters as if they were my own."

"They love you, too," Michelle said. "They love their Aunt Beth."

"So you guys have any theories about Terrance's death, then?" I asked.

"I wouldn't put it past Audra," Beth said. "I really wouldn't."

"Beth...really?" Michelle said.

I asked, "You think Audra killed Terrance?"

"Well, we all know it was an accident, but I'm saying is that I wouldn't put it past her. That's all I'm saying."

I said, "There've been some new developments down in

the Bahamas."

"What sort of developments?" Michelle asked.

"Sunny was murdered."

"You mean the guy who took us diving?" Michelle asked, her eyes wide.

"Yes."

"Who killed him?" There was a catch in Michelle's voice.

"The police are working on that. But they're close to coming up with the name of the murderer and the motive. Very close. And it's all connected to Terrance." I wasn't sure why I was lying about this. I guess I wanted to gauge their reactions.

Michelle's upper lip quivered while Beth kept rubbing her wrists over and over and staring into her coffee. It looked like her wrist was giving her pain.

Beth's voice was shaky when she said, "Maybe that was Audra, too?"

Audra. So quick for her to blame Audra.

Later, when we rose to leave, Beth's shirt rode up on her back a bit. And I saw bruises there. A row of them. Like red berries up her spine. Quickly, she pulled her shirt back down as she raced on ahead of us out of the restaurant. They had come in separate cars. This surprised me, although I wasn't quite sure why.

As she made her way to her car, I noticed how small she was compared to Michelle—small and sturdy, like a Jack Russell terrier. She moved ahead of us and got her keys out of her large bag. Michelle hung back. When Beth was well out of sight, Michelle put her hand on my shoulder and said, "There is something…"

I turned, but not before I noticed Beth staring at this exchange. It seemed that Michele saw this, too, and so she said rather quickly, "It was so, um, so nice to finally meet you. So nice."

Then she was gone.

Mom,

It was me. It was me, Mom, who broke into Audra's house and took all of Terrance's files. I had to. I thought about calling Audra and explaining the situation, but I decided not to. Something was happening, and I didn't need her to be a part of it, too. I didn't need to add to the craziness of things.

I found an unsecured basement window. Basement windows are the most vulnerable. That's the sort of stuff you learn when you grow up like me. Terrance told me he kept all of the stuff in a file cabinet in Audra's art studio. All I needed was to find this studio, and I'd be home free. He told me that Audra seldom checked the cabinet and thought his obsession was "ghoulish." If I was careful—and I'm always careful—I knew it might be years before she realized that anyone had even come into her studio, much less taken Terrance's papers. I needed them. She didn't. If I'm to carry on Terrance's work, I need them. I'd get his papers, and then I'd photocopy every single one. I had to make photocopies to give to Ben. I had a lot of my own papers. Terrance and I had shared a lot, but not everything. I knew Terrance had personal emails and things he wanted to protect me from. But the time has come now for me to carry on with his work. It's what he would have wanted.

I couldn't believe how huge and beautiful Terrance and Audra's house was. Each room was like an art show. Marilou used to do watercolor paintings, but hers were tiny flowers done with detailed precision. Marilou was embarrassed about all of her paintings and never wanted to show anyone. "It's just my little hobby," she used to say, hiding everything with her hands when you walked by. Francine had framed several of these and hung them in the living room, much to Marilou's chagrin. I have several of her paintings that I was able to grab and shove into my suitcase even as Social Services waited for me at the door.

But these paintings, these that Audra did were gigantic, vibrant and loopy. Great swishes and swashes of colors, ladies in dresses sitting on blankets playing stringed instruments, humongous trees, too giant and gaudy to be real, and everything green and vibrant, mountains, forests and mushrooms. The whole house was a gallery. I kept staring as I walked from room to room. I kept wishing I could show all of this to Marilou. She would love this place.

There was a set of stairs set into the second-floor hallway, and I climbed it and ended up in Audra's studio loft. It was a wondrous place with walls stacked with even more paintings and more on the walls. Easels and messy paints. Brushes in bottles.

The file cabinet leaned against a back wall, the only wall with no windows. Quickly, I went to it. It wasn't even locked. I'd brought along three of those cheap grocery store bags you can buy for a buck from Hannafords. I hoped I could fit everything in them.

So, Audra, I'm sorry if I freaked you out. Hopefully, you won't even notice that anyone was there. Purposely, I didn't even take the money that was sitting right there so you wouldn't notice it right away. I'm pretty good at sneaking around, covering my tracks. I've done it all my life.

And now that I am huddled in my motel room, I need to find the answers before it's too late. It's starting to make sense. Some of it.

Janice

CHAPTER 31

It wasn't until I had driven more than half an hour away from the coffee shop that I realized how deathly quiet it was. I always have music going in my car. Setting up a playlist from my phone into my car speakers is one of the first things I do when I set out on a trip. And sing along. I always sing along. Today I'm not even thinking of music. Beth's bruises were on my mind for one and Audra's sabotaged boat for another.

The stuffing box — should I have mentioned this to Beth and Michelle? Had someone been trying to kill Terrance, and this was the first "try?"

I had put a few scrapings of the stuffing box substance in a baggie and planned to take to my buddy Geoff. If there was anyone on the island who knew boats and compounds, it was Geoff.

Even though Ben was taking some time away, he was involved in this. I stopped along the side of the road and texted him:

I found out some important information. Some new stuff has come to light. Did you know that Wes and Marcus had some money go missing from the company? Do you think that's important? Apparently, they never went to the police about it. Pls call or text me, asap.

I pulled away from the rest area and headed north. I'd be home in two hours. I had no idea about the tides. That was the last thing on my mind while I was sitting in the coffee shop with Michelle and Beth. I had to admit that sometimes living at the end of an island was a hassle, but in a way, it was worth it. Once I was there, it was this little bit of heaven on earth.

On the outskirts of Portland, my phone buzzed. Ben!

At the first place I could pull over, I read the text. *Call me when you can talk.*

I did so. "I can talk," I said.

"Em." My name said stolidly and soberly. It was enough to stop me in my tracks.

"Ben?" I said.

"I'm taking some personal time."

"You already told me that." Why was his voice so strange? "I already know that. I'm sorry for texting you then."

"It's not that..."

"Oh?"

"My wife is here."

"Your wi..."

"She showed up yesterday."

I absolutely had no words. His wife? His *wife*? The way he called her by the possessive, "my" as in MY wife. Not "my ex-wife" or even her name. Not "Cindy showed up on my doorstep..." said in a slightly disparaging way, but "My wife is here."

"Em? You there?"

"I'm here."

"I'm sorry. I... We're working on things."

"Well, I'm glad you're working on *things*. That's wonderful for you that you're working on *things*." I could barely keep the sarcasm out of my voice. I gripped the steering wheel hard.

"Em, it's not like that... I..."

"Ben? Don't call me anymore, okay? Do not call me. Not even for police information stuff. Nothing. Until you get your shit together, don't call me."

I ended the call and threw the phone onto the passenger seat. It landed on the floor.

This was it. I was done. I couldn't do this anymore. My mistake? Getting involved with him in the first place. Hadn't my friends warned me about "becoming involved" with a married man? But I hadn't known he was married at first. He never told me, and he should have, right? Of course, he should have. It was *his* fault. He should have shared all of the horrible stuff of his past, even his son before we got involved. Before he kissed me the way he had. Good thing, I thought. Good thing it was only a kiss. One kiss. And didn't lead to more. One stupid kiss. He was married.

"Tell me, Em," my sailing friend Joan had told me almost a year ago. "You can't be that stupid, can you?"

Well, apparently, I can be. Tired of any playlist I could come up with, I found a pop station on the radio and turned it up loud. Real loud. And even though I hate modern pop music and don't know any of the words to anything, I sang along. If I screamed hard enough, if I kept it loud and angry, maybe then I wouldn't cry.

At home, I got my animals, had tea with EJ, and told him everything.

"Ben seemed so nice," he said.

"Some people are not what they seem."

"None of us are," he said. There was a sad look in his eyes. "Em, maybe you need to get the whole story."

"What whole story, EJ? And, what would be the whole story? He's married. I was a little interlude—no, I wasn't even that—I don't know what I was, and now she's come home to him, and all will be jolly. He's back with his wife. I did tell you that, right?"

He was quiet for a while, his lips pursed, his fingertips together on the tabletop. Finally, he said, "We all have a story. We all have some sadness we are working through. All of us do. Maybe listen to his whole story before you write him off completely."

"I have listened to his whole, complete story. And, I'm done."

Later that night, after a beer and many more cups of tea, I got to thinking about Wes and Beth. Was Wes an abuser? Had Beth known what Wes was like when she married him? Had she been like me and not known he was an abuser? She kept calling him her "salvation," but was she overdoing it just a little bit? Like Audra? Why were these women so hard to read?

Once I had calmed down a bit, I went to my computer and read Sunny's final message. The two words at the end jumped out at me. "Call Marcus."

I also remembered that Marcus had handed me his card and said, "Call me. Call me if you need to talk."

Marcus?

And then there was Michelle at the coffee shop, pulling me aside, as if she had something important to tell me, and then looking up at Beth and hurriedly saying how happy she was to meet me. Had there been more she wanted to tell me?

I pulled Marcus's card from the bottom of my bag. I looked at it. His name, email, and phone number. That was all.

I thought about it all night, and in the morning, plugged his number into my cell phone.

CHAPTER 32

Two rings. Three rings. I began to hope it would go to voice mail. What would I say? Hi! This is Captain Em Ridge. You told me to call you. Do you want to tell me why? Oh, and hey, Sunny told me to call you, too. And now he's dead. And your wife. She wanted to tell me something, too.

I was just about to hang up when the call was answered. A rather tired sounding, "Yeah?"

"Is this Marcus Downey?"

"Yeah."

"This is Captain Em Ridge."

"Hello." Not a note of surprise. It was as if he was expecting my call.

I said, "In Miami, you said to call you if I had questions. Also, Sunny sent me a message. He said to call you, too."

"I...um...I saw that, too."

"You saw Sunny's message? On Facebook?"

"Yeah. Everybody did. I saw where he said to call me. I wish he hadn't written it so publicly."

"Did you know Sunny is dead now? He was murdered. The police think it's something random, maybe a bar fight. But I know it's not."

"You're probably right."

"What do you know?" I asked him. "Why would Sunny tell me to call you?"

For a moment I thought I'd lost the connection.

"Marcus?"

"Wait a minute. Let me go outside here. Quieter out there. My kids are making a ruckus as usual."

Seconds later, he was back, and his voice was stronger.

"Sunny and I talked," he said. "After Terrance died, I began wondering about things. I went to Sunny. He was afraid he was going to be sued. I think he wanted to pick my brain. I ended up agreeing with him."

"Agreeing with him about what?"

When he didn't immediately answer, I asked, "Why did you give me your card?"

"Because I knew you and Sunny were friends. I was worried for you and for Sunny. I was right to worry."

I thought about that for a moment before I said, "What does all this have to do with Terrance and Audra? I had coffee with your wife and Beth. They told me about the missing money and that you suspected Audra and Terrance of sabotaging your company somehow."

His voice was even quieter when he said, "They told you that?"

"They did."

"I'm fairly sure it wasn't Audra and Terrance who did that."

"Who do you think it was then?"

"That's not important."

"You don't think it's important?"

"It was such a small amount. Terrance thought it might be just some little error, something that we didn't catch. He fixed it."

I was confused. "Beth said all this happened after Terrance was hired."

"No, it was around the same time. Wes didn't want me hiring Terrance for fear of what he might find. That was the bottom line."

"What would he have found? What happened to the money?" I asked. "Who took it?"

Very quietly he said, "Wes. Maybe Wes. Or Beth. Maybe the two of them together."

Wes!

He went on. "Wes and I have been close friends, all four of

us have been close. Wes and I are like brothers…"

"And Michelle and Beth like sisters. They told me all about it."

"I always thought Wes had my back. Well, maybe he did once upon a time. This work changed him. Our business together changed him."

"How?" I asked.

"Making money became the most important thing to him. So much so that I've been trying to leave this partnership, Michelle and me both. The cruise was Wes's idea. He thought it might heal the tension that was growing between us."

"And you wanted Terrance and Audra to come?"

"They were part of it now. Part of us. But it gets worse. We had an offer of a buyout. A pretty substantial one. I was all for it. But then I found out, well, actually it was Terrance who found out that the offer was bogus. A scam. They would have taken the company and our assets and we, Michelle and me, would have been left with nothing. Terrance came highly recommended, and we were hoping he'd figure it all out for us. A totally unbiased third party. That's what I was hoping for."

"But he ends up getting killed," I said.

"Michelle and I did something on our own. We hired a PI to get to the bottom of this buyout scam. He traced the IP address right back to Wes. Actually, Beth's computer. When I confronted Wes, he, of course, denied it, and by this time, the internet path back to her computer had been deleted. And we hadn't copied it. So I had nothing then. No proof. No proof to take to the police."

"Why are you telling me all of this?"

"I want as many people to know as possible. I think Janice knows something about this and that she might be in danger."

"Janice? What would she know?"

"I don't know. Just a feeling I have. Michelle agrees with me."

I had no idea what to say about this. "All I know is when

we met her on Eleuthera, she took one look at us and fainted."

I ventured, "She took one look at you four and realized she wasn't up for the job."

He was quiet for a minute. "Could be. That's what people are saying. I think it was more…" His voice trailed off.

"What more?"

"I don't know."

I took a breath. "I think Beth is being abused." I told him about the bruise marks on her back and wrists.

"There's something you need to know about Beth. She's not the victim here."

I was standing beside my big window and looking out at my sunny bay. "If she's being abused, she's a victim, period. No matter who she is."

He sighed into the phone. "If there is abuse going on, I would say that it's the other way around."

"What?"

"If there is any abuse going on, I would say that Wes is the one being abused."

His words shocked me. "I saw her bruises, Marcus. She wore a turtleneck to hide them, but I saw."

"You saw what she wanted you to see. I'm afraid that Beth has him tied around her little finger. He would do anything for her. She wants more money? He jumps. I think Beth's the reason he has gone all crazy about making more money. She's never satisfied. She wants something? He goes out and buys it even when they can't afford it. She has this hold over him that Michelle and I don't understand." His voice became quieter. "I don't understand."

"Wow." It was all I could think of to say.

"It started a while ago. Something was going on with them that I couldn't put my finger on. We were so busy. We were busy raising our daughters. But it was getting worse and worse. A few years ago now, I took him out for a beer and asked him what was going on. He told me that he and Beth had been trying for a child. Beth was on fertility drugs. It didn't work. He told me the drugs were changing her personality for the worse."

I stood at the window and watched a kayaker disappear around a bend on the calm water.

He went on. "She wanted children. They couldn't seem to have them, so she wanted IVF treatments. She was demanding them, demanding children, and blaming Wes. That's what he told me. Those treatments are expensive. That's when money started going missing. Because I suspected Wes but knew the pressure he was under, I didn't say anything. It kept happening. I confronted him, but in a sort of friend to friend way. He denied it, and I believed him. He became just as concerned as me in finding out where the money was going. I always felt there was something I was missing. Wes and Beth fight constantly. After Terrance died, Sunny witnessed one of their more heated arguments. Later, Wes went to Sunny and told him to forget anything he had heard."

"What had he heard?"

"Sunny told me he hadn't heard anything specific. Just something like, 'We have to see this through'"

"So, that's maybe what got Sunny killed?"

"I don't know," he said. "All I know is that Sunny was worried for his diving business and wanted to know what I thought. So I told him about their troubled marriage."

"Audra told me something," I said to him. "She told me that her husband had talked to her about 'blowing the lid off' something on this trip. Do you have any idea what she could have been talking about?"

Another pause. A long one.

"Marcus?"

"I don't know what she was talking about. It could be this whole money business, but if I were you, I'd stay away from Wes and Beth. Away from this whole thing."

"What? Wait..." But he had ended the call.

After the phone call, I took Rusty out for a walk. He was

hobbling, yet so happy to be out in the backwoods with me. I watched him and thought about what Marcus had said. Stay away from Wes and Beth. Something else occurred to me, too. Murder someone in another country, and you're sure to tie things up in red tape forever. Yes, the Bahamas were the perfect place for the murder of someone not Bahamian.

I picked up a stick and threw it for Rusty. He did his best to fetch it for me, tail wagging in joy while I wondered — would Sunny's fate be mine?

To my mother,

I never really believed it was Russell who killed you, not deep in my heart anyway. I know how much the evidence pointed to him. I know what Terrance always thought, how the police weren't even looking for him, and wasn't it strange that he disappeared at such a convenient time? But Terrance never met him.

I could never really get my head around it. I didn't believe, not entirely, what Francine and Marilou believed—that if you stayed with Russell, there would be hell to pay.

Because I had seen you. I had seen the light in your eyes. You were so beaming, so happy. You were different in those months that you knew Russell. You hadn't told me about him, but I could tell. I had also seen Russell that one time. I saw the way he looked at you. He wouldn't kill you. You were in love with each other. I knew that then. I still know it now.

When Terrance would email me, "How can you still think it wasn't Russell? He's the most logical choice. Who else is there?" I would reply, "It could have been lots of people— people in the restaurant where they worked. Did they check all of them? There was always this cook that Francine would argue with. What about that guy?"

"The police questioned them all thoroughly. They all had alibis."

"So did Russell."

"Leaving quickly from work can be easily arranged," he wrote.

"Yeah, for all of them," I wrote back.

Terrance remained fixated on this Russell person, and at one point, asked me to write down as much as I could remember about him. He wanted me to go back in my memory and tell him all of my impressions, however tiny and small— every detail about Russell.

I have only the two memories of Russell—the one time when you and he were cuddled close on the couch, and the other time when I only heard him but didn't see him. That first time, though, I noticed something. He looked back at you with such longing. Such love. I'm not making this up or imagining it. It is how I remember it.

Then there was the time when I heard all of you instead of seeing you. Again, no one was expecting me home so early. A friend's mother drove me home when classes were cancelled because of a water main break in school. Francine met me in the hallway inside our apartment building, eyes wide. "What are you doing here? Janice, why are you *here*?"

When I told her, she grabbed hold of my hands and said, "Let's go."

"Go where?"

"Just out. Do you want some ice cream? Let's go get some ice cream. We'll get cones and then we'll bring some ice cream home for later." She was talking too fast.

By now I could hear the yelling.

"What's going on?" I asked.

"Nothing. Let's just go."

"Where's my mom?"

"Let's go!"

"But my mom's in there! I hear her!"

"Janice! Now!" I had never heard Francine use that tone with me.

"Where's Marilou?" I asked quietly.

"She's at work. Now, come, come."

Loud voices came from inside the apartment. A woman— not you—was yelling, and then a man's voice, "No wait. We can all talk. We can get this straightened out."

I kept saying, "Who's in there? What's going on? Who's with my mom?"

And then I heard that woman saying, "Come on, Russell. Let's get out of here. I've had enough of her whining. Just enough!"

"No. No! Don't go!" It was your voice, and you were sobbing, crying.

Francine gripped my arm, took hold of my shoulders, and steered me down the stairs, out the door, and to the corner convenience store. She bought two ice-cream drumsticks from the freezer beside the checkout. We went outside and sat on a bench on the sidewalk and ate them in silence until they were gone. By the time we got back to the apartment, everything was quiet. You were in our shared room calmly reading a book, but your eyes were red like you'd been crying.

"Janice!" you said when you saw me. "Come here. Come sit beside me. Come sit beside your old mom." You closed your book and put it on the end table.

"Are you okay, Mom?" I asked.

"Here. Here." And you patted the space beside you on the bed. "I have something important to tell you."

When I cuddled in with you on your bed, I said, "What was all that yelling?"

"What yelling?"

"I heard some yelling before."

"Oh." You made a dismissive sound. "I'm okay. That was nothing. I'm fine since you're here. My precious angel."

"What do you want to tell me?" I asked.

You were quiet for a bit and said, "Later. Maybe this should wait until I'm sure."

"Sure about what?"

"Maybe this." You gave me a big snuggly hug then. I was glad you were smiling. "It's all going to work out. I just know it is."

In the night, when I got up to get a drink of water, I could hear whispering coming from behind Francine and Marilou's door. I went and stood with my ear pressed against it.

Marilou was crying. She was always the more sensitive one. "I told her," I could hear her saying, "I told her to stay away from him."

And then Francine. "She thinks they can work it out. If she's able to just get him alone, that is."

"I don't trust the two of them. I especially don't trust that woman."

"Well," said Francine, "I'm beginning to think she's more of a problem than Russell."

"You may be right."

Were they talking about you? What did all this mean?

There was more mumbling, then, more mumbling that I couldn't make out.

Russell wasn't around anymore after that, and you grew

sadder and sadder. The bits and pieces I was able to glean from whispered conversations were that Russell had gone back to his old girlfriend, the one he had before you. I guess she wasn't happy when you and Russell got together.

All of this—the murder, the dead picture of your face, cuddling in bed with you, all of this comes back at me with such force while I drive, drive, and think and piece things together. Little things. Big things. All of everything, and I am beginning to remember a whole lot more.

And I am astonished.

Jan

CHAPTER 33

After our walk in the woods, I packed up Rusty and put him in the car along with my Ziploc of stuffing box goop and headed over to the old ferry terminal. I found Geoff out in his yard, the engine cover off of an old Johnson outboard attached to a Boston Whaler, both of which had definitely seen better days.

"Hey," he said when I got out. Rusty also jumped out. I didn't even leash him because I knew he wouldn't go far.

"Hey yourself. You busy?" I got out the baggie.

"Not too. Seeing if I can get this old outboard workable."

"It yours?"

"Found it. On the mainland. Actually, it was going to be junked. Thought I could salvage it, fix it up, maybe sell it."

"Good for you."

I told him about my most recent survey and showed him the baggie of oily stuff. He climbed down from the boat, poked his finger into the bag.

"It's not Never Seize?" I said.

"Doesn't look like it. Wrong color. This here's a kind of pinkish." He brought it to his nose. "Where'd you get it?"

All I told him was that the owners had put "the wrong stuff" on their stuffing box and had nearly sunk the boat.

He looked at me. "Didn't the owners tell you what they used?"

I shook my head. "They didn't know." I didn't want to tell him the whole story. "Can I leave this with you?" I asked. "See if you might be able to figure out what it is?"

"Sure thing."

I didn't run off immediately, even though I felt all at loose ends and wanted to. If I was asking him to do me this favor, the least I could do was to spend some time shooting the breeze. So we chatted boats and engines and the crappy economy. Boaters always like to talk about the crappy economy.

Once home, I spent the rest of my day doing chores—cleaning, laundry, mopping floors, all that wonderful stuff, while all the time, trying to come up with some sort of connection between the murders of the three women and the more recent murders of Terrance and Sunny.

Later on in the afternoon, I made myself a double espresso and brought my laptop to life. I should leave this whole thing alone, I thought, leave it to the police, but curiosity mixed with equal amounts of fear was getting to me. The first thing I saw was that Michelle wanted to be my Facebook friend. I gladly accepted. This would give me immediate access to her life. I was especially interested in her "friends," namely Beth and Wes. Wes either didn't have a Facebook page or wasn't a "friend" of Michelle's, but Beth was.

Unfortunately, all Beth's photos and timeline were carefully private. I debated whether or not to request "friendship," but decided against it. Instead, I scoured Michelle's page and photos for hints. At this point, I had no idea what I was looking for. Proof that Beth was abused? What?

Michelle's photos were arranged in albums by date and event—*Trip to Aruba, Vacation to the Keys, Here We Are On Our Boat In Miami, The Four of Us Sailing Around Martha's Vineyard, With Friends! Cheers!*

Beth was in a lot of the pictures, as was Wes. I looked for more evidence of bruising on her body. Saw none.

In some of the photos, Beth wore the skimpiest of outfits—bathing suits, bikinis and tiny midriff bare tank tops. In others, however, she was clad from neck to wrist in long swimming tops, neoprene and stretchy turtlenecks. I tried to study the expression on her face in each photo.

There was nothing—no pictures, no specific album entitled, *Cruising the Bahamas*. That wouldn't be so strange, though. If someone died on a trip, would you really want to commemorate it with a Facebook album of here-we-are-having-fun pictures?

I noticed something else a bit odd. Michelle had requested to be my friend, yet her last timeline post was two months before their ill-fated trip had begun. Also, for the past year and a half, her timeline had ceased to be personal and were mostly re-postings of cute cats and inspirational sayings.

Except for one, one photo taken just before their Bahama trip. I checked the date. The six-person selfie was in the cockpit of *On Our Way*. Drinks and plates of cheese and crackers and nuts were on the small table between them. A typical sailing vacation picture. On the starboard side were Michelle and Marcus. She was sitting stiff and straight in a sky-blue bathing suit. One hand was on her husband's knee. She wasn't smiling. Neither was Marcus. Neither looked like they were enjoying it much.

Was there a reason for their grimness? Could the two of them have foreseen the tragic turn this trip would take?

Wes and Beth sat opposite. He was grinning with that glad-handing-happy-go-lucky way of his. Next to him, Beth's mouth was opened wide in a laugh. I zoomed in. No bruise marks. Nothing that I could see. I remembered what Marcus had said, "You saw what she wanted you to see." I zoomed in more closely. Beth was inclined toward Wes, her knee against his, but it looked as though he seemed to be leaning away from her. It was almost imperceptible, but I saw it.

At the stern were Audra and Terrance. The two of them were sitting close together. He was smiling at wherever joke had entranced Beth, one hand in midair when the photo was taken, the other holding his drink. Next to him, Audra sat still and straight her knees together, her face neutral. Terrance was "giddy" on this trip, full of "pent-up energy," according to Audra. She wore a sheer white bathing suit coverup that came above her knees. Underneath, her one-piece bathing suit was a pale shade of green. I judged by the cut of her geometric hair that this was early in their trip, maybe even the day they left. I studied the photo, hoping to get clues from the scenery as to where they were, but all I saw was a blue ocean. It could be anywhere.

I took a good-sized swallow of my coffee and wondered if Audra had a Facebook page. I searched. She did, but it seemed to be devoted to her art. Nothing personal. Nothing about Terrance. I looked but could not find him on Facebook at all.

I went back to Michelle's Facebook page and scrolled back, way, way back into her history to see if anything was interesting. Screen after screen I looked at, sometimes waiting several seconds for the old screens to load, way back before she even knew Terrance and Audra. Back then there were plenty of selfies, often of her and Beth, the two of them making faces for the camera. Best of friends then. Michelle and her daughters, a few of the entire family. Lots of Christmas photos, pictures of Beth, her arms around Michelle's daughters. All one big happy family, at least according to the photos.

I checked the dates. I grabbed a few sheets of plain paper and began writing things down. It looked to me that her personal photos stopped around the time Terrance was hired. Why would that be? I carefully wrote that down. I made lists, and then from the lists came a narrative. I wrote it down. Anything that came to me, I jotted it down. Notes. Thoughts. My experiences with them all. Descriptions. It all might make a kind of sense to me if I got it all down on paper. I stacked all the sheets beside my computer.

Wanting more information about Beth, I Googled her name—Beth Rhorson. I found nothing until I realized I might get someplace if I knew her maiden name. If they were childhood friends, maybe I could find a clue from Michelle's Facebook feed. They lived together when they were girls, before Facebook, but maybe Michelle knew Beth's family. I looked. I studied all of Michelle's friends that might have a connection to Beth. Some of their feeds were private. Some were wide open. It was a tedious job, and at one point, I wondered why the hell I was doing this in the first place. What did I hope to find? Wasn't this a job for the police? Why was I taking it so personally? I guess a good answer to that was that it was affecting me. Personally. My friend had died. I had two women wanting me to get advice from Ben. I felt sorry for Audra. I felt sorry for Janice. I didn't know who to believe.

I thought about all of this as I kept foraging about on the internet for information about Beth. Eventually, I found something that looked promising. Michelle had a friend Pete Hager, and together, they had one mutual friend, Beth. I clicked on his page and discovered he had listed Beth as his "sister." Ah! So this was Beth's brother!

I looked up Beth Hager. There were a lot of Beth Hagers, so that was of no help. Deciding that Beth was a derivative of Elizabeth I tried Elizabeth Hager and added Massachusetts. I found a photo that looked like a younger Beth Rhorson. The name was Lisa Hager. Both Lisa and Beth are diminutives of Elizabeth. I was getting somewhere. I zoomed in and looked at the eyes. It had to be her. It was her.

I kept looking, kept reading. I googled Wes Rhorson again and found the announcement of the business. Plus, I found another little tidbit of interest — there was a small article in a local newspaper, an obituary notice for Wes Rhorsen's mother who had died a year ago. Hadn't Beth told me that she and Wes had recently visited her? Maybe I'd heard her wrong. Maybe it was *her* mother. But I got the impression that she had no relationship with her real mother. That note got added to the growing pile beside my computer.

I also googled Francine Hinson, Marilou Robertson, and Virginia Strong. The only thing I found was information about the murders. I didn't have the benefit of all of Ben's printouts. I read all about the mysterious Russell. No last name, or none that I could find. I did find one thing that I read through twice. When Janice's mother first went missing and before her body was found, Francine had been quoted in the paper as saying that she feared Russell had taken up with his old girlfriend, and Virginia, heartbroken, had gone off by herself somewhere to grieve. I didn't have the benefit of the autopsy report that Ben had, but I found a fascinating fact in one of the news articles. It was speculated that Virginia Strong was pregnant when she was killed. Really? Did this matter? Was this important?

There was a rustling outside, a distinct noise. How long had I been at this? Had the wind picked up? I had been at this so long I hadn't noticed that it was full dark now. All of the curtains and drapes on my many windows were open. I heard it again. Footsteps. A whooshing sound. Rusty whined and stood from in front of the fireplace where he'd been sleeping. I got up, edged to the kitchen door, and flicked on all the lights. Rusty glanced toward the back door and continued whining.

"Rusty?" I whispered. "What is it? What is it, boy?"

This wasn't his, "I need to go out" whine. This was his "I'm very unhappy about something" whine.

I heard it again, a soft, deliberate tapping like someone was trying to gain access through my laundry room window. I picked my way toward my kitchen counter. Slowly, I reached for my wooden knife block and pulled the biggest knife I own, my chef's knife, the huge one I use for chopping veggies, the one Geoff had recently sharpened to within an inch of its life.

Now, there were soft footsteps on my porch. I stood there, trying to control my breathing. In out. In out. You're not safe. *Stay out of this. You could be in danger.* All the warnings came back to me. Terrance. Sunny. Janice's mother. Terrance's sister. Marilou.

"Emmy?" A soft voice.

I let out the breath I'd been holding.

"Emmy? You there?" A knock. I sighed, put the knife back into its appropriate slot and went to the door. There's only one person in the world who calls me Emmy.

"EJ." I opened the door on my back porch, and there he stood holding a foil-covered plate. "What are you doing here at this hour?" I said. "You nearly scared me to death!"

"Oh." He chuckled. "Sorry. I couldn't sleep. I saw your kitchen light on. I brought some food." He eyed me. "Are you okay? Still no word from Ben?"

"Come in. And why would Ben call me anyway? He's happily married now. I already told you all of that. I'll put on the tea."

He gave me a bit of a smile. "Actually, a beer might go down a bit more nicely."

"Sure. Beer it is, then."

He placed the plate on the table and took the foil off. On it were slices of meat and cheese. "Leftovers," he said. He eyed my computer and my sheaf of scattered notes beside it. "You working at something this late? You writing a book?"

"A book. Right. I should be, shouldn't I? A heartbreaking story of love gone wrong."

He picked up the top sheet where I had written about Virginia's pregnancy. He looked up at me.

"Actually, it's just this whole thing. Sunny's death. I wish I knew what the hell I was even thinking." I grabbed a box of crackers from a cupboard, receptacles for EJ's meat and cheese. They were for me only. EJ never eats crackers. "I thought if I got it all down on paper, it might make some sense."

He nodded. "Should be interesting reading." He put the top sheet back on the pile.

"Now that you're here," I said covering a cracker with a meat slice. "I could use your expertise, your wisdom of the ages."

I told him about my meeting with Michelle and Beth, about what I was learning online and what I was beginning to piece together. I showed him the Facebook pages that I'd made screenshots of, and the pictures and the news items and going over the key points in my notes.

EJ sucked his lips. "You need to go to the police with all of this. Emmy," he said.

"I don't know."

"At least Ben," he said.

"Ben is not a part of the equation. There will be no more 'going to Ben' ever again in my life."

"But Ben has all of those papers from Janice. He *is* involved."

"Right." I nodded. "And that is unfortunate."

"You need to be careful, Em."

"Don't worry about me. I'll be okay." I smiled over at him. "I can always go out to the shed and get your old gun."

He waved his hand. "That old thing."

"Do you even have bullets for it?"

He shook his head. "I have no idea."

"You could sell it to a collector."

"Maybe. But I don't need the money."

"Or donate it to the historical society."

"Well, there's that, I suppose."

"Yeah."

"Em, seriously. You need to be careful. This should not be taken lightly."

"I know."

After he left, I put the remains of the meat and cheese in my fridge, and went through the pages of notes, I grabbed a new sheet of lined paper and began writing about what I was beginning to think, beginning to fear, beginning to believe.

Just before I got into bed, my cell phone pinged. I grabbed for it and stared down at the text message in disbelief.

CHAPTER 34

Captain Emmeline,

I've got more important information for you. Meet me at the same rest area as before. Tomorrow morning. Early. 7:30. Don't bring Ben. Promise me you won't tell Ben. It's important that you don't tell Ben. Or anyone. Also, don't reply back to me. This number will be turned off after a while.

Janice

Janice!

I copied her text into a separate folder, and then just to be on the safe side, I printed it off and set it beside my computer with all my notes. Nope, no chance of me telling Ben. Don't worry about that, Janice. I wondered if I should tell EJ where I was headed, decided against it. He would try to persuade me not to go. I knew EJ.

I checked my phone for the tides and realized I'd have to leave my place by friggin' four in the morning to make the tidal road. If I was on the tidal road by four fifteen, I'd make it just at the tail end of the tide. Well, I'd do it. No way could I ask Geoff to ferry me over that early. If I told him it was an emergency, he'd be all concerned and want to know what the emergency was. No, it was better I just get the tide on my own. What I'd do is get to Portland, find an early-opening coffee shop and wait there until it was time to meet her. I had several novels downloaded onto my iPad I could read. Or not. I'd probably be too anxious to concentrate.

I set two alarms to wake me at four, but I didn't even need one. I slept in fits and starts and was awake before the alarm went off. Before I left, I jotted a quick note to EJ and stuck it on his door.

Had to leave for an early meeting that just came up. I should be home around mid-morning, but if I'm not, can you please feed my animals? Food is on the counter, or if you have any leftover meat, Rusty and Bear will love you forever. Especially Bear.

The air was blanketed with fog this early in the morning. Even though I am a Maine girl and used to the fog, this one felt suffocating. Normally, I like being out on the water this time of day. There's a certain magic in it as the beams of light begin to peak themselves through the dusk, frail at first, and then breaking the night into shreds. But on this morning, it felt claustrophobic, like I couldn't breathe. Even though it was still summer, I needed the heat on to clear the windows and remove the dampness.

I was the only car out here at this time of the morning, and I made it across the tidal road with minutes to spare. After driving around Portland, I did manage to find an early-opening coffee shop. It didn't look like much, but I went in anyway. Just coffee. I didn't want anything else. My stomach was in knots as it was. I sat and drank multiple cups and played solitaire on my iPad. I couldn't concentrate on reading, not even the news. At six thirty, I set off for the half hour drive to the meeting place.

At six-forty-seven, I pulled into the empty rest area. I drove into the same parking space that Ben and I had parked in just days before. I waited. I didn't move. A duck was on the pond. I watched its movements trying to quell the nervousness that seemed to pervade my entire body. I stretched my hands out in front of me. They were shaking. I clasped them together. I got out of my car. I was alone here so early in the morning. After umpteen cups of coffee and a very, very nervous stomach, I was glad there was a ladies' room nearby. I headed up to the building.

After I exited the ladies' room, I stood for a long time examining the huge map on the wall. "You Are Here," it proclaimed.

I am here. I am here in this strange place wondering what I'm doing and wondering how I got involved in this whole mess in the first place. I am *here.*

I longed to call Ben. The old Ben. The Ben who was simply my friend before our relationship got all cluttered up with his marriage, my feelings, my confusion, his being a cop and his son, and his wife who was now with him and probably waking up in his bed next to him. *Don't think about that.*

I walked away from the building. It was warming up, ever so slightly. I shivered, nevertheless. I wandered around the rest area, past the dilapidated picnic benches, past the one where Janice had given Ben the boxes.

I went back to my car, sat in the driver's seat and locked the doors. I checked my phone. Still too early. Twenty minutes before Janice was due to be here. Unless she was early. Please be early. Please be early, Janice, just so we can get this over with. Just so I know you're okay. I wanted to hear what she had to say and then go home just as soon as I could, back to my safe place on the island. I thought about all the notes I had left in a neat pile next to my computer.

Something about this whole morning was starting to not feel right. You're never completely alone in these rest areas, even the rural ones like this one. I got out and stood beside my car. I kept glancing at the cars on the highway, willing one of them to drive in and be Janice. Or the police. I willed a State Trooper to drive up here.

I walked back up to the building. My trepidation was turning to worry, which was turning into a kind of fear. She had said seven-thirty. What had happened? Where was she?

Seven forty. Seven forty-five. I kept looking at my phone. The text had said seven-thirty. I read it again. Emmeline. *Captain Emmeline?*

Something began to niggle at me. Emmeline. Janice knew me as Em. I didn't even think Janice knew my name was Emmeline. I had not mentioned that name to her—ever—I didn't think.

As I stood there thinking about this, pondering the name thing, a car pulled in next to mine on my driver's side. Too close. The cars were too close. Janice? I began walking down toward the cars. Slowly. Very slowly. *Janice?*

Emmeline. EJ called me Emmy, but to everyone else, I was just Em.

Except for one person.

M, like the letter? No, Em, short for Emmeline. I am Captain Emmeline.

Wes had said that to me on the dock in Florida. Wes knew my name as Emmeline!

A trap. This was a trap. I eyed the unfamiliar car, tempted to dial 911. But what if this was nothing but my crazy imagination? How stupid I would feel if I called 911 and this was some random guy getting out to walk his dog.

I held my keys in my right hand, my phone in the left. If I hurried. If I ran, maybe I could squeeze into my driver's side, lock the doors, turn the car on and get the hell out of here. But no, the cars were too close. I doubted I'd even be able to open the driver's side door. The passenger door then, and I'd climb over.

As I stood there taking too long to figure out what to do, the driver's door opened and out came a small figure in a dark hoodie.

That small hooded figure had to be Janice.

I headed down toward her. Janice!

A car length away, the hoodie was pulled down. It wasn't Janice.

"You," I said stepping back.

To my mother,

I know who killed you now. I figured it out. And I know why. I also know who killed Francine and Marilou, and even Terrance and Sunny all these years later. Francine and Marilou had it figured out. That's what got them killed. They were going to go to the police with what they had, but they didn't have time. When I went through all of the stuff that I found at Audra's house, I came across personal emails between Terrance and his sister. After I went through them all one by one, just like Terrance had, I figured it out. He must have, and it got him killed. Now I know. I am sitting here, this email beside me, and shaking. I'm literally shaking.

Here it is:

My dearest brother,

You asked how Marilou and I are. We're not doing well, not well at all. It was horrible the way Virginia died, and we're finding it hard. We have Janice with us and are happy to raise her. When Social Services asked who she belonged to, we said, "us" without a moment's hesitation. So, thanks for asking about us. Keep praying for us, too. And keep praying they find the monster who did this.

Marilou and I think we know who killed our friend, but the police don't seem interested in what we have. Don't ask me why—but I know. It wasn't Russell, as we had originally thought. Virginia was right. It was Russell's girlfriend who did this. Maybe they did this together. I don't know. That certainly could be the case. We plan to go to the police tomorrow.

Again, thanks, Terrance, for your thoughts and concern and your many prayers. We really do need them. Marilou is finding it especially difficult, but Marilou is such a gentle soul. She feels things so deeply. I worry about her. It is such a high-profile case and in the news all the time. And I know you told me they would, but the news is making such a big deal about Marilou and me. Our relationship. Like that was the reason Ginny was killed. We are thinking of moving, leaving it all and maybe heading out west. Marilou has family out there. We would take Janice, of course. She is part of our family now.

Before we do that, we might take you up on your offer and drive down and visit you. When things get a bit more settled, that is. You would love Janice. Such a sweet girl. We would love for you to meet her. She takes after her mother in so many respects.

Love forever,
Your sister, Francine

I had not seen this email before taking them from Audra's files that day. I'd only ever read the news reports. It makes me so sad to read these words from Francine. I have such brief but sweet memories of the two of them, the way they just took you and me in when we had nowhere else to go.

What Francine wrote to Terrance makes a lot of sense now. I have read the autopsy. I have read the emails. I remember that shortly before you died, you said you had something exciting to tell me, something that would change your life and my life, too.

I kept asking, "What, Mom. What?" Do you remember me asking that over and over? But your eyes were bright, and you kept shaking your head.

"Not yet," you kept saying. "Not quite yet. Everyone will know soon enough anyway."

I know now that you were pregnant. I didn't know this for a long time because, for a long time, I wouldn't read the autopsy report.

I'm here in a motel room now reading over these words. Because I don't know what to do, who to tell. Em? I don't want to put her in danger. Ben? I've tried. I've tried and tried, and his cell just keeps going to voicemail.

After I left the Clifford's farm, I headed back first to Boston, because I knew that's where the answers were. After I stole Terrance's papers, I drove up to Maine and found a motel. I ended up buying a cheap printer and a ream of paper at Best Buy. I stayed up half the night photocopying everything to give to Ben. And now, what was he doing? He has all of these papers, and I can't even get a hold of him.

I was right in not thinking it was Russell. It wasn't Russell, was it? It was that girlfriend of his. The one I heard you arguing with. She killed you. How come the police didn't look for *her*?

The police made a half-hearted attempt to find Russell, but Russell didn't move away, did he? All he did was drop out of sight for a while and then was back with a different name. He left you, Mother, and you were heartbroken. But I think he was heartbroken too. I had seen how much you loved him. I had seen how much he loved you.

I had seen him back then when I was thirteen—that one time.

And I saw him again, didn't I? I recognized Russell as he walked toward me on the beach that day.

And I fainted.

Your daughter, Jan

CHAPTER 35

"**Y**ou!" I said it again.

She was wearing the same black turtleneck she'd worn in the restaurant, high up on her neck, with the sleeves down her wrists and to the tops of her fingers. Her skinny jeans were black, and her boots came to her knees.

More to the point, she was holding a gun with both hands and aiming it at me.

Wes must be in the car, I reasoned. I glanced at the car, but with the way the early morning sun was shining on the windows, I couldn't see inside. I clenched my phone with my right hand, trying to cover the whole of it with my fingers, and all the while chiding myself that I hadn't called 911, or at least pre-dialed the number when I had the chance, and then all I would have to do now was to press the green call button. Why hadn't I at least thought of that? Still, she stood there without a word to me.

"Beth." I said her name now.

"Me."

"What do you want?"

"First of all, your phone."

"It's in the car," I lied.

"It's not in the car. I can see it in your friggin' hand."

"Oh."

"Yeah, oh," she said mimicking me.

I held onto my phone, my fingers tight around it. It was like I couldn't think to untangle them.

"Give it to me," she said, the gun still pointed at me. "Now. And don't think I won't shoot you."

She would. I was sure of it. Or Wes would. He would climb

out of the car, and then I would have two people after me. I held my hand out, uncurled my fingers, and watched my beloved phone drop to the pavement. Still holding the gun in one hand, she bent down and picked it up.

From inside the car, I heard a mumbled, "Run, Em, run!"

Janice? That's why Wes wasn't out here. He was in the car with his gun on Janice.

"You have Janice. You and Wes have Janice."

"Shut up in there," Beth yelled. "Just shut up, or you'll be dead, too." There was a note of desperation in her voice that wasn't lost on me. Maybe I could take advantage of this. All I needed was to keep my cool. Right.

Beth turned and chucked my phone toward the pond. I watched it wend its way through the air and plop way out there in the water. The duck flapped away at the splash. I keep my phone encased in one of those super-duper waterproof containers—I'm a sailor, after all—but buried in the bottom of the mud down there? It would be lost forever.

I shifted my weight from foot to foot and glanced down to the highway willing a patrol car to find its way up here. Why was there no one here? Why were we the only cars up here? And then I saw why. A couple of sawhorses were blocking the entrance to the rest area. Beth and Wes had obviously done this. It could be hours before anyone in authority realized that these were put there by mistake. I took a step backward so I could get a better view of the highway.

She said to me pointedly, "You run now, and Janice is dead."

"You've killed before," I said. "You and Wes both. You killed Terrance, didn't you? And Sunny. You guys weren't off taking care of a sick mother, were you? You went back down to the Bahamas for the express purpose of killing Sunny after you read what he put up on Facebook."

"Marcus told him. He and Marcus became such good chums."

"So you admit it?"

She shrugged.

I went on, "Why not kill Marcus then?"

"Don't think I haven't thought of it."

I said, "It began with Janice's mother, didn't it? And then Janice's mother's friends. You killed all of them."

I had figured out some of it, but I was clearly fishing at this point.

"For the record, I never killed anyone." She emphasized the word "I." "Virginia's death was an accident. She wasn't supposed to die."

From inside her car, I could hear the muffled calls of Janice urging me to run, run, run. But of course, I wouldn't. She was in there, in danger. Wes was probably holding a knife against her throat as I stood out here.

"Wes in there with Janice?" I asked. "Or should I call him by his real name and ask, where's Russell?"

Her mouth became a straight line.

"I know what happened," I said. "I know exactly what happened. The police do, too. They know I'm here and will be here any minute, too."

For a long minute, she looked at me and then said, "You lie."

"You were the girlfriend. You killed Virginia because you couldn't bear that Russell had broken up with you and gone to her. That's where it began, didn't it? You couldn't bear that Russell had left you and found Virginia."

The narrowing of her eyes told me that I was getting it right.

Quietly, she said, "I told you, Ginny's death was an accident."

I said. "That was no accident. She was dragged across so many rocks that her teeth were torn out. I read the autopsy report."

"She was dead before that."

"You couldn't bear the thought that Russell had found someone else, someone he loved more."

"Shut the fuck up and get in the car," she demanded. "Now."

"Why don't you just shoot me now and be done with it?" Saying this was a gamble, but I had a feeling that she and Wes wanted something from me, from Janice and me. Otherwise, there was no doubt we would be dead already.

I made no move toward the car. "Just tell me this much. How did Virginia die?"

"She fell." She said it matter-of-factly. "Her head hit the edge of the coffee table. It was an accident. She came to see Russell. I was with him when she showed up, raving and screaming like a mad woman. She was a madwoman. I don't think she expected that the two of us were back together again. She couldn't stand that. Wes and I wanted her out of our lives. For good. But she kept yelling, screaming. It was her fault. She pushed right in. We argued. When he pushed her away, she fell. That's when it happened. But he wanted me. Not her. Me. Me."

"She was pregnant," I said. "With Russell's child."

She stared at me for a long time, the gun still aimed at me. "Don't say that. It's not true."

"It is true. I read the report."

"It's not! It's not!"

"Just for the record, Lisa, I don't believe a word you're saying. I don't believe she fell and died accidentally. You killed her. You and Russell Then you ran off, and Russell became Wes, and you became Beth."

For a long time, she said nothing. I didn't hear anything from the car, either, and I had this idea that Janice was listening intently. I had no idea what Wes was doing. I would have expected him to be out here by now.

"He is Wes now, and he loves me. I had him way before *she* came along. He was mine before, and he's mine now."

"Your salvation," I said, remembering how she'd described him in the coffee shop.

"He was mine!" Her voice was becoming louder. "No one

but me. Mine." She had both hands on the gun now and began talking quietly. "So much blood. I've never seen so much blood. Russell. He was. He was holding her by the shoulders. He was trying to talk sense into her. He was coming back to me. He had to tell her that. He was! He was! I went there, and there she was. The two of them talking. Like making plans. I didn't want them talking the way they were. Laughing. Like friends. Like they had a secret that didn't include me. Russell was only going back to her because of the baby. I knew that."

"I thought you said you were at the apartment with Wes and she showed up."

"No! I don't know! It all happened so fast, I don't remember it exactly. I told Russell there had to be another way. She could get an abortion. We could *make* her get an abortion, couldn't we? But she'd been brainwashed. *Brainwashed!*" Spittle was forming at the corners of her mouth.

"Brainwashed?" She was making no sense.

"Brainwashed by those two lesbian bitches she lived with. Those perverts. Living together like they did. Putting all these ideas into her head."

I stood stock still. The force of what she was saying sent a shiver of terror down my entire body. Very quietly, I said, "And so you killed them, too."

"They deserved to die. Ask anyone. For what they were. And what they did to Virginia."

"Oh, you mean like taking in a homeless single mother and her young daughter?" My fear was turning to a kind of rage.

"Get in the car," she said. "Get in the car now!"

She went over and opened up the back door and motioned for me to get in. From inside, I heard Janice yell, "Run! Em! Run"

I slid in beside Janice whose wrists were tied on her lap with cable ties, and her hands seemed to be tied to the seatbelt with yet another set of cable ties. We two were alone. Wes was not here.

With one deft movement, Beth had secured my hands. She

closed our door and locked it. While Beth made her way around the front of the car to the driver's seat, I whispered to Janice. "It's going to be all right. I have a plan. Don't say anything."

I really didn't have a plan, but I didn't want her to worry.

I noticed something about Janice. Her signature name tag seemed to be missing.

"She wants something," I whispered. "Or we'd be dead already. We'll find out what it is."

She had time simply to nod before Beth climbed into the driver's seat and started the car.

"What do you want with us?" I asked as she backed up the car.

"The papers," she said turning to face us in the back seat. "Terrance and Janice collected letters and articles and police reports. I want them all."

The papers? Frantically, I tried to think of something.

"I know you have them. Take me to them," she demanded.

"For your information," I said. "Most of that stuff is online anyway. You could just Google everything."

"Not everything. There are emails and police communications and even some news articles that have been taken off the web. I've looked. I want the autopsies. I want the autopsy reports."

"What do you want them for?"

"I need them! We need them!" she yelled.

"You and Russell."

Janice's eyes went wide when I said this.

"Yes. Russell and me. We need them."

"Okay," I said quietly. "I put them out on an island for safekeeping."

"An island?"

"Right." I would take them to my place. Then I would get us all aboard my sailboat where I would have the advantage. I always have the advantage on my own boat. Yes, maybe we could do this thing. Janice and me together, both of us sailors.

"Just head out onto the highway and turn right. I'll direct you the rest of the way."

"You better be telling me the truth."

"Of course."

We travelled pretty much in silence until we hit the tidal road, now covered with fast, swirling water.

"What is this?" She growled. "Some kind of joke?"

I said, "It's a road. We have to wait here for a few hours."

"What the hell are you talking about?" She picked up the gun she had placed on the seat beside her. She waved it in my face.

I fought to remain calm. "See that land over there? That's an island, and this is a road. We can only drive over at low tide, which will be in two or three hours at the earliest."

"Are you fucking kidding me?" She turned to face me in the back seat.

"We have to wait for the tide." I was coming up with a new idea, an even better one.

She sighed loudly and muttered, "This is so stupid."

And that is how we happened to be sitting there, the three of us, for the next two hours, while I thought and planned and wondered and prayed for someone, anyone to come along. A police officer would be nice right about now.

But it didn't happen.

Eventually, finally, after both Janice and I got out ostensibly for pee breaks, but at which time I presented my plan, the ocean receded enough so that we could cross.

"Okay," I said quietly, "You can drive across, just keep to the middle. If a car comes, you may have to back up, but that seldom happens. They'll see you and not drive down. You can see the whole road from the island side, but not this side, so it's sort of an unwritten rule that the island side traffic gives way to the mainland traffic."

"Be quiet!" she yelled. "You're talking too much."

"Stay in the middle." She was driving too fast. "Are you crazy? Beth, you're going to get us killed! You can't drive this fast on this slick road."

"Shut up," she said. "Those papers damn well better be there."

"Just take that fork to the right now."

We passed Jeff and Valerie on their way out. Even though they didn't know Wes and Beth, they waved. Everyone waves on this island. I stared at them, frowning and making a face, trying to get their attention, but of course, they didn't see me, or if they did, they would think I was just being weird.

And then we were at my house. "Park over there," I said, directing her to park on the far side of the house. I didn't want EJ to see me. I hoped he was sitting in his front room drinking tea and gazing out his window to the sea. That was the only variable. The last thing I needed was for him to get caught up in this. I didn't want him seeing us going into his shed. Because that was my plan now. Somehow get her in there and lock her in the shed. If I could get to EJ's gun, so much the better.

"You see that big old house there? An old guy lives there. Crazy old coot, deaf as a post."

Beth parked, then came around and still holding the gun, untied me.

"Janice?" I said.

"She stays. We get the papers and then leave."

"And then you kill us."

She grinned.

The two of us made our way toward the old wooden shed. I opened the door.

I said, "They're in that metal cabinet over there."

We climbed over the junk on the floor, the tires and bottles and boards and nails.

"Give me the key to it then," Beth demanded and held her hand out.

"It's a combination lock."

"Then give me the friggin' combination."

"I can't. It's tricky. You'll never get it open. I have to do it."

"Forget it then." She made for the door.

"Look, if you want those papers, this is how it has to be."

"Okay then. Geez."

"You'll have to cut these cable ties from my wrist."

"Okay. But I'm right behind you with the gun."

"I'm well aware of that, Lisa."

"Shut up! Don't call me that! Lisa is dead!"

My plan was to reach in, grab that old pistol, get her in a corner, and then run out and lock her in. The thing was, her gun was loaded. Mine, although bigger, would not be.

The lock was there but hung on the hasp. I looked at it frowning. I know I'd fastened the lock after Ben and I had looked at the gun. I know it! I opened the cabinet door wide. It was empty. The gun was gone! It simply wasn't there.

"It's not here," I said confused, turning to Beth. "I don't know…I don't understand."

"The papers?" Beth peered in.

"I don't know what happened," I said. "I don't understand. It…they were here. I swear it."

At that moment, EJ appeared in the doorway, hair askew, plaid shirt tucked half in and half out of old dungarees, the gun held high, a wild look on his leathery face. At his side, Rusty growled fiercely, and beside him stood Janice, her hands still tied in front of her.

"Git off my property or I'll shoot!"

CHAPTER 36

With the barrel of the gun, he roughly shoved Janice in front of him. Her hands were still cable-tied in front of her. "Who is this little one? She was in your car screaming her head off. The three of you, get against that far wall."

I gave Janice a barely imperceptible nod. She could have run, I saw but didn't, which made me wonder what EJ had told her. EJ waved the gun around dangerously, and I wondered if he had magically found bullets for it.

Beth backed away and raised her handgun and held it on him. "I'm stronger than you, old man!" she said.

"Beth," I whispered in a low voice. "He's nuts. I told you he was an old coot. You're not stronger than that crazy old man. Believe me. I know. I know firsthand."

"Drop that gun!" He snarled. "You think that little gun of yours is a match to this one? This one is from the war, girlie. And I know how to use it! Don't think for one minute that I don't. I've killed many a man with this tricked-out gun."

Beth did not lower her gun, and I feared that she would shoot him. I knew she could. "Beth," I warned. "Be careful. He's killed before. He has a reputation on this island."

Next to him, Rusty growled at us ominously. It was like he knew what was expected of him. I was so thankful he hadn't run to me, tail wagging.

He said, "Against the back wall. Now!"

From the porch, I caught a whiff of meat cooking. EJ was probably roasting a whole roast or chicken in his outdoor cooker. "You smell that meat..." I whispered to Beth. "He eats roadkill and whatever he finds. I told you, he's crazy."

Without missing a beat, he said, "Roasting a couple of

coons."

Beth gasped.

"Now drop the gun, missy."

If the situation weren't so grave, I would have burst out laughing.

"Why the hell," she asked me quietly, "would you put those papers on his land?"

"You see that house back there? My late husband grew up there. That kayak is his." I pointed. "I thought it would be safe. This guy, though, this guy has gotten crazier as the years go by. I didn't know he'd gotten this bad. I haven't seen him in ages."

"I don't trust that dog." She raised the gun to shoot Rusty. I gasped loudly.

"I swear, Beth, if you shoot that dog, he WILL go nuts. Him and that old dog? They are inseparable. I would do as he says. Trust me, I'll get us out of here. I think I can handle him. I sort of know him. But, if I were you, I'd pitch that gun toward him on the ground."

"Shut up and drop the mother-fuckin' gun or I WILL shoot and don't think I won't!" he yelled at Beth. Now I really did look at him with wide eyes. I had never in all the years of living next to EJ hear him use language like that. I didn't even know he knew the words.

Finally, Beth did. I kicked it away. He picked it up. Now he had two guns. Well, one technically. Still holding the gun on us, he pulled out a length of grimy rope from his back pocket.

Beth whispered. "He's old. We can take him. It's three healthy young women against one old man."

"You really have a death wish, Beth? Are you that crazy? Oh, I forgot to tell you, this guy lives out here is one of those survivalists. He has hundreds of guns stashed away all over this property. Probably there's a couple of knives in his pockets. Man, the stories my late husband would tell me. I think he even makes his own ammunition. He's not kidding when he says that gun is tricked out."

"Get up against the wall! All three of you. And shut up!"

He tied the three of us with amazingly good knots to nails in the shed wall, while all the time I wondered how he had come to be here?

When we were tied up sufficiently, he sat down on a broken chair and just looked at us. He put a piece of straw between his teeth. Now, I almost *did* burst out laughing.

"Now we wait," he said.

"For what?" I asked.

"You three are trespassing. I called 911. They're on their way. Some police guy named Ben took my call."

He winked at me.

CHAPTER 37

Ben was the first to push through the door of the shed. Moments later, two other officers came, a young male officer I didn't recognize and a woman I had met once. They must have come in two cars. Ben whispered something to EJ who handed him both guns. Ben gave them to the woman officer who took them back outside. Without looking at us. Ben headed directly to Beth who was hollering loudly. "Get that guy. He's nuts. Totally nuts. He was going to kill us. Hey, what are you doing? Handcuffing *me*? What the hell? It's that guy you want."

Over her screaming, I could hear Ben reading Beth her rights.

She was being arrested, I heard, as an accessory to the murders of Virginia Strong, Marilou Robertson, Francine Hinson, Terrance Hinson, and for the murder of Sunny Love.

The *murder* of Sunny Love? Had she gone down there on her own and killed Sunny? I knew he had to have had some really strong evidence to arrest her.

"I never killed anybody!" Spittle formed at the edges of her mouth. "It was an accident! Virginia was an accident! That had nothing to do with me!"

Ben led her to the waiting police car. I heard him say, "We have your husband already in custody. He's told us everything."

"He's lying. He lies about everything. Don't believe him." And then more faintly, I heard, "But he loves me. He loves *me*."

Ben came back into the shed and undid my knots.

"Quite an ordeal," were his first words to me.

"Quite," was all I said, even though I had a million questions. How did EJ know to call him? How did EJ know to show up the way he did with his gun? Then he undid Janice's knots, and both of us were free. He said, "We've got Wes in custody, but I'm going to need the two of you to come down to the station and make statements."

Outside, Ben said to EJ, "That gun loaded?"

"You kidding me?" He took off his suspenders and slicked down his ruffed hair with the palm of his hand. "I don't think they even make bullets for it anymore. It's more a collector's item."

"Still, we've got to take it into evidence. You'll get it back. Probably soon."

"Fine. Just let me go turn off my meat cooker."

I was shivering uncontrollably and leaned against the shed wall to steady myself.

"You three can ride back with me to the station."

I said rather tonelessly, "My car's out at a rest area."

"We can help you get that."

"And my phone's gone."

With Ben's help, Janice climbed into the front seat of the waiting police car. The other patrol with the still screaming Beth was pulling out onto the road to head back to Portland.

EJ and I climbed into the back seat. And then Ben was backing out of my driveway and heading down the island road. "You guys can thank EJ. He called us right away."

"How did you know?" I said to EJ.

He sighed, licked his lips. "I got up early. I often don't sleep. I heard something early on. You leaving. Something just didn't sit right. I kept thinking about it. You seemed quite upset last night. I think that's why I didn't sleep. During the night, I made up my mind. I was going to come over and demand that you go to the police. If you wouldn't, I was going to go behind your back and call Ben. And so," EJ continued, "at around seven, I got your note. I went into your kitchen and began reading all those papers you wrote. Then I called

Ben."

"We've been trying to reach you since then," Ben turned in the front seat to face me.

I said. "By that time, my phone had unfortunately taken a swim in a pond."

But EJ went on. "I kept calling Ben. I kept saying that you were in trouble somewhere. I skimmed through all the notes beside your computer. I remembered my old gun. You reminded me of it when we talked. So, I went and got it. I was sitting there on the porch with it when you showed up with that woman. I didn't recognize the car but thought I should go investigate. I heard you talking and then decided to go into action."

He said he got the idea about dressing like an "old coot" from our last conversation. He ran his fingers through his hair until it was standing straight up, grabbed some old suspenders and rolled one pant leg up, and headed outside. "I could tell that woman was up to no good," he said.

"EJ, that was so brave of you, considering her gun was loaded, and yours was not."

"She wouldn't have any idea about that, now would she?"

"She could have shot you."

"I knew Ben was on his way. I called him as soon as that unfamiliar car rolled in. When she took you both into the shed, I went over and listened to what she was saying."

"I'm glad you did that, EJ," Ben said. "But you should have waited in your house. What you did was dangerous."

"It worked, though," he said.

In the front, Janice was still shivering. She said, "I was so scared." She paused. "Beth somehow found my number, and she called me, said she had to meet with me. I had no idea what she wanted. So when she came to pick me up in the middle of the night, I went with her without even questioning. Sometimes I'm so stupid."

"No, you're not," I said. "You're very brave."

When we got to the police station, the three of us were

taken into separate rooms. A female officer came with coffee for me and took my statement, recording it and writing down the pertinent information. I was forced to remember and go over every little detail. I was tired. I realized I hadn't slept much the night before, well, maybe the past few nights. The police station coffee was settling oddly in my stomach.

I learned that what I had suspected was true. Beth and Wes, or Russell as he was then named, were together, but Beth was demanding and cloying, and when he met Janice's mother, Virginia, at the café where she worked it was like a breath of fresh air to him. The couple fell in love. But Beth was not going to let go without a fight. She would stop at nothing to get him back. She stalked him, sat outside of his house for hours, wrote him notes, called him so much, he changed his number several times. When Russell and Virginia found that Virginia was pregnant, they decided to leave the city and get married. The three of them would make a family someplace — Ginny, Russell, and Janice. And, of course, eventually, the new baby.

When Beth found out that Virginia was pregnant, she was livid. She confronted them both at his apartment where she took a swipe at Virginia. When Russell stepped in to stop her, a scuffle ensued. Virginia fell and hit her head on the cement block bookshelf.

There were discrepancies in both Beth and Wes's statements. Did Beth push her? Or was Wes trying to keep Beth from pushing her? Was that how it happened? Their stories differed, Ben later told me. But Ginny died then, and Beth ended up convincing Wes that it was his fault and that she was going to go to the police and turn him in unless he came back to her. If he married her, she wouldn't tell the police that he was a murderer, and together, they could easily cover up the crime. They would make it look like a horrific murder by dragging her body across the stones and leaving it partially uncovered near a quarry. Wes felt he had no choice. He went along.

Francine and Marilou, however, figured it out and confronted Wes, and after harping on him day and night, they managed to get the truth out of him. They were going to the police, but Beth convinced Wes that he had to kill the women before they did that. After that, he and Beth were forever glued together.

It was the same with Terrance. Through emails and documents and research, Terrance was finally able to piece together most of what happened. Because of it, Beth declared that he had to die. She coerced Wes into doing the deed. When the three guys were on their last dive, when Marcus was off behind one of the reefs, Wes came out, grabbed Terrance from behind, and yanked out his mouthpiece. Terrance fought back and kept his teeth clenched tightly onto the mouthpiece until it broke away from the regulator. When Terrance drowned, Wes grabbed the loose mouthpiece and took it to the surface. This was the black cable tie that I had found down there. Marcus related some of this to Sunny. It was Beth who flew down to the Bahamas and killed Sunny, keeping hidden on the island the whole time. She had demanded that Wes go and kill Sunny. This time, he wouldn't. He said he'd had enough. Why did she pretend to be abused by her husband? So, that the blame would fall on him and not her,

All of this was told to me by Ben later that afternoon when he drove me to the rest area to get my car. "Wow," was all I kept saying.

Before I got out to retrieve my car, he said, "Wait…"

"What?"

"I need to tell you something."

"Something more on Beth and Wes?"

"My wife is gone."

I looked at him.

"No, I mean she's gone. Really gone."

I waited.

"She came out to see me. I told you that part. Her visit lasted barely two hours."

I really didn't know what I was supposed to say to this.

"Em, I'm sorry. It's truly over with my wife."

"Um…"

"She walked in the door carrying divorce papers. I read them over and signed them. It's over, Em. It's completely over. We ended it. She's gone."

At that moment, I realized just how foolish his wife — his soon-to-be ex-wife — was in letting him go.

EPILOGUE

"You know I get seasick, right?"

"Oh, come on." I'm grinning at him now. "You're the great and mighty sailor. You should know this boat like the back of your hand."

"I had a lot of other things on my mind then," he says.

More than a year ago, Ben accompanied my sailing friend Joan and me when we sailed this very boat north from Florida to Maine. Now, my Uncle Ferd was on his way here to pick it up. He would be taking off shortly for points north — way north, Iceland, Greenland. My uncle has been just about everywhere on this boat. He asked if I would take it out to make sure all systems were a go. And that's how Ben and I happen to be aboard *Wandering Soul* on this most glorious of fall days.

It has been two weeks since Beth and Wes were arrested. Michelle and Marcus were brought in for questioning, as was Audra, but they were released. It's been all over the news, as you can well imagine.

It was Beth who tried to sabotage Terrance's boat, *Myriad*, thinking it was a good way to get rid of them both. It was a tube of Chapstick, plain old ordinary Chapstick affixed to the stuffing box. Something that simple had almost killed us.

As for the missing money, that was a kind of false flag, thought up by Beth, to get Terrance out and away from the company before he could uncover the truth. Terrance discovered the link between Russell and Wes and had been trying to figure out how to get more information to see if his theory was correct. When they advertised for the job, Terrance saw it as his way in.

The wind is picking up a bit, and I decide we need to let out the jib a bit. Ben is at the helm, not a bit of seasickness about him now. When the boat is sailing even again, he says, "You ready for some lunch?"

"Sure." I brighten.

Since this whole thing broke apart, Ben and I have spent almost every day together. We have talked long and hard about our feelings for each other, hours together, hours on the phone.

Ben came into my life at a time when I was vulnerable. My husband, Jesse, had died, and I was lonely. He helped solve Jesse's murder, and that brought us close. Was what I was feeling for him just a rebound from Jesse? Or something more? We talked about that.

And then there was him. He had taken the job in Maine after a major trauma of his own. So, here we were, thrown together at a time when we were most vulnerable. Maybe that's why we kept backing away from each other in turns. First, it would be him, and then it would be me.

We talked about that, too. We wanted our relationship to be more than two damaged souls clinging to each other. We needed to be sure. Over long cups of coffee, I told him about my fears. I was sure I couldn't bear to lose another husband to violence and could he, a police officer, guarantee that?

I remember what he said. "There are no guarantees of anything in this life, Em. But why live in constant fear?"

What could I say to that?

"And don't think I don't have the same fears," he said. "I see you take off in a boat, and then in the news, I'm reading about some hurricane or other. You don't think that worries me?"

"So what did you bring?" I ask him now.

"A new Mexican restaurant opened up near me, and I've been told they're good. I've got a whole bunch of stuff."

"Ah, that's the wonderful aroma emanating from down below."

Ben goes down to retrieve the small cooler. Up in the sunshine, he extricates little containers of delicacies. He places each of the offerings on clean plates on the cockpit table. One bite into the burrito and I am hooked.

"Did I tell you I once crewed on a boat to Mexico?"

"Please don't tell me you went through a hurricane."

I laugh. "Well, it was only a tropical storm, and we were just at the edge."

A gust of wind hits at the boat, and I stumble into his arms laughing. We stay that way for a long time.

To you, mother,

It's over. All of it. I know who killed you, and I know why. It's in all the papers. My name, too. I've had reporters call and even come to try to talk to me. I'm not used to being in the spotlight, and I'm not very good at it. The reason I fainted when I saw the couples in the Bahamas was that I recognized Russell! I had only seen him once and from a distance, but there was something about him that sent me into shivers of fear. I recognized him! But not right away. It took me some time to put the pieces together.

I need to get away from all of this. Maybe that's why I'm drawn to life at sea. You get to be on your own with nobody bugging you about anything.

I'll be leaving soon. Skip and Sue want me to come down to Florida. So, I'll be driving their car back down. They want me to skipper their boat permanently. I think I will like that. It has the added benefit that I can get in hours towards my captain's license.

When I told Em I was leaving, she invited me out to her place. I think she wanted to show me her boat and her uncle's boat, and perhaps erase the horrible memory of the last time I was out there.

When I got there, we ate Mexican food out on her front porch that she bought from some new restaurant. We ate it while she told me she admired my sailing ability and that if I needed a reference, she would gladly provide it. She told me all the pitfalls, too, like the loneliness at times, the feeling that we, of all people, have an easy way to run away from all our problems.

"It's so easy to be tempted to do that," she told me. "Don't."

"I'll be careful," I said.

I asked what she was going to do now, and she said she would still do what she wanted, delivering boats, but that the call of the land was getting stronger, and she was thinking of putting down more roots here. Literally. She wants to clear the brush, plant a little garden. "I'll have to get some topsoil," she said. "There's good soil on the island in amongst the trees. I'll borrow EJ's wheelbarrow."

She told me about her next job where she will be delivering a big catamaran to Bermuda, but as she was talking about it, I was getting this idea that she was very wistful. Like something in her didn't want to go. Like she just wanted it to be over.

Maybe that happens. You do one thing for a long, long time, thinking that there is nothing else you want to do in your entire life, and you can't see yourself stopping for any reason. And then things change, and you no longer feel you want to keep doing that thing. Right now, I can't think of anything I'd rather do than sail, but who knows?

We drank beers on her front porch and looked out at her uncle's boat. Still there. Her uncle was coming next week for it, she told me.

"You know," she said. "For the first time, I don't envy him. Do you know he has a daughter in Portland he hardly ever sees?"

"Really?"

She told me about it.

When we said goodbye, I gave her a long hug. I'm going to miss her, although I know we'll keep in touch. "Will you be coming to Florida in the winter?" I asked. "To work on boats?"

"I'm not sure this year. I might just stay home. Take up skiing again. Maybe snowshoeing. Jesse and I used to snowshoe all around this island."

So that's how we left. Maybe things are changing for her. Maybe things change for everybody.

I have to tell you something else that's weird—my name tag fell off when Beth had me in the back of her car, and since that time, I haven't put one on. Em must have noticed, but she didn't say anything. Although I did see her looking at my jacket every now and again.

I don't know what that says about me. I've worn my name tags forever. It began in one of the foster homes I lived in before the Cliffords. One of my foster caretakers could never remember my name. She could remember everyone else but me. So I put a sticky of my name on my shirt and wore it every day.

Then I found a small pin with my name on it at one of those gift store places. I bought several in different styles. It got so that without my name tag, I felt like I was invisible, that nobody would know who I was. That nobody would care.

Even at the Clifford's, I wore name tags. By then, I was so used to it, I couldn't imagine not doing it. I had this idea that the only person in the world who would remember my name was you.

There is one more place I want to visit before heading south. I'm going to drive up to see the Cliffords. They called me when my name was in the paper and wanted to know if I was okay. They told me they thought about me all the time. Mom, I wish you could have met them.

I started this journal, these letters to you when I decided I finally wanted to figure things out after Terrance died. But now, even though it's over, I wonder—is it okay if I write to you every now and again?

Your loving daughter,

Janice

ABOUT THE AUTHOR

Linda Hall spent the early years of her writing career as a journalist and freelance writer. She also worked in the field of adult literacy and wrote curriculum materials for adults reading at basic reading levels. In 1990 Linda decided to do something she'd always dreamed of doing, she began working on her first novel. The book she wrote, *The Josiah Files* was published in 1992.

Since that time she's written twenty more mystery and suspense novels and many short stories and essays.

Most of her novels have something to do with the sea. Linda grew up in New Jersey and her love of the ocean was born there. When she was a little girl Linda remembers sitting on the shore and watching the waves and contemplating what was beyond. She could do that for hours.

Linda has roots in two countries. In 1971, she married a Canadian who loves the water just as much as she does. They moved to Canada and have lived there ever since. A lot of the beautiful summer days in New Brunswick are spent on their kayaks.

For more that twenty years Linda and her husband Rik sailed the coast of Maine and New Brunswick. Both Linda and Rik have achieved the rank of Senior Navigator, the highest rank possible in CPS. The U.S. sister organization is the U.S.P.S. Linda's Senior Navigator diploma hangs proudly on her office wall. What this all means is that she knows how to use a sextant and can 'theoretically' find her way home by looking at the stars.

Rik and Linda have two grown children, seven grandchildren and one very spoiled cat.

CONNECT WITH LINDA

Email:
linda@writerhall.com

Website:
http://writerhall.com

Facebook:
http://www.facebook.com/writerhall

BOOKS BY LINDA HALL

Em Ridge Mystery Series

Night Watch
The Bitter End
The Devil to Pay

Short Story Collection

Strange Faces

Whisper Lake Series - Harlequin Love Inspired Suspense

Storm Warning
On Thin Ice
Critical Impact

Shadows Series - Harlequin Love Inspired Suspense

Shadows in the Mirror
Shadows at the Window
Shadows on the River

Fog Point Series

Dark Water
Black Ice

Teri Blake-Addison Mysteries

Steal Away
Chat Room

Coast of Maine Novels

Margaret's Peace
Island of Refuge
Katheryn's Secret
Sadie's Song

The Canadian Mountie Series

August Gamble
November Veil
April Operation

Stand Alone

The Josiah Files

www.ingramcontent.com/pod-product-compliance
Lightning Source LLC
Chambersburg PA
CBHW020359210626
46816CB00006BB/2035